OTHER BOOKS BY TARA WYATT

If you like small town romances that bring the heat

(and a hint of magic):

GOSSAMER FALLS

Just Like Magic

One Enchanted Evening

Good Luck Charm

If you like stories where the villains are the heroes:

KINGS OF HELL'S KITCHEN

Tease Me

Tempt Me

If you like Standalone Companion Novels

about One Big Family:

THE PRESCOTTS

Stupid Love

Snow Job

Love Bug

Bad Intentions

Side Effects

Burning Up

Until You

Skin Deep

If you wish Hallmark movies had some spice:

THE GRAYSONS

When Snowflakes Fall

Like Fresh Fallen Snow

Until the Sun Sets

If you like baseball players:

DALLAS LONGHORNS SERIES

Stealing Home

Wild Card

Caught Looking

Moon Shot

Hit and Run

Scoring Position

If you like MMA fighters:

THE BLOOD AND GLORY SERIES

co-written with Harper St. George

Dirty Boxing

Take Down

No Contest

If you like bodyguards:

THE BODYGUARD SERIES

Necessary Risk

Primal Instinct

Chain Reaction

If you don't want to commit to a series:

Royal Treatment

Nailed

Stripped

Little Blue Lines

For complete information on all of Tara's books,

visit www.tara-wyatt.com.

ONE *Enchanted* EVENING

TARA WYATT

A *Gossamer Falls* NOVEL

"Sarah knew what wishes
were made of—ephemeral
hopes and dreams that no
act of wanting could bring
to fruition, no matter how
ardent the wisher's desire.
And yet, when she'd stood
beneath the falls, touched
by the mist, it had seemed
to her that the air had
shimmered with possibility.
With the hope that the
magic of a wish just might
be real."

The Legend of Gossamer Falls,
written by Mary Elizabeth Axton,
published 1890

Rosalie Crawford had always been certain in her beliefs. In her view of the world. From a young age, she'd known that things like true love and magic —the kind you'd find in fairy tales—weren't real. They were the stuff of childhood fantasies, tales spun to amuse and entertain. They weren't real life. She knew, because she'd experienced the realities of life up close and personal, and she'd seen no evidence whatsoever of true, lasting love, or magic. They were as real to her as Santa Claus, or the tooth fairy.

And yet, somehow, she'd ended up working for Carrie Clark, one of the world's most famous singer-songwriters, who spent most of her time pouring her soul into songs about love and soulmates and bone-deep connections. As her head of PR, it was Rosalie's job to not only market Carrie, but her songs. To make the world wish they could experience love the way Carrie sang about it.

And it was because of her job that she was on her way to

a small town about ninety minutes north of New York City that was purportedly full of legends and magic and wishes for true love granted. Carrie had read about Gossamer Falls in a magazine, and had instantly swooned over the town's magical reputation. Once the idea of filming a music video there had taken hold, it had been all but a foregone conclusion.

So, Rosalie was headed to Gossamer Falls to scout it out and find out if filming a music video there was even a possibility. Not exactly a PR job, but everyone on Carrie's team had an official title that came with nebulous, constantly shifting duties. Rosalie didn't mind, most of the time; it kept things interesting, as far as she was concerned, even if some of the things she was expected to do were a little below her paygrade.

She shifted uncomfortably, sliding against the too-warm leather seat in the borrowed sedan. She didn't have her own vehicle, spending most of her time in Manhattan, where Carrie lived—when she wasn't in Malibu, or Nashville, or London, or Paris. Glancing back and forth between the road and the sleek dash, she looked for the control for the heated seat. She needed to turn it down or off before she cooked herself. Even through her thick camel coat and jeans, her skin was becoming uncomfortably hot and prickly.

She jabbed at a few buttons, and the relief was almost instant when she found the right one. Tightening her grip on the steering wheel, she refocused her attention on the road ahead. She'd left Manhattan over an hour ago, which meant she should be arriving in Gossamer Falls in about ten minutes, give or take.

The sky had been clear and brilliantly sunny when she'd taken the keys from Trevor, one of Carrie's business managers, but as she'd driven, thick, purplish gray clouds had blotted out the sun, darkening the sky. It was going to snow, and soon.

As if on cue, thick snowflakes started to fall from the sky, batting against the windshield like fluff, and she fumbled for the wipers, flicking them away. She slowed her speed, wondering if the car was fitted with winter tires.

She glanced at the in-dash navigation, watching for her exit. Through the swirling flakes, she spotted the sign for Gossamer Falls, flicked on her signal, and took the exit ramp from the 9D. The ramp curved gently, and she saw what looked like a bay to her left, although it was hard to tell through the curtain of white. With both hands on the wheel, she slowed to below the speed limit, squinting through the flakes as she made her way into the small town of Gossamer Falls, named for the famous waterfall just north in the Hudson Highlands.

Rosalie grinned as she slowed the car even further. Snow clung to the branches of the trees, frosting them with fluff. Following the GPS's prompting, she carefully turned onto Chestnut Avenue, passing by a charming antique shop with a vintage Art Deco display in the glowing front window. A few pedestrians walked up and down the snowy sidewalks, flakes clinging to their knit hats and coats. Even though it was just past three o'clock—her meeting was at three-thirty—the street lights had already flickered to life, casting a gentle glow on the road and sidewalks. Snow fell softly but steadily from the sky, seeming to stick to everything it touched. Even though the city was less than two hours behind her, the snow here felt different. Gentler and cleaner, somehow. Maybe it was the way it didn't instantly turn to gray slush the moment it landed on the streets or sidewalks.

She drove past cute boutiques with displays of cozy sweaters, and small restaurants, front windows quiet between lunch and dinner. She came to a slippery stop at the corner of Chestnut and Main, waiting to turn right onto Main as snow-dusted pedestrians crossed the street. Her gaze caught on another boutique, this one with a white and gold sign emblazoned with the name Wild Flower Clothing Co, the window display featuring chunky cardigans, delicate sweaters, plaid maxi skirts, and a sweater dress in an absolutely stunning shade of burgundy.

If she had time after her meeting, and the shop was still open, Rosalie was totally coming back here. If Rosalie had had to name a weakness—under duress, of course—she'd say clothing. She had a closet full to bursting back in her Manhattan apartment, full of elegant, glamorous, sophisticated clothes. Nothing made her feel more vibrant or alive— or successful—than pulling on a buttery soft cashmere sweater, or rolling on a pair of pure silk stockings. To boot, she had an extensive lingerie collection, and always wore a lacy, matching set under her clothing. Yes, it was superficial and materialistic and probably not the best use of her incredibly generous salary, but it made her happy.

"Oh my God, that scarf," she said, leaning against the seatbelt, peering through the snow. "And those boots. And those earmuffs!" She made the kind of sound usually reserved for eating something delicious. Or sex.

She huffed out a breath at the thought of sex. It had been

a while since anyone had seen her in that fancy lingerie she loved so much. Which was fine, because she wore it for herself and she wasn't looking for a boyfriend. She was never looking for a boyfriend. Casual flings were fine. Casual flings were fun and safe.

A horn tooted behind her, and she made her turn, not realizing she'd been holding up traffic.

"Sorry," she said with a little grimace, holding her hand up in a wave as she turned onto Main. On her right, she spotted what looked like a coffee shop, and she briefly caught the scents of cinnamon and chocolate as she passed, wafting as if by magic through the car's vents. Her mouth watered appreciatively, and she realized that she hadn't eaten anything since her oatmeal that morning. Okay, she now had two stops to make after her meeting.

Hemlock Square, her destination, was ahead on the left, buildings with Tudor-style facades lining three sides of the square. She pulled into the small parking lot, crossing her fingers and toes that she'd find a spot. There was one left, right in front of the municipal building on the far-right side of the square. According to the website she'd consulted, it housed the tourism office where she was meeting her contact person, along with the small town's city hall, munic-ipal offices, a post office, a small courtroom, and the police station.

She parked, gathered her overflowing, oversized purse and stepped out of her car and into the gently drifting snow. Now that she was off the highway, the snow didn't seem nearly so dangerous. The flakes were still thick, but fell in slow swirls before landing gracefully among the thickening carpet of white.

The municipal building was a three-story brownstone with triangular arches over the colonial-style windows, which were lined with empty flower baskets. The front door looked heavy, and was painted a bright, cheery red. Lights glowed from behind the windows. It looked like something out of a movie set, not an actual town hall in small-town upstate New York.

Carrie was going to flip over this place. Rosalie already knew it in her bones, and she hadn't even seen the famed waterfall yet.

She made her way to the entrance, reaching for the door's handle when it swung inward so suddenly that she stumbled slightly. A uniformed police officer stood on the other side, his phone pressed to his ear. He shot her a rueful smile, showing off a dimple in his left cheek, and then stepped back as he held the door for her, tipping his head to indicate that she should go ahead.

"I'll have to check the records to see what information we have. I'll send you anything I find before the end of the day," he said, his voice pleasantly masculine.

She stepped inside, and their gazes collided. Gorgeous blue eyes pinned her in place, and her eyebrows inched up her forehead as unexpected heat pooled low in her belly.

Well, *hello*, officer. It was a fact that she was an absolute sucker for a man in uniform.

Then he winked and stepped through the door and out into the snow, not missing a beat in his phone conversation.

"What in the Hallmark Channel is this place?" she asked no one in particular, shaking her head slowly.

The lobby of the building was warm and cozy, with a set of leather furniture gathered around a fireplace in the far corner. A placard hung on the wall, listing all of the different offices and locations in the building. She scanned down the list, finding the tourism office, and set off down the hall, her boots clicking softly over the polished floor. At the very end of the hall on the first floor, she came to a door with a frosted glass window, vinyl letters declaring that she'd found the Gossamer Falls Tourism Office.

She checked her watch, noting that she was still a bit early, and she debated whether or not to wait in the lobby for ten more minutes or just knock. The decision was made for her when the door opened, revealing a tall woman in her early to mid-thirties—Rosalie's age—in the midst of shrugging on a thick brown coat similar to Rosalie's.

"I'm sorry, I know I'm early—" she started, but the woman cut her off with a shake of her head, snapping the door to the office shut behind her.

"No, you're perfect. It's best if we leave now, before the snow starts to really come down. I'd hate for you to come out from the city and not even get the tour of the falls you were promised. My Jeep's just out front." She wrapped a vibrant red scarf around her neck and then stuck out her hand. "Indy Greer. I'm the manager of the tourism office here, among other things."

"Thanks so much for taking the time to meet with me," said Rosalie, shaking the other woman's hand. She was striking, tall and confident with dark hair and gleaming skin.

"Of course!" said Indy, rummaging through her purse and retrieving a set of keys as they walked back down the hallway. "Honestly, we're thrilled that someone as cool and famous as Carrie Clark has even heard of our little town. How did we end up on her radar?" she asked with a slightly arched brow. She opened the building's front door and held it open for Rosalie.

"She saw an ad in a magazine, did some googling, and was intrigued. Not just by the scenery, but by the story surrounding the town."

They walked carefully down the snow-covered steps, taking their time. The snow was still falling steadily but gently from the sky, sticking to everything it touched. Indy inhaled and then turned to Rosalie, a smile lighting up her round face, emphasizing her wide mouth and high cheekbones. Snowflakes clung to her thick lashes, which framed her light green eyes.

"Don't you just love the smell of fresh snow?" she asked. Rosalie blinked, sniffing tentatively at the air.

"I wasn't aware that snow had a smell," she said.

"Close your eyes and breathe in."

Rosalie grinned. Indy was a little offbeat, but there was also something about her that Rosalie liked. So, she closed her eyes and inhaled, deeply and slowly. The air had a crispness to it, the cold air rushing into her lungs. "I smell...pine, I think. And something clean and fresh that I can't identify. Like...a cold forest." She opened her eyes to find Indy smiling at her.

"Now you know what snow smells like." She tipped her head to the right. "I'm just parked over here. And don't worry, I've got snow tires on and all-wheel drive, so we should be fine." She peered up at the sky as they walked, Rosalie having to take two steps for every one of Indy's wide strides just to keep up. "Were you planning on driving back to the city?"

Rosalie nodded. "After our meeting, yes."

She glanced up at the sky again. "I'd check the weather reports and 511 for road conditions before heading out." She unlocked a dark blue Jeep, tossing her bag into the back as she settled into the driver's seat. Rosalie quickly scooted up into the passenger's seat, glancing nervously at the sky.

TWO

Once Rosalie had buckled her seatbelt, Indy pulled out of the parking lot and turned right onto Main, leaving Hemlock Square behind them. She adjusted the knob for the heater and then looked over at Rosalie. "We have a great hotel in town, if you do decide to stay. It's called the Shephard Inn, run by the Shephard family since the 1940's. January's usually fairly quiet, so I'm sure they have a room available."

"I'll keep that in mind," said Rosalie, eyes fixed on the cheerily glowing storefronts. "What's the population of Gossamer Falls?"

"Just over 2,300 at last count."

They drove slowly down Main, passing by shops and restaurants, and the coziest looking pub Rosalie had ever seen. It, like much of the town, looked like something out of a movie set, with its black lacquer façade and scrolling name in fancy gold serif. She sat back in her seat self-consciously when she realized she was practically pressing her face to the glass of the window. She wasn't normally one for small towns—her favorite place on Earth was Paris, after all—but there was something about this one that appealed to her.

She pointed at the pub through the window as they passed. "Pour Decisions is a fantastic name for a pub," she said, and Indy laughed.

"If you decide to stay, you should wander over for a drink. It's only about a ten-minute walk from the hotel. I highly recommend the spiked hot chocolate. The bartender even toasts the marshmallows on top with one of those little torch thingies."

"I'm always game for anything that involves a little torch thingy," she said, her gaze still trained on the snow falling from the soft gray sky. They continued down Main, passing by a small, old-fashioned looking grocery store, a gas station, and signage for the train station. Indy turned right onto Foundry Bridge Road, her tires sliding slightly in the accumulating snow.

"Is it...are we...are we crazy for going out to see the falls right now?" asked Rosalie once her stomach had settled back down where it belonged, even though Indy didn't seem the slightest bit fazed by the slippery roads.

She shrugged. "I mean, maybe a little. But you came up from the city, and this is important. We're talking about Carrie freaking Clark possibly coming to our town, after all. I'm under strict instructions to do everything in my power to make this happen." She exhaled, blowing a lock of errant hair out of her face. "It's just a little snow. It'll be fine. I'm not putting your life in danger. I promise." But she eased off the gas a little as they wound their way out of the town and toward the Hudson Highlands. Snow-covered pine trees loomed ahead, looking like a fairy tale forest. The Hudson

River churned to their left—the river almost never froze over completely—but the water was sluggish and slow. Rosalie shivered and snuggled into her coat.

"How much do you know about the legend?" asked Indy, two hands on the wheel, her eyes glued to the windshield and the snowy road ahead.

"Not much," answered Rosalie honestly. Magic and fairy tales weren't really her thing, so she'd avoided digging into the town's allegedly magical history. "Carrie read the story after hearing about the town, and she mentioned something about the falls and true love, which is totally up her alley." Carrie's alley, not Rosalie's. Definitely not.

"Carrie. Ha! It's so surreal to hear you talk about one of the most famous women in the world so casually. Honestly, a part of me can't quite wrap my head around the idea that she might actually be coming to our town. God, I have so many questions I want to ask you, but in the name of professionalism and focusing on not sliding off the road, I won't." She glanced over at Rosalie. "Today, anyway."

Rosalie smiled, but truth be told, sometimes she got a little sick of answering questions about Carrie Clark. Sure, it was interesting that she worked for Carrie, but Rosalie often found her job title eclipsed everything else about herself. It felt hollow, sometimes.

Indy blew the same lock of sleek, dark hair out of her eyes again, and then continued. "So, the legend is based on a famous short story published in the 1890s. It was written by a woman named Mary Elizabeth Axton, and it's about a Civil War widow who visits the falls—just like Mary Elizabeth herself did—in an effort to escape her grief and get her feet back under her..." At this, Indy trailed off for a moment and then cleared her throat. "A-anyway, she visited the falls under the light of the full moon and felt as though her tears were being kissed away by angels. She felt soothed, hopeful, even. She felt as though the angels were grieving with her, and this healing energy opened her heart to the possibility of a new love." She paused again, and Rosalie had the feeling there was more she wasn't saying.

She snorted softly after a moment. "A new love. Right. Anyway, in the story, the widow meets a handsome doctor, and they're engaged before the next full moon." She said the last part all in a rush, almost like ripping off a verbal Band-Aid. "The legend surrounding the town grew from that story, and we transitioned from an industry town—there used to be a foundry on the edge of the bay, hence the name Foundry Bridge Road—to a tourist destination. People started coming to visit the falls, believing that if they were kissed by the mist under the light of the full moon, their true love would be revealed to them before the next full moon. The legend and its magic spread, and now we're one of the top tourist destinations in the state."

Just then, they slid to a stop beside a small guardhouse with a snow-dusted placard that welcomed them to Gossamer Falls. Indy powered down her window, and a flurry of snowflakes gusted inside. The man inside the guardhouse slid open his window.

"The hell you doing out here, Indy? It's supposed to keep snowing all afternoon. Roads are gonna get worse," he said with an assured nod.

"Clint, this is Rosalie," she said, tipping her head in Rosalie's direction. "She's with Carrie Clark's team."

The man's bushy eyebrows rose, almost disappearing into

his knit ski hat. "Oh, Carrie Clark! Well, why didn't you say so?"

"Just did, Clint," said Indy, glancing over at Rosalie and rolling her eyes slightly.

"Right, right. Okay, head on in and use the main parking lot. Stick to the main paths, don't go down near the creek. It's frozen over, but you know how slippery those rocks get."

Indy saluted him. "Will do. Thanks, pal." She powered her window back up. They drove down a narrow road, gravel and snow crunching beneath the Jeep's tires, passing by wide, open areas that were currently covered in snow, but probably ideal picnic spots in warmer weather. Indy pulled the Jeep into a parking spot, cutting the ignition.

"Well, here we are," she said, pushing open her door. Rosalie did the same, stepping out into the cold. Immediately, the sound of rushing water filled her ears. Towering pines soared up to the sky, clumps of white frosting the dark green branches.

"It doesn't freeze?" Rosalie asked, following Indy down a gently sloping hill and to a wide, paved path that was thankfully cleared of snow and covered in a mixture of salt and sand.

She shook her head. "The creek does, but the falls themselves don't. They're 215 feet tall, making Gossamer Falls taller than Niagara Falls. The force of the water prevents it from freezing."

They walked side by side, salt crunching beneath their boots, mingling with the sound of the falls, which grew louder as they approached. A set of stairs opened on their left, and Rosalie followed Indy down, clinging to the railing.

The light felt...different here. Brighter, yet softer. More diffused somehow.

As though she could read her mind, Indy said, "The air is damp here, especially in the winter. The mist from the falls crystalizes, giving the air that gleam you're noticing. Some of the locals call it fairy frost."

"That's cute," said Rosalie, making a mental note to tell Carrie about the fairy frost. It was exactly the kind of ephemeral alliteration the songwriter lived for. She opened her mouth to ask another question, but it flew out of her head as the falls came into sight. The water looked like a stream of silver pouring out from the jagged, snowy rocks, thundering down into the creek below. The basin wasn't frozen where the waterfall landed, but the rest of the creek was, glinting in the light like a silvery ribbon. Bare trees swayed gently in the wind, frozen branches clicking together and adding another dimension to the sound surrounding them.

"Wow," she said, a puff of white escaping her lips. "This is incredible."

"Glad you think so," said Indy. "We've never had anyone film anything here, so if she decides to use this location, Carrie Clark would be the first."

Rosalie made a mental note to tell Carrie that, too. Slipping off her gloves, she pulled her phone out of her coat pocket and started snapping pictures and taking short snippets of video.

"In better weather, we're able to get much closer to the falls. On the night of the full moon, there are always people here, ready to get kissed by the mist and make their wishes for true love." She turned to Rosalie, an earnest expression on her face. "I want you to know that we'd be beyond thrilled to have Carrie film her music video here. If she decides to come, we'll make sure she has anything and everything she needs. We can have a local construction company build ramps to make it easier to get equipment in and out, have trailers in the parking lot, and work with local law enforcement to ensure she has the security she needs."

At the mention of law enforcement, Rosalie's mind drifted back to the smoking hot officer she'd nearly run into earlier, replaying that flashing dimple, the flirty wink. Despite the snow gusting around her, heat simmered low in her belly.

Rosalie pushed the thoughts away and nodded. "Noted." She looked around again, sighing softly as she took in the sparkling mist, the gently swirling snow, the soothing sound of the falls, the crisp scent of the air. Breathing it all in, she couldn't deny that this place was special. She could see why people thought there was magic in the air. "Ultimately, it's not up to me, but if it were, I'd choose to film here. And honestly, I'll be shocked if Carrie doesn't feel the same way after seeing these pics and videos I'm sending her. Knowing that the town is excited to have us and willing to work with us is a big plus, too."

Indy tapped the tips of her fingers together in an excited little clap. "Excellent. Whatever we can do to make it happen, just let me know."

They spent a few more minutes looking at the falls, and Rosalie made sure she had plenty of images and video to send back to Carrie. Clouds even darker than before appeared on the horizon, low and heavy. The wind picked up, gusting snowflakes into her face, and she wrapped her coat tighter around herself. A chill that hadn't been there before now permeated the air. Crunching boots sounded behind them, and they turned to see Clint, the man from the guardhouse.

"You all better head back," he said, raising his voice to be heard over the wind. "There's a weather advisory in effect, and we're going to shut down for the day."

Indy nodded. "No problem. I think we're just about finished up, right?" she asked, glancing over at Rosalie, who nodded. Satisfied, he turned and headed back toward the main path, and Rosalie and Indy followed, wind swirling around them. By the time they got back to Indy's Jeep, Rosalie's cheeks and nose were frozen.

"Listen," said Indy as she turned the car on and cranked the heat, which Rosalie was grateful for, "if you want, I can drive you straight to the Shephard Inn, unless you have something in your car you need to get? I don't think you should be on the roads in this weather."

Rosalie hefted her large bag. "Thankfully, pretty much my entire life is in here. And yeah, I'd appreciate that. I think you're right; I'd better not drive back tonight." Rosalie hated driving in the best of conditions—it was one of the many reasons she didn't own a car. The idea of white-knuckling her way back to the city through a snow storm was a hard pass.

Indy nodded and carefully steered them back out to the road, snow crunching beneath tires, wind whipping snow against the windshield. She turned on the radio just in time to catch the weather forecast.

"...adjust your plans, or your driving if you need to be on the roads tonight. Road conditions are deteriorating rapidly, with accumulating snow, and reduced visibility thanks to blowing snow. If you're on the roads, be sure to slow down, leave plenty of room between vehicles, watch for tail lights, and be prepared to stop. We're expecting a solid eight inches before morning."

Indy sighed, shaking her head. "I wish *I* was expecting a solid eight inches before morning."

Rosalie cracked up. "Right? That would be amazing." Because while Rosalie didn't believe in true love, and as a result didn't really put much stock in serious relationships, she did like sex. A lot. And it had been a while since she'd gotten off with another person present. It had been even longer since she'd had *good* sex. The kind that reminded you that you were alive. The kind that felt like a gift. The kind that left her sore and smiling.

"Amazing, miraculous, and pretty much next to impossible."

"It must be hard to date in a small town like this," she said. "Although I don't know that Manhattan's that much better. Everyone has this constant FOMO vibe, always on the apps, always stringing someone along while they wait to see if something better pops up." Which was one of the many reasons Rosalie wasn't interested in dating. She'd seen the shark-infested waters that made up the dating pool. No way was she jumping in only to get bitten. She was smarter than that.

Indy nodded. "I can see how too many options can be just as paralyzing as too few. And you're right, it is hard in a small town like this. There aren't a ton of single people, and having grown up here, I can tell you that most of them are single for a reason. Or off limits, like family friends, or whatever." She paused, her fingers curled tightly around the steering wheel. "Plus, there aren't exactly a lot of thirty-two-year-old widows in town, so I'm a bit of an anomaly."

Rosalie's eyebrows rose as her heart panged in her chest. "You're a widow?" she asked softly.

Indy nodded. "Yeah. My husband died of brain cancer about two years ago."

"Oh. I'm...I'm sorry," said Rosalie, completely at a loss for what to say. She'd never met a widow her own age before, and she was from Manhattan, where people didn't really open up to strangers about personal stuff. "That must be... hard." She felt uncomfortable, not because of what Indy had shared, but because she had no idea what to say.

Indy sighed. "Thanks. Honestly, I've accepted and made peace with it. It's super unfair and it sucked enormous ass, but he's gone. I'm still here, but everyone in town walks on eggshells around me. It makes me feel...untouchable, I guess." She glanced over at Rosalie, a smile pulling at her lips as two pink spots appeared on her cheeks. "Anyway, that's enough oversharing." She laughed self-consciously and shook her head. "You're just easy to talk to, I guess."

"Oh, well. Thanks."

Changing the subject, she pointed out a few shops and restaurants as they drove down Main again, past Hemlock Square, and up into a quieter, residential area. Rosalie noticed that all of the streets appeared to have tree-themed names: Oak, Pine, Cedar.

"I have a little place on Pine," said Indy as she turned onto Cedar. "And the hotel is just up here at the end of the street."

Rosalie nodded, but then frowned. "Should I have called first?"

"Nah. They'll have a room. And if they don't, my guest room is yours if you need it."

"Wow. Um, thank you. That's very generous of you, and frankly, trusting." When Indy's head swung in her direction, she continued. "I mean, how do you know I'm not a crazed axe-wielding psycho?"

Indy laughed. "No offense, but I think I could take you."

Rosalie grinned. "Fair point." Rosalie was barely over five feet and had exactly zero muscles.

The houses lining Cedar were colonial-style, many with warmly glowing windows. It was only about four-thirty, but it felt much later, thanks to the encroaching darkness of the storm. Indy turned down a large, winding drive at the end of the street, a sprawling mansion with gleaming lights shining like a beacon up ahead. It sat on top of a gently sloping, snow-covered hill, and even through the streaming snow, Rosalie could make out a gabled roof, French windows, and twin chimneys on either side of the mansion, each with a plume of smoke rising from it, promising the warmth of a fire. Not a simulated one, but a real, live, crackling one.

Yes, please.

Indy carefully pulled around the circular drive and under a porte cochere, sheltering them slightly from the falling snow. Cutting the ignition, she hopped out, clearly planning to come inside with Rosalie.

They stepped into the hotel, the front door falling closed behind them and shutting out the storm. The hall they'd entered was wide, with gleaming wood floors and warm, soft lighting. To the left was a dark wood staircase with an elaborately carved banister. A small reception desk was tucked beneath it, and past the desk, at the end of the hallway, was a room that seemed to be made of nothing but windows. It currently looked like a snow globe come to life, given the conditions outside.

A young woman stood behind the reception desk, eyebrows raised as she spotted them. She was extremely pretty, with long, dark brown waves falling past her shoulders, sparkling blue eyes, and high cheekbones.

"Hey, Indy," she started, then stopped when her gaze landed on Rosalie. She looked her over slowly, a shrewd, assessing expression on her heart-shaped face. She muttered something under her breath, something that sounded like "interesting." Then, a smile spread slowly, transforming her expression and only enhancing her delicate beauty. "Hi, I'm Autumn Shephard, the manager," she said, extending her hand across the desk to Rosalie. "Welcome to the Shephard Inn. I assume you're looking for a room?"

Rosalie nodded, a little surprised that this young woman was the manager, but Indy cut in before she could say anything.

"She's part of Carrie Clark's team, here to check out the falls as a potential music video location."

Autumn's mouth fell open as she stared at Rosalie. "Oh, well. In that case. Let me double check that our best room is available."

Rosalie held up a hand. "I really don't need anything fancy. It's just for tonight, until the storm passes."

Autumn ignored her completely, fingers flying across the keyboard.

"Our two best rooms are available," said Autumn, nodding triumphantly. "Would you like—"

"I'll take the smaller of the two," said Rosalie quickly, feeling a little embarrassed at the fuss they were making over her. Normally, this was the kind of behavior reserved for Carrie, and she basked in it. Then again, she'd been world famous before finishing high school, so she was used to it. Rosalie, however, was not. She turned to Indy. "Thank you so much for the ride to the hotel, and for taking me out to see the falls. I'm going to send everything I have to Carrie once I get settled, and she'll be making a decision soon. I have a feeling we'll be in touch."

"Great," said Indy, rocking back on her heels. "You have my contact info if you have any questions. Have a safe trip back to the city tomorrow, and I look forward to hearing from you." She turned to Autumn. "I'll see you around, babe."

"Yeah, let's get coffee or something next week."

"Sounds good. Text me." Indy waved and headed back out into the snow, a little flurry sneaking inside the hall as she stepped out.

"Okay, so, I've got you in room ten, which has an amazing view, and is personally one of my favorites," said Autumn, bringing Rosalie's attention back to the reception desk. "Do you have any bags?" she asked, peering over the desk.

Rosalie shook her head, adjusting her large purse on her shoulder. "No. I was planning to head back to the city after the meeting, but I guess Mother Nature had other ideas."

Autumn grinned, something twinkling in her eyes. "Mmm. I guess so. Hang on a sec," she said, and disappeared into a small room behind the reception desk marked "office," emerging a few minutes later with a paper gift bag. "Here. To make your stay as comfortable as possible." Rosalie took the bag, peering inside. There was a toothbrush and travel-sized toothpaste, a hairbrush, a soft pink scrunchie, a mini deodorant, and a package of makeup removal wipes. There were also a couple of vouchers for local businesses, including a free drink at Pour Decisions.

"Thank you," said Rosalie, feeling oddly touched. Of course, this was something an upscale, boutique hotel like this did for their guests all the time and it didn't mean anything. But still, it was nice to feel...cared for. It wasn't a feeling she experienced often, she realized.

"Of course! If there's anything else you need, just let me know. Here's your room key. Take the stairs here," she said, gesturing to the massive staircase behind her, "and it's the last room on the right, way at the end of the hall. If you're hungry, we have a restaurant just through the lounge," she said, pointing straight ahead and into a cozy looking lounge with a crackling fire and leather furniture. "Our chef is currently on leave, but his replacement is killing it."

Rosalie nodded and turned to go, wanting to get settled into her room so she could get some work done before figuring out what to do for dinner. She kept thinking about that pub she'd seen with Indy, so maybe she'd venture out into the snow to check it out. She didn't know why, but she felt almost compelled to go there. Strange. Maybe it was just the power of suggestion, since she'd seen the voucher in her gift bag.

"Oh, one other thing," Autumn called out, and Rosalie turned back. "We have two friendly ghosts on the premises.

So, if you see, smell, or hear anything a little strange, it's probably just one of them. Don't worry—they're friendly. Helpful, even."

Rosalie's eyebrows rose. Autumn had said all of that with such a straight face, but she couldn't be serious, could she? Ghosts? This had to be a joke she played on unsuspecting guests.

"Oh—okay," she said, uncertain what to say in the face of Autumn's earnest expression. She seemed friendly and sweet, but maybe she was just as crazy as the guy on the subway who claimed to be Jesus. She backed away slowly, then turned towards the stairs, hurrying up them.

Crazy manager or not, the hotel was absolutely beautiful. The carpet was lush beneath her feet as she walked down the hallway, large windows between the rooms looking out onto the sprawling grounds and the forest beyond, everything covered in a blanket of pristine white.

She found room number ten easily, slid her key into the lock and opened the heavy wood door, which relented with a soft creak. The floor was hand-scraped wood in a warm reddish-brown color, and covered with patterned area rugs. A king-sized bed sat in the middle of the room, looking snug and inviting with its fluffy white duvet, layered blankets, and tasteful arrangement of throw pillows in cream and soft yellow tones. A chandelier made from the branches of a birch tree hung above the bed. Across from the bed, a flatscreen TV was mounted to the wall, and to the right was a large floor-to-ceiling window that looked out onto the hotel grounds and the forest. A gas fireplace was nestled into the corner, ensconced in arched stone.

To the right of the large window was a doorway that led

to a small living room, with a loveseat upholstered in soft chocolate brown leather, a matching armchair and a large ottoman, all oriented around the window, which faced the same direction as the one in the bedroom. Bookshelves lined the walls, full to bursting with books both old and new. Which was good, because Rosalie liked to read, but didn't have anything with her.

She walked back into the bedroom and then into the bathroom, which was hiding behind a sliding barn door next to the fireplace. The bathroom was done in gleaming white subway tile and sage green paint. A large soaker tub sat directly beneath a set of skylights, and Rosalie was already envisioning taking a book from the shelf in the other room and enjoying a long, hot soak.

Just then, she heard a thump from the other room. Her heart pushed up into her throat as Autumn's words about ghosts came back to her, but logically she knew it was probably just the sound of a guest moving around in another room, or the old pipes rattling. But still, she found herself moving back into the sitting room. She gasped when she saw a book lying on the floor. She went completely still when she saw that it was a worn copy of *Wuthering Heights* by Emily Brontë, one of her all-time favorite books.

"What is this place?" she whispered, bending down and tracing her fingers over the softly frayed edges of the book.

She could've sworn she heard someone whisper the word *home*.

THREE

J ack Shephard wasn't normally a huge fan of snow. Not because he didn't like the white, fluffy stuff, but because snow usually meant road closures, accidents, power outages, and other emergencies that meant he was out in it when everyone else was snuggled up at home with a warm drink and a good movie. As the chief of police for Gossamer Falls, he usually didn't have that luxury.

But not tonight. Tonight was one of the rare occasions where he wasn't only off duty, but he wasn't even on-call. Now, he knew there was a chance he might get called in if things got particularly hairy, which was why he was limiting himself to one beer tonight, even though he wanted to down a whole keg.

He wanted to drink until he couldn't feel the hollowness in his chest that was threatening to swallow him up if he didn't get a handle on himself. He wasn't going to, but the idea of drowning his sorrows was an appealing one.

"I can't believe Norah's engaged," said Jack's brother

Beckett from behind the bar at Pour Decisions. "I mean, I can because she and Ian have been solid for a while now, but still. Shit, man." He wiped out the inside of a freshly washed pint glass and stowed it on the shelf behind him.

"Yeah," said Jack, because for once, he was truly at a loss for words. There was a time when Norah had been everything to him. His high school sweetheart, his first love, his first *everything*. They'd married young, fresh out of high school, mostly because Jack had enlisted in the Army, and he'd wanted the peace of mind that came with knowing she'd be taken care of should anything happen to him. She'd never been thrilled about his military career, and instead had stayed behind, going to college, visiting when she could. They'd been married, but living entirely separate lives. While she'd been studying, graduating, and getting her career going, he'd been living on Army bases between deployments to Iraq and Afghanistan. After eight years, he'd come home to Norah and to Gossamer Falls and become a police officer.

He'd come home to a stranger, in all honesty. In the time they'd been a long-distance couple, they'd both changed. Grown up and evolved and become different people. But Jack hadn't seen that as a set back. He'd seen it as an opportunity to fall in love with his wife all over again.

And for a few years, things had been great. They'd reconnected, both physically and emotionally, and Norah had gotten pregnant. The day Chloe was born—eleven years ago now, holy fuck—was still one of the happiest days of Jack's life.

But by the time Chloe was four, they'd grown apart again. They'd felt like two people standing on either side of a giant boulder, trying to wrap their arms around each other. Intentions didn't matter when there was so much other shit in the way. It was a distance that, in the end, had proven to be insurmountable, despite their efforts. Despite a year of counselling and trying everything Jack could think of to save it. But it hadn't mattered, because when Chloe was in first grade, Norah had told him that she cared about him very much, and she'd always love him as Chloe's father, but she wasn't in love with him anymore, and hadn't been for some time. She didn't want to break up their family, but she also knew that they both needed to move on because they weren't happy.

Still, Jack had held out hope that they'd get back together. That with time, Norah would see that Jack still loved her.

When she'd started dating someone else, about three years ago, Jack had been forced to face the reality that the only woman he'd ever loved had moved on.

And so he'd moved on, too. Mostly with tourists from out of town, because while he wasn't looking for a relationship, he enjoyed sex. A lot. But even still, his reputation among his family was greatly exaggerated. It had all started when his older brother Adam caught him sneaking out of the hotel early one morning, and one assumption had led to another. Yes, Jack had fun when the opportunity arose, but his reputation as a bit of a manwhore wasn't exactly true. But, for now, he was happy to let the rumor stand because then his family left him alone about dating and love and all that shit. He wasn't interested in putting his heart out there again. It had already been through a blender once. He wouldn't survive if it happened again. Besides. He had Chloe, he had his family, he had a job he loved. He'd be downright greedy to wish for more.

Beckett poured a pint and set it down in front of Jack, not saying anything. He flipped one of the TVs over the bar to the Rangers-Penguins game, and then ran a cloth over the gleaming wood.

"Care to make it interesting?" he asked, tipping his head in the direction of the TV. Everyone in the Shephard family was a Rangers fan, with the exception of Beckett, who cheered for the Penguins. Their mother denied it, but he'd clearly been dropped on his head as a baby. There was no other explanation.

Jack sipped his beer. The bar was pretty quiet tonight, thanks to the snow. A fire crackled in the fireplace, and a few people were gathered around tables. He shrugged. "What did you have in mind?"

"Loser has to shovel Mom's driveway tomorrow morning," he said, grinning.

"You're on." Jack fucking hated shoveling snow. The Rangers had better win.

Beckett turned up the volume on the TV slightly, and when the game went to commercial, Jack glanced around the pub again. He was always on alert; it was a habit that had been drilled into him in both the Army and the police academy, and one he didn't know how to switch off. He took in the colorful tapestries hanging on the wood paneled walls, the gleaming parquet floor, the stack of split logs piled neatly next to the fireplace. Mismatched tables and chairs were spaced throughout the pub, most of them empty. Two guys in their twenties sat at one of the tables, each nursing a beer, talking and watching the game. An older couple, the Herberts, sat on the long couch by the fire, talking softly while she knit and he flipped the pages of a newspaper, neat glasses of brandy in front of both of them.

Jack sipped his beer, glancing up at the screen and grimacing when the Rangers took a penalty for roughing. "Fuck me," he muttered, shaking his head. There was a tightness in his chest, a heaviness across his shoulders that he couldn't seem to shake tonight. The news that Norah was engaged to Ian wasn't surprising. He'd seen it coming. And yet, he still felt like he'd just been plowed over by a truck. He'd barely mustered up the energy to drag himself into the bar tonight, even though he wanted Beckett's company.

"You're not my type," Beckett quipped, smirking at him. "But she might be." He tipped his head in the direction of the front door. Jack could tell that it had just opened with the gust of cold air sliding along his back.

Jack didn't turn and shook his head. "Not looking tonight."

Beckett arched an eyebrow at him. "Just look. I promise, you won't regret it."

With a roll of his eyes, Jack turned on his stool. A woman stood just inside the bar, stamping her boots on the mat and brushing snow off of her expensive-looking coat. She turned, and Jack's heart dropped into his stomach for a second as he stared. And stared. And stared.

"Told ya," said Beckett, but Jack didn't even respond. He was too busy drinking in long espresso-colored hair shining sleekly in the soft lights, huge, luminous eyes, an upturned nose, a heart-shaped mouth, and a long, delicate neck. Her cheeks were pink from the cold, and snowflakes clung to her hair. She looked like a woodland fairy, just emerged from a winter wonderland.

He sighed and turned back to the bar, taking a long pull on his beer. As tempting as it was, he didn't need a gorgeous tourist tonight. He needed to be in his feelings so he could move forward and be the dad Chloe needed him to be. In fact, he could probably do with fewer gorgeous tourists in general. Chloe was in middle school. She was starting to notice boys, according to his sister Autumn. The last thing he needed was for her to notice her dad's less than exemplary dating patterns.

"Not gonna go for it?" asked Beckett, tilting his head. Just then, the Penguins scored, and he rapped his knuckles on the bar and shot Jack a smirk. "Oh, I am so not shoveling tomorrow."

"We'll see about that. Don't get cocky, it's just the first period."

"Seriously, though. If you're not interested in Little Miss Gorgeous over there, I think I might be."

Jack shrugged. "Go for it, man." And yet...the words tasted slightly bitter in his mouth. "I'm not up for company tonight."

"Because you didn't take your little blue pill?" Beckett smirked at him and Jack tossed a coaster in his direction. It sailed over the bar and landed on the floor.

"Hey, I'm thirty-eight, not fifty. Jesus Christ."

"You're closer to fifty than twenty."

Jack flipped him off.

Beckett just laughed. The second youngest in the family,

he'd always been a shit who lived to terrorize his older siblings. And yet, he was always there when he was needed. It was just the Shephard way. There were six Shephard siblings in total—Adam, Jack, Oliver, Finn, Beckett, and Autumn—and they'd always been close. They'd somehow grown even closer after the unexpected death of their father a couple of years ago, rallying around their mother and holding each other up in the face of loss.

Well, everyone except Finn, who'd taken off without a backward glance the minute their father's funeral was over. When he thought about Finn and the way he'd run off, Jack tried to look at his brother's actions with empathy. But deep down, Jack was angry. It felt like Finn had abandoned their family when they needed him most. His actions felt selfish and immature, and that was *not* how things were done in the Shephard family.

"What the hell you thinking about him for right now?" asked Beckett, a hint of a growl creeping into his voice. If Jack was angry at Finn, Beckett was livid. They'd been best friends growing up. Any mention of Finn had Beckett stomping around and growling. Jack's anger was nothing compared to Beckett's.

"Just thinking about our family and stuff. Just thinking in general."

"I'm telling you, thinking is not what you need tonight." He moved to the other side of the bar to take an order from the two guys in their twenties who were wanting another pint.

Jack glanced over his shoulder again, but the woman wasn't anywhere to be seen. He took it as a sign to forget about her and just watch the damn hockey game.

Rosalie's walk from the Shephard Inn to Pour Decisions had been snowy and cold, but also somewhat peaceful. The snow was still falling steadily, but the wind had died down, taking the worst of the chill out of the air. There were no cars on the streets, and only a handful of pedestrians. The streetlights glowed softly, illuminating the path of the gently swirling snowflakes. Everything was blanketed in white, like a visual hush over the world.

The inside of the pub was even cozier than she'd hoped, and she looked around as she stamped the snow off of her boots on the rug in the entranceway. A fire crackled merrily in the fireplace, and a few tables were occupied with people watching the Rangers game, or chatting quietly amongst themselves. Soft jazz music floated through the speakers, and the scent of woodsmoke hung in the air.

The bar itself was long and took up the majority of the space along the back wall. Bottles lined the backlit shelves, and she could smell the warm, yeasty scent of beer mingling with the woodsmoke. A lone customer sat at the bar, his back to her, his attention on the hockey game as he chatted with the bartender.

She noticed a display of black and white photographs on the wall to the right of the bar, so she wandered in that direction, eyes scanning over the images. The frames were an eclectic mix, and each picture showcased a part of the town's history. There were photos of the old foundry that Indy had mentioned, the original town hall, a catastrophic flood in the 1920s, the opening of the train station, and of course, the falls themselves, all in varying sizes and levels of historical graininess. She spent several seconds looking at each one. She wasn't normally into history, but there was something about this place that interested her.

Mixed in with the photos were framed newspaper clippings about the town and surrounding area, including one from the late 1940s about the opening of the Shephard Inn. She moved closer, peering at the yellowed paper in the dim light, eyes roving over the building that looked much the same today as it had nearly eighty years ago. A couple stood proudly by the front doors, beaming from ear to ear. God, they looked young. She squinted to read the caption below the photograph. "Mr. and Mrs. Nicholas and Mary Shephard are the proud owners of the Shephard Inn, which opened its doors to guests last week."

"Nicholas and Mary," she murmured to herself, goosebumps dancing over her arms. Maybe she was so interested in this place and the people because of the deep roots visible nearly everywhere she looked. Roots were something she'd never really had, and for a long time, she'd been convinced that she didn't want them. But now, in this small town where everyone seemed to know everyone else's name, where neighbors were friends, and a collective history bound everyone together, she was thinking that maybe she'd never wanted them because she didn't understand what they actually were.

When she was a kid, her parents had moved around a lot as her dad bounced from job to job, always chasing some impossible dream, and she'd lived in Brooklyn, Newark, Queens, Yonkers, Hoboken, Flushing, and Manhattan before the age of ten.

Then her dad had left, and it had been just her and her

mom. Her mom who'd fallen apart when her husband had left, leaving Rosalie to pick up the pieces, giving her a front row seat to a shattered marriage. From a distance, she'd watched her dad remarry and have more kids, and then ten years later repeat the cycle, abandoning that family as well for a much younger woman. She'd never met her grandparents, had lost touch with her father a long time ago, had a politely strained relationship with her mother, and had a handful of first cousins she barely knew and probably wouldn't recognize if they walked past her down the street. And because of that, she'd thought that roots were something that tied you down. She didn't want to need anyone. Now, she could see how they were something that connected you.

Not that she had anyone to connect with, but still. It was a nice concept, and one she was finding she could appreciate now, seeing it all in action, even if it didn't exactly work for her life.

From the very end of the hallway, a glimmer of light caught her eye, and she turned in that direction. She laughed softly when she saw the old-fashioned fortune telling machine. It was a large wooden box with smudged windows showcasing a mannequin dressed as a witch inside, a glimmering placard with the name "Esmerelda" running along the top. She was dressed in sparkly purple robes and held a glowing crystal ball in one plastic hand. The instructions said to put a quarter in the slot, press one of the buttons labeled love, career, or money, and then place your hands on the crystal ball attached to the front of the machine.

A jolt of excitement raced through Rosalie, and she glanced over her shoulder. No one was paying her any attention, so she fished a quarter out of her purse and slipped it into the slot. It landed inside the machine with a soft clank and then the entire thing lit up, playing eerie, carnival music. It was so delightfully cheesy that she found herself grinning. While she was all quiet luxury on the outside, she had a deep fondness for kitsch of any kind.

"Make your selection," came a sultry woman's voice tinged with record fuzz. Rosalie stared at the options for a moment. Her finger hovered over the career button, the most natural, and most obvious choice, but at the last second, she pushed love. It felt almost like a compulsion, like a weight on her hand guiding her to that button.

"Place your hands on the crystal ball," said the woman's voice, skipping once on the word "crystal." Rosalie did, and immediately felt a warm tingle make its way up her fingers, through her hands, and up her arms. The buzzing sensation spread, coursing through her body until she felt almost light-headed with it. All soft and glowy and warm.

A grinding sound pulled her back to reality, and she glanced down to see a small piece of yellowed paper sticking out of the machine. She pulled her hands away from the still glowing ball to retrieve her fortune, frowning in disappoint-ment when she read the three words printed in an old-fash-ioned looking type.

AROUND THE CORNER

"Around the corner?" she said out loud, scrunching her face up. "Lame." That didn't tell her anything at all. Around what corner? Love is just around the corner? She laughed at herself and tucked the scrap of paper into her pocket. So silly. The vibes in this town were getting to her. With her hand still in her pocket, her fingers brushed against the edges of the voucher she'd brought with her, and she made her way back down the hallway and toward the bar. The spiked hot chocolate was calling her name.

FOUR

J ack sipped his beer, his eyes on the hockey game. As
though if he focused hard enough on it, the Rangers
would come back and win.

Beckett leaned his hip against the bar, polishing
another glass, his eyes on the screen. "You know where
Mom keeps the shovel, right?"

"Fuck you," he muttered, shaking his head as a grin
threatened to surface.

"Already told you, you're not my type," said Beckett,
standing up straighter as a customer approached.

It was the woman from earlier. Jack could tell just from
the glimpse he got of her in his peripheral vision.

He forced his attention back to the hockey game.

"Welcome to Pour Decisions. What can I get you?"

She placed a voucher down on the bar and slid it across.
"I've heard very good things about the spiked hot chocolate,"
she said, her voice sultry with a slight raspiness to it. That
voucher meant she was staying at the inn. Definitely a
tourist. A tourist with a sexy as hell voice.

Nope. No. Not going there tonight.

Beckett took the voucher and grinned at her. "One spiked hot chocolate, coming right up." He set about making the drink with quick, efficient moves designed to show off, and the woman leaned on the bar, watching. "So, first time in Gossamer Falls?" Beckett asked, all easy charm.

Hockey. Watch the hockey game.

"Yeah. It's beautiful here. I wasn't planning to stay, but with the snow..."

"Oh yeah, you shouldn't be driving in this," said Beckett, flashing her a killer smile as he worked. "Especially all alone."

The woman burst out laughing, and it was as though someone had beamed sun directly into Jack's stomach.

"Wow, so subtle and smooth," she teased, and Beckett's cheeks actually went a little red. Jack grinned into his beer. No, wait. Hockey. He was supposed to be watching hockey. "Next, you're going to tell me that I'm too pretty to sit alone, so I should sit here at the bar so you can keep me company."

Beckett frowned as he toasted the marshmallows on top of her drink and Jack bit his lip to keep from laughing out loud. "Uh...well, I wasn't..."

She laughed again. "The young ones are always so easy to fluster."

"Maybe it has nothing to do with age, and more to do with you," said Beckett, perking right back up as he slid her drink in front of her. She ignored him completely and reached for her drink.

"Oh my God, this looks amazing. Your cheesy attempt at flirting is forgiven if this is half as good as it looks." There was a pause where Jack assumed she was taking a sip—not that he'd know because he was watching the hockey game—and then she moaned softly.

Fuck. No. He was trying to be good tonight. To not use sex to numb the shit he didn't want to feel. Growth mindset and all that shit.

"Okay, you're forgiven." She took another sip and then laughed to herself. "Maybe my fortune wasn't about a man but about this drink."

"What fortune?" asked Beckett, leaning on the bar.

"From your fortune telling machine in the back there."

"Esmerelda?" Beckett scratched at his head.

"Yeah. I put my quarter in and my fortune just said 'around the corner.' It was supposed to be about love, but I guess chocolate is an adequate substitute."

Beckett froze, a bewildered expression on his face. "Uh... about that machine..."

"What?" she asked, and Jack allowed himself to glance over. Fuck, she was pretty. And of course, she had a tiny bit of whipped cream clinging to her lip, which made his mind go to absolutely filthy places.

Stop. Hockey.

Beckett cleared his throat. "It doesn't work. It's not even plugged in, because when it's on, it shocks people."

She laughed. "Uh huh. Sure."

"No, I'm serious."

"Serious about messing with tourists." She started to laugh again, but it trailed off at the look on Beckett's face.

"I swear, I'm not."

She paused, then gave Beckett a deeply skeptical look before retreating around the corner. She came back a moment later, huge brown eyes—not that Jack had noticed how pretty her eyes were, because he wasn't looking—on Beckett.

"You unplugged it."

He shrugged. "I've been behind the bar the entire time. Ask him," he said, tipping his head in Jack's direction. Jack sighed, not wanting to be dragged into this. He appreciated what Beckett was trying to do, and on a different night, maybe he'd let Beckett play wingman. But not tonight.

"Has he really?" she asked, sliding onto the stool next to Jack, her hands wrapped around her mug.

Even though he wasn't looking for company tonight, Jack also wasn't rude, so he turned to face her, holding up two fingers. "Scouts honor. He's been back here ever since you walked in."

She blinked slowly as she studied his face, and heat crawled up his spine. "You're the cop," she said softly, openly staring at him. When he didn't say anything, mostly because he seemed to have a hard time connecting his tongue and his brain when he was looking at her, she continued. "You held the door for me earlier today, at the town hall. You were just leaving, and you were on the phone..." She trailed off, spots of pink appearing on her cheeks. "You winked at me."

The moment came rushing back to him, and a small smile pulled at his lips. "I remember."

She swallowed and then took a sip of her drink, her eyes darting back and forth between Jack and the hockey game. "Thank you. Again. For holding the door."

"You're welcome," said Jack, rubbing a hand over the back of his neck. How did he, who flirted with *everyone*, have no words right now? "You, uh...I hope you liked the town hall." He cringed inwardly. Beckett's eyebrows rose as he watched, hiding a laugh disguised as a cough behind his fist.

"Is the machine really broken?" she asked. "Because I swear, I put a quarter in and got this." She pulled out the small scrap of paper she'd allegedly gotten from the machine and dropped it onto the bar.

"It's really broken," said Beckett. "But maybe old Esmerelda's got some real magic in her."

She looked up at him, her eyebrows knitting together. "Real magic?" Jack could hear the skepticism dripping from her voice.

"Sure. The town's full of it."

"Full of something," she muttered, taking another sip of her drink.

Jack picked up the slip of paper, tracing his fingers over the printed ink. It was still fresh. The woman was telling the truth. As he touched the paper, a warm tingle made its way up his arm.

Having grown up in Gossamer Falls, Jack was well-versed in the town's mythology. For the most part, he didn't put much stock in it. It was just a story, designed to entice tourists to visit the town. After all, he'd been to the falls with Norah under the light of the full moon way back in high school, and look how that had ended up.

Then again, he didn't exactly have an explanation for why the unplugged and broken machine was spitting out fortunes, even if they were nonsensical ones. And he'd watched his brother Adam fall hard and fast just this past fall after his now-girlfriend Hazel had visited the falls on a whim. Adam hadn't believed until Hazel had come into his life.

It was probably easy to believe in magic when you were falling in love, though.

Just then, the Penguins scored on a breakaway, and both Jack and the woman said, "Oh, come on!" in perfect unison. She looked over at Jack, gesturing at the screen. "That was *so* offside. Unbelievable."

"Right? Where the hell was the whistle?"

She shook her head. "We should *not* be losing to the Penguins. They're one of the worst teams in the Metropolitan Division."

A smile spread across his face. "You're a Rangers fan, huh?"

She nodded, eyes still on the screen. "Oh, yeah. I love hockey, and the Rangers have been my team since I was a kid."

Jack swore he felt his heart thud somewhere down around his feet while a funeral hymn played at the death of his resolve. He didn't know where the night was going, but he knew he was done pretending he wasn't intrigued as hell by this woman.

He could talk to her, right? Talking still counted as being good. Talking wasn't sex. And besides, talking about hockey wasn't sexual at all. Hockey talk wasn't flirting. It was fine. This was fine.

He held out his hand. "Jack."

She took it. "Rosalie." Another wave of heat shot down his spine at how small and soft hers was.

Oh, God. He was so, so fucked.

FIVE

Rosalie grinned into her drink, her eyes darting back and forth between the Rangers game and the gorgeous man on the stool beside her. It turned out that hot cop—Jack—was even hotter up close. He had dark blond hair verging on light brown, and bright blue eyes with lines that fanned out around them when he smiled. He was tall and built, and moved with a kind of masculine confidence she found very, very appealing. She was used to Wall Street types in Armani suits showing off their Philipe Patek watches. There was a ruggedness to Jack that she found immensely attractive. Maybe it was the stubble coating his sharp jaw. Maybe it was the way he was wearing jeans and a navy blue sweater, simple and clean, but clearly not trying to show off. Maybe it was his big hands with thick fingers. They were roughened and strong, hands that knew work.

Whatever it was, it was working for her. Big time.

"Yes, go!" he said, eyes on the TV screen. She raised her hands as the Rangers forward skated through the defense towards the net. He executed the most beautiful drop pass she'd ever seen, and the winger wristed it right into the net.

"Yes!" she screamed, slapping her fist against the shiny wood of the bar. She turned to Jack, whose face was lit up, his smile transforming him from sexy to stunningly gorgeous. He lifted his large hand, and she smacked it in a high five.

"That's what I'm talking about," he said, and pointed at the bartender. "You might be shoveling after all."

The bartender smirked, and it was in that moment she noticed the resemblance between them. The same blue eyes, the same sharp jawline.

"Who is shoveling what?" she asked, sipping her drink.

"Our mom's driveway. See, Beckett here," said Jack, jerking his thumb in the bartender's direction, "is a Penguins fan. So, we made a little bet. Loser shovels tomorrow morning."

"So you're telling me that we have yet another reason for wanting the Penguins to lose tonight?"

"Yes," said Jack, sipping his beer and shooting Beckett a look. "We do." Beckett just grinned and shook his head as he put a few glasses away. Jack turned to her, and she couldn't seem to stop staring at his broad shoulders, his big hands, his thick thighs. "So," he said, swiveling slightly on his stool. "What brings you to our little town?"

"Work, actually."

His eyebrows rose slightly, because he'd clearly had her pegged as a tourist. "What sort of work?"

"I do PR and some business management for Carrie Clark."

His eyebrows rose even higher, his head tilting.

"Seriously? I'd heard a rumor that she might be filming a music video here, but that was months ago."

Rosalie shrugged. "You can't believe everything you hear, but that one's on the money. I came out here to scout the location and make sure it would work."

"And?"

She shrugged again. "I think it's a great spot to shoot the video. I sent back footage and photographs, and I met with someone from the tourism office today, and she assured me that the town wants Carrie to come film here. So, we'll see. Ultimately it's her call."

"Must be wild working for someone so famous," he said.

She laughed. "I don't know about wild. I've been working for her for a few years now. I was starstruck at first, I'm not gonna lie. But I got used to it after a while. I mean, yeah, she's super famous, but she's still just a person, you know?"

"How did you wind up working for her?"

"I actually started out working for Atlantic Records. When I was doing my MBA—" At that, he let out an impressed whistle, which had her ducking her head and biting her lip for half a second— "I interned for them in their sales and marketing department. After graduation, they hired me to work on the US marketing team. After a few years, I jumped to Warner Music, and I worked my way up to VP of PR. Then Carrie poached me," she said, laughing and shaking her head. "Now I just work for her. It was a change, going from a ton of clients to just one, but it hasn't been boring, I can tell you that much."

"I bet," he said. "So you're from the city?"

She nodded. "Yeah. Born and raised, bounced around the boroughs a bunch growing up. But New York is home. Carrie travels a lot, and I usually go with her, and don't get me wrong—getting to see the world is a huge perk of the job. But it's always nice to come home, too." She finished off her drink and slid the empty glass away from herself. "Are you from here?"

He nodded. "Yeah."

"And have you always been a cop?" A little wave of heat worked its way over her skin at the memory of Jack in his uniform. God, men in uniform were hot. They just did it for her. The authority, the discipline, the alpha male-ness of it. Delicious.

"Not always. I was in the Army for eight years, joined the police force when I came back home."

Her heart thunked into her stomach, and she found herself reaching across the bar, her hand landing gently on his forearm, which was firm and warm even through his thick sweater. "Thank you for your service," she said, meeting his eyes. She meant it.

A small smile pulled at his lips, and she got the distinct impression that his time in the military wasn't something he wanted to talk about.

"And have you always been a Rangers fan?" she asked, deftly guiding the conversation back into less fraught waters.

He flashed her a grateful smile. "Yep. Since I was a kid. Always watched the games with my dad." Sadness flickered across his face. "He died a couple of years ago."

"I'm sorry. I...I haven't lost a parent...like that. But it must be hard."

"It is. Fuck, I'm sorry. Here I am, talking to a gorgeous woman, and I'm being a fucking Debbie Downer."

She laughed. "I think Debbie Downer might be a bit

extreme." Her cheeks felt flushed at his compliment. "Did you ever play?" she asked, pointing up at the screen where the next period was just starting.

"Yeah, I did. Still do. There's a rec league a couple of towns over."

"What position?"

"Defence, usually."

Beckett wandered back over, effortlessly scooping up her empty glass. "Can I get you another one?"

She glanced over at Jack, who was nursing his pint of beer. She had a feeling him being here was more about watching the game and hanging out with his brother than drinking. "You know what? I will take another, but let's make it a beer. The spiked hot chocolate was delicious, but I don't think I can do two sweet drinks in a row."

"Sure. What would you like?" he asked, gesturing at the taps.

"I'll take a pint of Blue Moon, thanks."

He winked at her, looking very much like a younger version of Jack in that moment. "So, you two are brothers, huh?"

"For our entire lives. Well, my entire life," said Beckett, pouring the pint and sliding it across to her.

Jack tipped his chin at Beckett and then tapped his own chest. Beckett nodded, and Rosalie had to admit that she was fascinated at the easy, wordless communication between the two of them. She'd never had a sibling, and that whole dynamic was intriguing. Most of the time she was glad she'd been an only child, because having a younger sibling would've meant yet another person Rosalie had to look after when her dad peaced out, but sometimes she felt like she'd missed out. Times like now.

"What just happened?" asked Rosalie, taking a small sip of her beer.

"He told me to put your beer on his tab," said Beckett, punching something into a touchscreen behind the bar.

"Oh." She turned to Jack. "Thank you. You didn't have to do that."

He shrugged. "I know. But I wanted to." He leaned in closer, bringing the scent of his clean, masculine cologne with him. Her belly dipped and swirled, and then flopped over on itself. "You saved me from having to spend the entire game talking to this guy."

"Anything for a fellow Rangers fan."

"You heading back to the city tomorrow?" he asked, and a little jolt of excitement charged through her. Was he putting feelers out? God, she hoped he was putting feelers out.

"I am," she answered. "As soon as the roads are clear."

"You must be staying at the Shephard Inn."

"I am," she repeated. "You know it?"

He laughed softly. "It's the only hotel in town, and it was founded by my grandparents. You probably met my sister Autumn when you checked in."

Her eyebrows rose slightly. "Oh, Autumn's your sister? Your family runs it?"

He nodded. "For over eighty years now." Again, the idea of deep roots struck her, and she felt...untethered. Like something meaningless just floating, unconnected to anything else. She took a long sip of her beer, doing her best to ignore the weight on her chest.

"So, you've got a brother and a sister," she said, but he shook his head.

"I've got *four* brothers and a sister. I'm the second of six."

She almost choked on her drink. "Six? Wow. I can't even...I mean, I'm an only child, so I can't even picture what it would be like to have so many people around all the time."

"Annoying as fuck," said Beckett.

"Where do you fall in the six?" she asked. He was definitely younger than Jack by several years.

"I'm Shephard kid number five. Autumn is the baby."

"Do you all still live here?"

"All except one," said Jack, and with the way Beckett's jaw tightened, she had a feeling they'd inadvertently waded back into choppy conversational waters. Well, if there was anyone who was good at brushing messy things like feelings under the table, it was Rosalie. God knew she had thirty-four years' worth of practice.

"Still, you must know each other really well," she said, tracing her fingers up and down her pint glass, gathering condensation. Jack's gaze followed her fingers, his Adam's apple bobbing as he swallowed. "What do you think Beckett would be doing if he wasn't a bartender? Not that there's anything wrong with being a bartender," she added quickly.

Jack smirked. "He thinks I don't know this, but he's got a brochure for the police academy tucked away somewhere in his apartment."

Beckett laid his hands on the bar, arms spread. "I don't want to be a beat cop, I want to be a homicide detective."

Jack laughed. "I mean, yeah, that's how it works. You graduate as a rookie and they hand you a detective shield and a bunch of cold cases." When Beckett sighed, Jack shook his head. "You work your way up to it. Like how I worked my way up to being the Chief."

Rosalie's eyes widened. "You're the Chief of police?"

"He has a staff of four," interjected Beckett. "I don't want to give out parking tickets. I'm just really into murder." He opened and closed his mouth. "Not...wow, that sounded bad. Not in a creepy way."

"What's the non-creepy way to be into murder?" asked Rosalie. Jack shifted closer, his knee brushing against her thigh.

"You know, true crime shit."

"Maybe you should start a podcast," she said. "Could be fun."

Beckett blinked, and then shrugged. "Yeah, maybe."

She'd been about to ask another question when the Rangers had another breakaway, stealing her attention for a minute.

"Damn," Jack ground out when the goalie made a killer glove save. "At least they're back in it."

"Okay, question for you," she said to Beckett once the excitement had died down. "What's something Jack did growing up that your parents never found out about?"

Beckett tipped his head back and laughed. "Oh, man. I've got a few."

"Come on man, don't make me look bad," said Jack in an exaggerated stage whisper.

"Well, there was the time when he and our older brother Adam cut school. Adam's twelve years older than me, and Jack's ten. So these two, they cut school and where do they decide to go? These super cool guys? The zoo a few towns over. And I happened to be there with my first grade class on a field trip. When they knew I'd seen them, they threatened to feed me to a lion if I told."

Rosalie smacked Jack's arm. "What kind of loser cuts school to go to the zoo?"

"The kind without a car and without much money who hadn't studied for his chemistry test."

"Or there was that time he smashed a window playing hockey inside. Never fessed up to that one either."

"Wow, hockey and zoo animals. Definitely a bad boy." Rosalie grinned at Jack, who grinned back.

Beckett laughed. "Jack doesn't have a bad bone in his body. He's basically Captain America." He stepped out from behind the bar to clear some tables, leaving Rosalie and Jack alone.

"What's something you did that your parents never found out about?" he asked. Rosalie looked down into her beer.

"I'm gonna be honest, Jack. While I love hearing about your family, mine's a bit of a touchy subject for me."

He eyed her appraisingly, and she braced herself, ready for the pitying expression. But it wasn't there. Just a gentle understanding. He nodded.

"Fair enough. God knows we've all got our shit." He rubbed a hand over his chest as if trying to soothe an ache there.

She laid a hand on his thigh, leaning in close. "So let's not think about the shit we all carry around with us tonight. It's snowing, the Rangers might come back, and I'm having fun."

He swallowed thickly. "You got a boyfriend back in the city?"

"Nope."

He grimaced. "Shit. Husband, then?"

She laughed. "Definitely not. I'm very, very single. Are you?"

Please say yes, please say yes, please say yes.

"Very single."

Their eyes met, and for several seconds, they just stared, not even reacting when the Rangers scored to tie the game.

SIX

Despite the way it had started out, tonight was turning out to be a pretty freaking great night. The Rangers had come back and won the game in OT, meaning Beckett would be the one hauling his ass over to Mom's first thing tomorrow morning. And then there was Rosalie…if he was reading the vibes right—and he was pretty sure he was—she was into him. But there was more to it than a sexy woman flirting with him. There was something about *her.* It was the rasp of her laugh, feminine and sexy. It was the way talking to her felt like the easiest thing in the world. It was the way he wanted to know more about her. Hell, if they spent the entire night just sitting here *talking* he'd go to work an exhausted but happy man tomorrow.

It sounded trite and cliché, but Rosalie was different. Or maybe she just made him feel different. And that difference was creating a pull he hadn't experienced in a very long time.

It was strong enough that it was making him rethink his resolution to go home alone tonight.

"You paying tonight, or am I just adding this to your tab?" asked Beckett, wiping down the bar. It was after ten, the game was over, and the customers were filtering out into the snowy night. Technically the bar closed at eleven, but with the snow and everyone heading out, Beckett obviously intended to close up a little early.

"Tab," said Jack. "I'll clear it up next week."

Beckett just shrugged. "No worries. I know where you live."

Jack chuckled. He usually ran a tab at the bar. He and Chloe had a Thursday night tradition of nachos for dinner at the pub, and the majority of his bill was food, not alcohol. He enjoyed a drink, but being the police chief in a small town meant he could never fully let loose. At least, not with booze.

Rosalie returned from the ladies' room and glanced around. "Oh...are you closing up?" she asked, and Jack didn't miss the note of disappointment in her voice.

Beckett nodded. "Yeah."

"Well..." she said, her bottom lip caught between her teeth. "It was nice meeting you both." She shrugged her coat on, and everything inside Jack's chest went tight. She was about to walk out into the snow, and that would be that. He'd probably never see her again.

That thought was enough to push him to his feet as he pulled on his own heavy-duty winter coat. "I'll walk you back to the hotel," he said, wondering if she could hear the hope and the need in his voice.

She smiled, and when her gorgeous brown eyes met his,

he swore the heat in the room rose by a few degrees. "And they say chivalry is dead." She said goodbye to Beckett, who waved and then gave Jack a covert thumbs up. Jack fought back the instinct to roll his eyes. But then again, why wouldn't Beckett assume Rosalie wasn't just another conquest?

But she wasn't. They'd barely touched, and somehow, Jack already knew that. He couldn't explain it. He felt... magnetized towards her.

Which was bad, right? Shouldn't the fact that he was feeling shit mean he should keep his distance?

He'd picked up women before. Dozens of times over the past few years. So why did he feel like a tangled up mess tonight? A mess of feelings and thoughts, hope and fear? It didn't make any sense.

He gestured for her to proceed him, and he held the door for her, once again winking at her as she passed, just as he had earlier that day. Except this time, she stopped in front of him, an adorably sexy smirk on her lips.

"You keep winking at me like that, and I'm going to start getting ideas, officer."

"What kind of ideas?" he asked, his blood heating and starting to move south.

"The kind that would make me a very..." She moved closer, arching up on her tiptoes to whisper in his ear. "Bad girl."

Oh holy fuck. He couldn't remember the last time he'd wanted a woman this badly. Alarm bells started to go off somewhere in the recesses of his brain.

He laughed. "You're fucking adorable, you know that?"

She laughed too, her cheeks going pink. "Glad you think

so." She moved past him, stepping out into the snow. Jack was mesmerized by the way it clung to her hair, falling softly around her. The entire street was silent, blanketed in white, not a single car or pedestrian to be seen. It felt as though the two of them were alone together in a snow globe, trapped inside some kind of glittery miracle.

Because that's what tonight was. Jack already knew. It was a perfect, pristine moment in time.

They started down the street, snow falling around them, the occasional gust of wind whipping the snow around their faces. Instinctively, Jack reached out and took her hand in his. She didn't take it back, instead giving his hand a soft squeeze he barely felt through their gloves.

"So, what's it really like, working for one of the world's biggest pop stars?" he asked. He wanted to know everything about her. She'd mentioned that family was a touchy subject for her, so he decided to go the work route instead.

"I…it's a job, you know? I do a lot of the same type of work for Carrie that I did for the music labels. It's just a narrower focus. I will say that the job has much blurrier lines than my previous roles, but I don't mind, mostly. Sometimes I wish it was more challenging, with room to grow, or…" She trailed off. "I don't know. I do like it. And Carrie's become a friend, of sorts."

"You must have all kinds of stories," he said, his shoulder brushing against hers as they trudged through the snow.

"I do. But I also signed an iron-clad NDA when I started working with her, so my lips are sealed."

"Fair enough." There was a beat of silence, and then he asked her, "So, what do you do for fun? When you're not working?"

There was a pause, and he glanced over at her, wondering if maybe she hadn't heard him. But he could see that she was deep in thought. Finally, after several more seconds, she shrugged.

"I…don't know. I mostly just work."

"Oh, come on. There must be something. A hobby, your favorite way to unwind."

"What do you do for fun?" she asked, turning the question back on him.

"I play hockey, spend time with my family. I work out. I volunteer at a local food bank."

She looked over at him, a playful glint in her eyes. "You really are Captain America, aren't you?"

Blood rushed to the tips of his ears. "No. I'm really not." He was a divorced Army vet who slept around too much. He was far from perfect or heroic. Which was why he was supposed to be trying to turn over a new leaf.

He still could. He could walk Rosalie back to the hotel to make sure she got back safely and then call it a night.

He could. He should.

"Tell me about the food bank," she said, her shoulder brushing against his again.

"It's in Stony Ridge, the next town over, out of the Presbyterian church there. It's open every Saturday morning, and it's almost entirely volunteer run. We solicit donations, and keep a log of all of the enrolled people. Over the past few years, more and more families have struggled to make ends meet. The goal is to give everyone who comes a three-day supply of food, and not just processed junk. But actual nutritious food—fresh fruit and vegetables, meat, eggs, milk, bread. And beyond that, we have a small section with items they can choose to add to their hampers."

"How many families are enrolled?"

"Over fifty now."

"Wow. That's...a lot."

"Aside from actually distributing the food, my main role is drumming up donations from local businesses, looking for non-profits who might give us a grant."

"That's a lot for a volunteer position," she said, tilting her head. "Have you thought about—"

Her words ended in a shriek as she slipped on a patch of ice, arms and legs flailing. Acting purely on instinct, Jack's arms shot out, wrapping around her waist to steady her. He hauled her flush against him to keep her upright. Everything inside him went completely still—his lungs, his brain, his sense of time—with the exception of his heart, which slammed against the cage of his chest with an intensity that almost scared him. She made a soft whimpering sound, her pupils huge even in the dim light cast from the streetlamps.

"You okay?" he asked, his breath puffing out in a white cloud.

"Yeah. Thanks for the save."

Slowly, he released her, making sure she had her balance before reluctantly dropping his arms to his sides. They started walking again, and she slipped her hand back in his, as though it belonged there. Effortless and natural.

God, none of this was unfamiliar territory. Flirting, going home with a woman. So why did it feel so foreign?

He realized then that it was because he cared. Oh God, he cared. And he didn't want to care. He didn't want to feel...

anything. The reason for hot, meaningless sex was to forget about feelings.

Okay, yeah. Definitely going with the whole "walking her back and saying goodnight" plan. It was the only thing to do, for so many reasons.

"Anyway, I was going to say that you should look into working with a charity navigator. They usually work for non profit foundations and might be able to make some connections for you, with grants and gifts in kind."

His eyebrows rose. "I'll look into that. I didn't know that existed."

She sent him a teasing smile. "Gossamer Falls might feel isolated, but you're not that far from the city. There are resources."

"You think Gossamer Falls feels isolated?"

"A little, yeah. I'm a big city person. Don't get me wrong, your town is very charming. Earlier, I compared it to something out of a movie. And maybe it's the snow, but it feels...I don't know. Very far from the city."

"Hey, I'll have you know that we've had electricity for over ten years now. Internet coming soon. Oh, and we just got these things called fax machines..."

She knocked into him, laughing. "Okay, okay. Point taken."

Another easy silence fell between them, permeated only by the crunch of their boots in the pillowy snow.

"What's your favorite song?" she asked suddenly, glancing at him.

"Hmm, tough question. I have to pick just one? Because I definitely have favorites. But they sort of fall into different categories."

"Interesting. Continue."

"As long as you don't judge me for being basic."

"I would never. Seriously, I'm a super basic bitch, and I'm fine with it. I love pumpkin spice lattes and those big salads you get at the Cheesecake Factory. I had a Marilyn Monroe print in my first apartment. I love rom coms and pop music. I have a star tattoo on my foot. I was obsessed with *Sex and the City*. I love musicals and the beach and I literally barfed when I met Ryan Gosling. I am the queen of the basic bitches, and I kinda love it."

Jack found himself grinning from ear to ear. Rosalie had money and clout and a job most people would kill for, but she wasn't full of herself. She was down to earth and didn't have a pretentious bone in her body.

"A star tattoo, huh?"

"Yep. Got it when I was nineteen and I thought I was super posh and sophisticated." She pointed at herself. "Basic bitch. And I don't care. I don't think people should be shamed for liking what they like. I don't believe in the concept of guilty pleasures. I mean, honestly, I could go on a whole rant about the patriarchy and feminism, but I'll spare you." She bit her lip. "So. Favorite song?"

"Do you know the song 'Skate' by Silk Sonic?"

She nodded. "Yeah. Great song."

"It's my go-to when I need a pick me up. It feels like…"

"Like sunshine in song form," she finished for him, and he nodded.

"Exactly."

"What else?"

"I do love classic rock. Led Zepplin, The Beatles, The Rolling Stones."

"Can't go wrong with the classics."

"Happy by Pharrell Williams when—" He cut himself off. He'd been about to say when he was hanging out with his daughter, but he had a rule that he didn't discuss Chloe with women. Ever. He'd gotten caught up in their conversation and had forgotten his own boundaries.

"When what?"

"When I feel like dancing." He cleared his throat. "What about you? Favorite songs?"

"My all time fave is 'I Wanna Dance with Somebody' by Whitney Houston. It's about...life, you know? It's about love and sex and dancing and all these things that make us feel alive. And that song...it's the best of the best. Whitney was the greatest female pop singer of our time. Maybe ever. The range, the power in her voice...it gives me goosebumps, every single time. It's actually a super hard song to sing, and she sings the hell out of it. It's dynamic and fluid and passionate. There's an urgency to it we can all relate to. And ultimately, that's the power of pop music. It's infectious and relatable and unifying, all at once. It's why I love it."

"Wow," said Jack softly. Mentally, he added *might be a genius and is definitely way smarter than me* to the growing list of Rosalie's attributes. "That's...astute and insightful and frankly, kinda fascinating. What other songs do you love?" He could listen to her talk about music for hours.

"'Dancing Queen' by ABBA, obviously. 'Like a Prayer' by Madonna. Anything by Prince, or The Beatles."

"Can't go wrong with The Beatles," he said. "They were one of my dad's favorites, and they were always playing on weekend mornings while he cooked breakfast and Mom got to sleep in." A pang of grief hit him square in the chest, so visceral and sharp that he actually winced.

Rosalie squeezed his hand. "I'm sorry, Jack. I'm sorry."

"Thanks," he said, swallowing down all of the pain and the loss that suddenly felt as fresh as the day he'd lost his father. He cleared his throat and directed them down the street towards the hotel. His heart picked up its pace, hammering away in his chest at the sight of it, glowing softly through the snow on top of the gently sloped hill.

"Favorite Beatles song," she said. "Yours, and his."

"His was 'In My Life,'" he said, his throat getting tight. "And mine is 'Come Together.'"

"Great choices," she said, leaning into him slightly as they started the ascent up to the hotel.

"Yours?"

"'Here Comes the Sun.' I like how hopeful it is. Plus, George was always my favorite Beatle."

They reached the front doors of the hotel, standing together under the porte cochere, sheltered from the snow. The wind seemed to intensify, and Rosalie turned to him, looking up at him through her long lashes. Snowflakes clung to hair, making it go wavy in sections.

"Thank you," she said, "for the drink, and the company and conversation, and for walking me back."

"You're welcome." He stepped a little bit closer, lifting his hand to brush a lock of hair away from her eyes. "Although I'm the one who should be thanking you. Honestly, today was kind of a shit day." It was as much an admission as it was a reminder to himself that he shouldn't be doing anything with Rosalie. He was trying to be good. Trying, being the operative word.

"And what kind of night is tonight?"

"The kind I wish didn't have to end." Even though it should. Gorgeous, smart, funny Rosalie was doing something to him. Something he should probably run from.

She made a show of checking her watch. "Are you going to turn into a pumpkin at midnight or something?"

He laughed. "Not exactly." An idea lit up his brain, and he stepped away, taking her hand and reaching for the front door. "Come on. I want to show you something."

SEVEN

R osalie knew three things for certain about Jack
Shephard.

1. He was sexy as hell.
2. He was a good man, who cared about his family
   and his community.
3. He was *impossible* to read.

One minute, she thought he was going to kiss her. The next, he was pulling away, uncertainty written all over his gorgeous face. Now, she had no problem whatsoever making the first move—as long as she was sure of the vibe. And with Jack, she wasn't sure. He seemed into her, but maybe he was just being nice. For once, she really couldn't tell. One minute he was telling her that she was fucking adorable with his eyes lingering on her mouth, her neck. The next, he was quiet and distant, as if lost in his thoughts.

They stepped into the quiet lobby of the hotel, the door whooshing shut silently behind them. The front desk was empty, with a small sign that read "ring bell for service" standing at attention. The light was on in the small office behind it, so *someone* was around. But still, it felt as though it was just her and Jack, alone together in this beautiful building.

He took her hand and started guiding her down the main hallway, past the lounge on her right and the front desk and sweeping staircase to her left, their footsteps cushioned by the lush rug below. Up ahead, she could see the sun room, the windows a black screen with white flakes dancing everywhere. The faint scents of cinnamon and woodsmoke hung in the air, and once again, she wondered if this place was real.

"What did you want to show me?" she asked softly.

"I mentioned that the hotel was founded by my grandparents, back at the end of the Second World War, yeah?"

She looked up at him as she nodded. He was somehow even more gorgeous in profile, all strong, square jaw and full lips. The blond in his hair glinted in the low light. The straight line of his shoulders was broad and firm, as though he could carry the world on them.

"I grew up here," he said, leading her directly into the sun room. "When my grandparents retired, my parents took it over. My mom stepped back once the family got larger, but she would still help out from time to time. My older brother, Adam, started running the hotel with my dad, and he took over when Dad..." He cleared his throat and pushed a hand through his hair. "When my dad died."

"I don't think I've seen your brother around yet," she said, tilting her head as she studied Jack. Again, she couldn't read him. One minute he was all flirty banter, and the next, he was telling her childhood stories.

In that moment, she could hear Carrie's voice in her head, telling her to relax and go with the flow for once in her life.

"He stepped back a few months ago to focus on his writing career. He and his girlfriend are writing a book together, and Autumn was ready to take over. It's what she's always wanted."

"She seems very good at it," said Rosalie.

Jack shook his head slightly, as though realizing he was rambling. "Anyway," he said with a rueful smile, "my brothers and I used to play a lot of hide and seek here, especially on rainy days. Want to see my never-fail winning spot?"

"Sure," she said, a slight hesitation going through her. This whole *walking her back to the hotel thing* wasn't going at all the way she'd expected.

He winked at her, sending butterflies flapping through her stomach, and then took her hand. Heat curled up her arm, and she suddenly wondered if she'd been misreading him all night. Maybe any flirtiness she'd perceived had been because of her own reactions to him. And who could blame her? He was sexy as hell, sweet and funny, with a warmth and kindness she hadn't found in most of the men she'd dated.

He led her across the sun room to a bookshelf nestled against the far left wall. He reached out a hand, and then dropped it suddenly, turning to her.

"Now, you have to swear on your life you're not going to

tell anyone about this. Only me and Autumn know about this spot. No one else."

She put her hand over her heart. "I solemnly swear that I won't tell a single soul about whatever it is you're about to show me."

"Good. I mean, you seem trustworthy enough, for a New Yorker."

Her mouth fell open in mock anger. "For a New Yorker? Well, if that's how you feel, maybe I should just go," she said, taking a step back.

He reached out and circled a hand around her wrist, tugging her against him. Oh God, he was hard in all the right places. Solid and warm.

"I can't let you go. You already know too much," he said, his gaze dropping to her mouth. Her heart pounded erratically in her chest, and she was back to thinking he wanted to kiss her. He sucked in a breath, and she was pretty sure he was just as affected as she was at being pressed together.

Slowly, he took a half step back from her and then tugged on the spine of a book. It was a worn copy of *The Secret Garden*, the cover a faded green cloth with gold filigree type. There was a faint click followed by a soft creaking sound, and then the entire bookshelf swung inward.

"Whoa," she said, a tingle racing over her skin. A fleeting scent of roses seemed to fill the air for a second, almost like a gust of perfumed air.

Jack led her inside the tiny room, letting the bookcase/door fall closed behind them with another quiet creak. A narrow floor-to-ceiling window looked out onto the darkened fields behind the hotel, snowflakes occasionally catching the light from the sconces on the outside of the hotel. Dusty bookshelves covered the walls, lined with ancient looking books. A small step stool sat in the corner, along with a chest of drawers. A dried up poinsettia sat on top of it, along with several framed family photos.

Rosalie felt as though she'd stepped into another time, or another world. She felt as though they were completely shut away from everything, surrounded by books and snow and…Christmas decorations.

"I'm surprised someone decorated in here," she said, eyes roving over the fake pine garland strung along the middle shelf of the bookshelves, laden with red and green Christmas ball ornaments. A wreath sat on the back of the secret door, matching the garlands.

"I'm not. This is one of Autumn's favorite places, and she's nuts for Christmas. In fact, I bet…" he trailed off and moved a few feet away, clearly searching for something. "Aha." There was a quiet click, and suddenly the room was illuminated in softly glowing fairy lights.

For a moment, Rosalie was speechless, frozen in the beauty of the moment. Everything was bathed in soft, golden light, including Jack.

"Oh, wow," she whispered, swallowing thickly. "Thank you for…sharing this with me." She felt oddly emotional, and she cleared her throat.

"You're welcome," he said, his voice low and husky as he stepped closer to her. With the way the light played over the chiseled planes of his face, he looked like some kind of god. One she wanted to drop to her knees and worship. He took another step closer. "I'm glad you like it. I couldn't let you go without showing it to you."

Disappointment shot through her, cold and sharp, and

she sagged against the bookshelf behind her. Talk about whiplash. She tilted her head back slightly, and then frowned.

"Is that...mistletoe?" she asked, peering up at the rounded ball of white-tipped greenery. Jack looked up, a grin spreading across his face.

"Mmmhmm."

"It's January 12th."

He stepped closer, slipping an arm around her waist. "Right on both counts."

Kiss her

The words seemed to shiver in the air, but Rosalie didn't know where they could've come from beyond her own imagination. Jack froze for a second, his gaze roving over her face, lingering on her mouth.

She looked up at the mistletoe and then back at him, allowing herself the luxury of sliding her hands up his chest. They still had their coats on, but even through the thick layers of fabric, she could feel that he was all hard muscle beneath.

"Well," she said, practically batting her eyelashes at him. Screw it, she was shooting her shot. If he didn't want her, he was going to have to stop sending mixed signals and tell her to her face like an adult. "It *is* tradition."

He grinned at her, a sexy tilt of his lips that had her heart crashing against her ribs. "Can't mess with tradition," he whispered in a husky voice, slowly lowering his face towards hers. She held her breath, letting it out on a whooshing exhale when he closed his mouth over hers.

Gone was any hesitation she'd perceived on his part as he

kissed her softly and gently. He groaned, his grip on her tightening as he swiped his tongue over her bottom lip.

"Okay?" he asked, pulling back slightly.

"So very okay," she said, curling her fingers into the thick fabric of his coat.

"Good."

She moaned softly as he kissed her again, deeper this time, his tongue swiping into her mouth. Her hands skimmed downward, looping around his waist, and she opened for him, wanting more. Sparks shot through her as his tongue slid languidly against hers. His lips were firm and warm and...perfect. Achingly, beautifully perfect. It felt as though the entire evening had been leading up to this moment, where Jack kissed her in a secret room full of books, glowing softly with warm light.

Not just the evening. Everything. This entire snowbound trip. She couldn't explain it. Maybe it was just lust. Maybe it was the fact that no one had kissed her like this—hot and sweet and full of need—in a very long time.

Maybe it was Jack. She barely knew him, but she couldn't deny that she felt drawn to him in a way she didn't fully understand.

He stroked his tongue against hers, kissing the absolute daylights out of her. She moaned, clinging to him. He pulled her even more tightly against him, and even through their coats, she was sure she could feel him, hard and long, against her stomach.

He broke the kiss and buried his face in her neck, the collar of her coat scraping against his jaw as he kissed the skin there.

"Fuck, you taste good," he murmured, kissing his way up

to her ear. Her toes curled in her boots when he scraped his teeth over her earlobe. "So soft and sweet."

"Oh God," she moaned, the scrape of his teeth over her skin making electricity dance through her. "Upstairs."

He pulled back just enough to press his forehead to hers, and she got the distinct impression there was some internal war going on that she wasn't privy to.

"I...shouldn't."

She rolled her lips inward, frowning slightly as she studied him. They were still wrapped around each other, and despite his words, he hadn't moved to pull away.

"Why shouldn't you?"

His eyes shot to hers and he shook his head, but he didn't offer her an explanation.

She placed her palms on his cheeks and kissed him again, intending for it to be short and sweet, but they quickly got swept up in each other's mouths again, and before long, they were devouring each other, the kiss turning hot and deep.

"I'm not looking for anything beyond tonight, Jack," she said, scratching her nails down his neck. "I'm headed back to the city tomorrow. I'm not looking for promises or a boyfriend. You don't need to worry about leading me on."

"I'm not worried about that."

"Then what is it?" she asked, leaning back against the bookshelves. Just then, there was an ominous creak, and the door to the alcove swung outward—despite the fact that it had swung *inward* when they'd first entered—and she tumbled backwards, taking Jack down with her. They landed on the floor with Jack sprawled on top of her, most of his weight braced on his arms. She looked up at him, and she swore the heat that passed between them was so visceral that the air shimmered. She shifted her legs against his and he groaned softly.

"Will you still respect me in the morning?" he asked, sexy grin firmly back in place.

She laughed and winked at him. "Promise."

EIGHT

The feeling of Rosalie beneath him was enough to shred the last of Jack's reserve. He was in full on *fuck it* mode at this point. He'd tried to be good. He'd tried to go home alone tonight. But clearly, the Universe or fate or whatever the fuck had had different plans for him.

For them.

She slid her leg against his again, and heat poured through him, making his blood run through his veins like lava flowing from a volcano.

Distantly, those alarm bells kept going off as he stared down at her, mesmerized by her gorgeous brown eyes, her sweet mouth, her cute little upturned nose. He liked her. A lot. Not that he didn't like the women that he normally went home with but this...was different. He couldn't explain it. There was a pull, a magnetism, and it was throwing him off. It was making him want things he knew weren't in the cards. It was fucking with his head.

He kissed her once more, a brief nip of her lips and then he rose, offering her his hand to help her up.

"Oh, you don't want to have sex right here on the floor?" she asked, her raspy voice scraping over his skin like velvet. He needed to hear her say filthy things in that voice. His name, her moans as he made her come.

"I'm not much of an exhibitionist," he said, tugging her against him. "I want you all to myself." Blood rushed to his cock as images of everything he wanted to do to her flashed through his mind.

She let out a shaky laugh and then, with her hand nestled in his, started leading him toward the stairs. The wood creaked beneath their boots, but the hotel was otherwise silent. Rosalie tilted her head as they walked, a pensive look on her face as she studied the walls.

"I hope these walls are thick," she commented, pulling her room key out of her coat pocket. They reached her room, and she leaned against the door jamb, her eyes bright and twinkling with sexy mischief. "I've been told I can get pretty loud."

He leaned in, caging her against the door. His heart banged in his chest, throbbing in time with his cock. "You a screamer, Rosalie?" he asked, dragging his nose over her cheek. He nipped along her jaw and down her neck. Fuck, how did she taste so good?

"I think with you I might be," she answered, her fingers unzipping his heavy winter coat and sliding around his waist. "Should we find out?"

He grabbed the key card from her and smacked it against the lock. There was a soft beep and the door swung inward. They stumbled inside, a mess of hands and mouths, something warm and sweet sitting right in the center of Jack's chest.

There was no way he could tear himself away from Rosalie now, even if those alarm bells were still going off. Maybe they were there because he was breaking his promise to himself about turning over a new leaf. But it was fine. He could turn over a new leaf tomorrow. After Rosalie went back to the city.

Why did that thought make his chest clench like he'd just been punched? He barely knew her. He didn't even know her damn last name, and he wasn't planning to ask.

Maybe this all just felt different because of his tangled emotions about Norah's engagement.

Yeah, that was probably it.

He moved to pull her against him, wanting more of her now that they were alone in her hotel room. Normally, this would be the part in the hook up when he switched onto autopilot, which he knew sounded absolutely terrible. It wasn't something he was proud of. It was just a habit after years of having meaningless sex.

But Rosalie surprised him, pushing him against the closed door and kissing him, her mouth soft but hungry against his.

"We're definitely going to find out," she murmured, her hands sliding down over his chest and ghosting across the bulge in his jeans. Then she shrugged out of her coat, letting it fall onto the ground without a care. She took one step back and peeled off her blue and cream striped sweater, revealing the sexiest black lace bra he'd ever seen.

"Oh fuck," he breathed. He couldn't move. He couldn't

stop staring. She was gorgeous. Sexy as hell. Confident and pretty and just as into this as he was.

"You like?" she asked, smoothing her hands up over her breasts. He could see the outline of her nipples through the lacy fabric. It looked delicate and expensive. Luxurious.

"Let me show you just how much."

She grinned, and more of that honeyed warmth poured through him. He loved how sexual she was, how into this. He felt...wanted. And he realized that he was usually so focused on getting a woman to go home with him, on making her feel wanted that he'd never once examined why it wasn't more of a two-way street. Not that the women he'd hooked up with in the past didn't want him—they clearly did—but they hadn't made him feel seen and wanted the way Rosalie did. She wasn't just along for the ride. She was right beside him in the drivers' seat, and damn, that was a turn on.

He flung his coat off and reached for her, sliding his hands under her ass and lifting her against him. He was probably a foot taller than her, and significantly larger, which made it easy for him to manhandle her the way he wanted. She instantly wrapped her legs around his waist as his mouth crashed into hers, the kiss hot and messy and full of need and lust. Jack's skin felt warm and tight as he squeezed her ass, rocking her into him.

"Oh, wow," she breathed. "You like *a lot*." She rubbed against him, his straining cock nestled against the apex of her thighs. He buried his face in her neck, gorging himself on her scent, on the soft sweetness of her skin. She moaned, and then said, "Oh, God, Jack," in her husky, raspy voice, and he swore his cock actually jerked in his pants.

Bed. They needed to be on the bed. Now. Trailing kisses from her collarbone to her jaw, he started walking them toward the bed.

It was as though Rosalie was taking over every one of his senses, flooding him with her scent, her taste, her voice, her stunning beauty, her impossibly soft skin. It made him want in a way he hadn't experienced in a very long time.

Maybe ever.

He tumbled her down to the bed, and she landed on the soft mattress with a laugh, reaching for him, winding her arms and legs around him. Fuck, he was so hard he could barely think.

"Your turn," she said, her hair fanning out around her, the chocolate hue of it contrasting with the white duvet. She toyed with the hem of his sweater, and he quickly rose to his knees. Reaching behind his head, he tugged it off in one go, tossing it to the floor, and then doing the same with his plain white undershirt.

Her eyes went wide, her bottom lip caught between her teeth. "God, sometimes I wish life had a rewind button," she said, reaching out and skating the tips of her fingers over his abs. "I would love to watch you do that again and again."

He knew she was being flirty and cute and sexy, but something about her words—the reminder that this was just for tonight, maybe—had a pang shooting through his chest.

"You want me to put it back on?" he teased, smirking at her.

"Don't you dare, Jack Shephard. Don't you fucking dare cover this up."

He laughed and eased down on top of her, kissing her again, deep and thorough, drinking in her soft moans and the way her legs moved against his, the slight scratch of her lacy bra against his bare chest.

"This bra is ridiculously sexy, but it needs to go," he said, tracing her beaded nipple over top of the fabric as he kissed her neck, her throat, her collarbones, beneath her jaw. She arched into him, but he kept his touch gentle and teasing, wanting to make her as crazy as he felt.

She pushed up onto her elbows and reached back to unclasp her bra. It popped open and she shrugged out of it, revealing her breasts. Perfect handfuls, topped with dusky pink nipples begging for his mouth.

She cupped them, as though offering them up to him. "Please," she said softly, and the need in her voice almost undid him.

He lowered his head and placed an open mouthed kiss on each perfect nipple, sucking each briefly. She moaned, her back arching, her hands releasing her breasts and spearing into his hair. He cupped both of them and kissed each nipple again, moving back and forth, sucking a bit longer and a bit harder with every pass. He kissed between her breasts, and then swirled his tongue over her nipple. She pressed into him, her hips moving.

"You like when I suck on these pretty tits?" he asked, squeezing a little harder. He swiped his thumb back and forth over her hard nipple, playing with it. She whimpered, hips moving again.

"I mean, it's okay, I guess." She bit her lip, mischief once again dancing in her eyes.

He grinned and let out a little growl as he rolled them so that she was on top of him, her breasts brushing against his mouth. He sucked one nipple into his mouth while tugging gently at the other. She jerked against him, hips writhing. He scraped his teeth carefully over her nipple, then soothed the scrape with his tongue in long, hot sweeps.

"Oh shit," she said, her voice shaking.

"Just okay?" he asked, moving his mouth to her other breast and giving it the same treatment while sliding the wet nipple of her other breast between his first two fingers.

"It's...fine," she sighed, her eyes fluttering closed when he cupped them and jiggled them gently in his hands. Fuck, he could play with her tits all night, nothing more, and go home happy in the morning.

Morning. Was he staying? He didn't normally. But then the idea of not soaking up the entire night with Rosalie seemed insane. Certifiable.

He brushed his lips across her nipples, back and forth, and she gasped softly, so he did it again and again until she was practically dry humping him.

"Oh God, it's so good," she conceded, and he rewarded her by sucking her nipple back into his mouth while massaging the other breast. Little sounds of pure bliss fell from her lips.

"You like my mouth on you," he said, his voice a little rougher, and it wasn't a question this time.

"I do," she admitted on a shaky moan. "So much."

He grinned, her nipple resting against his lips. "Good girl."

At that, she met his eyes, more of that mischief shining out at him. "Oh, I'm anything but a good girl...*officer.*"

Pre-cum streamed down his dick at her words. Goddamn, but this woman was going to ruin him. They still had pants on, and he already knew that for a fact.

He rolled them again so she was underneath him, and then pinned her wrists above her head. "So what does that make you, Rosalie?" he asked, keeping his tone deliberately stern. Fuck, he was hard. He could probably cut through diamond right now.

"A very bad girl."

Heat seemed to spark in the air. "Do you need to be punished?"

She shrugged nonchalantly, playing up her petulant role.

He grinned darkly, dragging his nose up her neck and to her ear, where he nibbled and then said, "I think you *want* to be punished." She whimpered and he tugged on her earlobe with his teeth. "I was going to let you go with a warning, but I don't think you want me to let you go. I think you want the punishment."

"Duh, because I'm a bad girl."

"You got a sassy mouth, Rosalie. I think we need to put something in it."

NINE

Rosalie's eyes gleamed with excitement as Jack rose and made his way off the bed, moving around to the foot of it. He snapped his fingers and pointed at the spot in front of him. "On all fours. Right here." She sat up, starting to move towards him, when he barked, "And lose the jeans. Bad girls don't keep their pants on, do they?"

She bit her lip as their eyes met, heat sparking and flaring through him. Slowly, without breaking eye contact, she rose to her knees and unzipped her jeans, pushing them down over her hips to reveal the sexiest, tiniest black lace thong Jack had ever seen in his life.

Jesus Christ. She was going to murder him with this lingerie. He'd never thought of himself as a lingerie guy, but Rosalie was proving him wrong.

Or maybe it had nothing to do with the scraps of lace, and everything to do with her.

She kicked off her jeans and settled on her knees, her legs spread. His heart knocked against his chest, his dick throbbing. The tiny slip of lace between her thighs didn't leave much to the imagination.

"Look at you," he said, his voice gritty. "Bare and wet, just like I knew you would be."

She grinned naughtily and slipped her hand into her panties instead of moving to the end of the bed as he'd instructed. Openly defying him.

He let out a dark laugh and then circled back around the bed, fisting his hand into her hair and tugging just hard enough to put her on all fours. He strode back to the end of the bed, his hand going to the front of his jeans.

"Crawl," he ordered, flicking open the button of his jeans and then lowering the zipper. She made a low humming sound and did as she'd been told, breasts swaying, ass in the air as she crawled across the bed. He slipped his hand back into her hair, urging her even closer. His blood was so hot it felt as though it was burning him from the inside. "Take my cock out," he said, his balls throbbing eagerly. Fuck, it was going to take everything he had not to come in her pretty mouth.

She let out a soft moan as she slipped her hand into his boxer briefs and closed her fingers around him, stroking slowly. She teased her fingertip over the tip, smearing his pre-cum all over the aching head of his cock.

"Take it out, Rosalie," he growled. With a little purring sound, she did, shoving his pants and boxer briefs just low enough that he sprang free. With one hand still in her hair, he fisted his cock, stroking himself roughly and then squeezing the base, trying to temper the heat already building low in his gut. "Open," he ordered, and she did. He tapped the head of his dick against her tongue, then traced it over her lips. Good fucking God. Everything about this was so fun and dirty and...*different.*

Still gripping his cock, he slid it between her lips, fucking into her mouth. "Now suck," he snarled. "Show me what a bad girl you are. Show me what that sassy mouth can do."

She moaned, long and loud, as she sucked him deep. Pleasure flared down his spine, pooling low in his gut at the wet slide of her lips and tongue over his hard length. She looked up at him as she released him with a pop, licking all around his sensitive head.

"Holy fuck," he breathed, his chest heaving. The sight of Rosalie on her hands and knees, licking at him eagerly, was almost enough to undo him, right then and there. He tightened his grip on her hair. "Suck it like you mean it, Rosalie," he said, doing his best to sound stern.

She sucked him so deep that he swore his vision faded at the edges and then eased back, dragging her wet, swollen lips over him. "You want me to suck you dry, officer?"

Jack groaned, cock jumping against her lips. Rosalie grinned again, that naughty pull of her lips that made him want to fuck her until neither of them could move.

"You want to come in my mouth?" She stroked him and then feathered kisses up and down his length. "You want to watch me swallow your cum?"

He slid his hand from her hair and down the length of her spine, grazing his fingers against the fabric of her thong. Then, he slid them lower, dipping between her perfect cheeks and gripping the string, pulling her towards him while working the thong against her. She gasped.

"Less talking and more sucking," he growled, pulling hard on her thong. She whimpered and took him back into her mouth. "Deeper. All the way. There you go. Now we're getting somewhere."

She gagged slightly but he didn't ease up, thrusting slowly in and out of her delicious mouth. His breaths were nothing but ragged pants, sweat beading along his hairline as she worked him with her lips and tongue, up and down, deeper and deeper, moaning and choking.

"That's it," he said, still pulling her onto him with his fingers twisted around her thong. "We'll make a good girl out of you yet."

She moaned again, and his cock started to swell and pulse, his balls throbbing in time with his wild heartbeat. He yanked her off his cock, red and wet and pulsing angrily. Rosalie sucked in a gasping breath, wiping at her streaming eyes and wet mouth. Her eyes were bright with excitement and lust, and he grinned down at her, brushing a strand of hair out of her eyes.

"Why did you stop me?" she asked. He didn't miss the way she was rubbing her thighs together, and his mouth watered at the thought of tasting her.

"Because that was only the first part of your punishment. I think we're making progress, but you haven't learned your lesson yet."

She grinned up at him, playing with her breasts, and fuck, her confidence was so sexy. He was playing the role of bossy cop, but she was taking what she wanted from their night together, and he respected the hell out of her for it. She was a woman who knew what she wanted and went for it.

And in that moment, Jack realized that he was actually having fun. That he wasn't just going through the motions of a hook up. That he was actually in the moment, and loving every single second.

He started to move around the bed, ideas bouncing around his skull about where he wanted to take their little game next, when his jeans tangled around his ankles. He flailed his arms helplessly for a minute before hitting the floor with a hard thump.

"Oh my God, Jack! Are you okay?" asked Rosalie, peering at him over the edge of the bed. Their eyes met, and it was as though something cracked open inside him. With his hands over his stomach, jeans around his ankles, he burst out laughing, and once he started, it was as though he couldn't stop. The laughter spilled out of him, and Rosalie joined in, laughing until fresh tears leaked from her eyes and she couldn't catch her breath.

"I'm good," he managed, toeing off his boots and kicking free of his jeans before climbing over top of her on the bed. "Now, where were we?"

"I think you were about to fuck the bad girl right out of me," she said, her voice going sultry again. She reached for his cock, which was still hard, but some of his earlier arousal had cooled, which was probably a blessing, given how close he'd been to coming in her mouth.

"Mmm," he said, urging her onto her back and sliding her thong down her legs. "Hands above your head."

This time, she did as she was told, no sass, and he deftly tied her wrists together with her thong. She pulled against it gently, frowning in mock outrage.

"Did you just handcuff me?"

Instead of answering her, he pushed her thighs further apart, taking in the glistening pink of her pussy. Slowly, holding her gaze, he slid one finger inside her. She was hot and wet, fluttering around him, and he clenched his teeth.

"Oh, fuck," she moaned, back arching off the bed, thighs spreading even wider. She looked so sexy, so beautiful, so pretty and so very his in that moment that he couldn't help himself. He leaned down and kissed her. She brought her tied wrists down over his neck, holding him close, kissing him back, tongues and lips melding, teeth nipping. He kissed her, and kissed her, and kissed her, until she was completely soft and pliant beneath him.

"Rosalie," he said, his voice rougher than sandpaper. "You make me feel crazy. I don't think you have any idea what you do to me."

He slid his finger free, wetness trickling out of her. He gathered it up and massaged it in, playing with her. She bucked against his touch, her breaths fast and shallow.

"More. God, I need more." She nipped his bottom lip, hard.

He slid two fingers inside her this time, fucking her slowly, scissoring them. "You're a tight little thing. Need to get you ready for me." He sped up slightly, the wet sound of the slide of his fingers filling the room. "You like this."

"Wow, do you have a genius level IQ?" she asked, full of sass again.

He laughed, but didn't change what he was doing. "Need to find another way to shut you up," he murmured, pulling his fingers away and sliding down her body until he was between her thighs, his mouth inches away from her swollen pussy.

He never wanted to forget the sight of Rosalie spread for

him, wrists tied with her thong, lips swollen from sucking him. It was dirty and hot and fun and perfect.

For once, it was actually worth remembering.

"You seemed to enjoy teasing me," he said, blowing a stream of air over her clit. "I think it's my turn for a little teasing."

She started to say something, but it dissolved into a moan as he sucked her clit into his mouth, polishing it gently with his tongue. The taste of her exploded across his tongue, tangy and feminine. Sweet and thick, like honey.

"That's not teasing. That's trying to make me come on your face," she panted.

"Are you complaining?" he asked, nipping at one of her outer lips with his teeth.

"Oh, shit," she hissed. "No, I—"

He cut her off by sucking her clit back into his mouth as he slid two fingers inside her, curling them up and stroking over that small rough spot inside her.

She made a sound that was something like, "unnngggghhhhaaaaaaaahhhhhhnnnnn," her hips writhing as he sucked and licked, fucking her with his fingers. He kept going until her clit was swollen and his fingers were covered in her juices, until she was flushed and bucking on the bed.

"Yes! Fuck, you're good at that. Oh my God," she said, her voice thin and shaky. "Oh, God. Jack! Yes, Jack!"

The sound of his name seared through him, and it was so hot and perfect that it was almost enough to make him forget about the game they were playing.

He wanted more of those moans, those screams, his name said in that sexy, raspy voice. Wanted so much more than tonight. He barely knew anything about her. But what he did know was that for once, he wanted to know more. To know everything.

He slid his fingers free and moved back, stopping what he was doing.

"What? No!" she said, the torment he was causing obvious in her voice. Ah, she thought his sudden stop was part of the game. Truth be told, it wasn't.

He rubbed a hand over his face, the taste of her still fresh on his tongue. He grinned at her, an almost rueful expression on his face. "Oh, did you not get there?"

She made the most adorably frustrated grunt. "Please, Jack. Please don't stop."

But he stood from the bed and reached for his pants, finding his wallet and pulling a condom out. "I had to. If I don't get inside you in the next ten seconds, I'm going to lose my fucking mind."

She laughed softly at that, then shot him a sassy look. "But I haven't come yet."

"Don't worry," he said, tearing open the condom. Her eyes followed his movements as he tossed the wrapper onto the bedside table and then rolled the condom down his straining length. "You will."

He reached down and unwrapped her thong from around her wrists, tossing it to the floor. "On all fours. I want your ass in the air."

She was too turned on to do anything but obey at that point, and he could see her pulse jumping in her throat. Could see the flush spreading across her chest. She glanced over her shoulder at him, her hair a mess around her pretty face, and Jack swore his heart stopped for a second.

"I'm so ready," she said, her voice shaking. "Fuck me. I want you hard and deep."

He smacked her ass, a loud crack in the otherwise quiet room, and she let out a guttural moan. "I said ass up." She lowered her upper body to the mattress, pushing her ass into the air.

He settled on the bed behind her, hips level with her ass. He gripped her hips and pulled her back, his cock nestled against her cheeks. "I want you to know something," he said, sliding slowly back and forth.

"What's that?"

He leaned over her, grazing her shoulder with his teeth, the shell of her ear. "You might be a bad girl, but I think you're fucking perfect."

"Jack," she whispered, and then he lined up the head of his cock with her entrance and slammed into her.

"Fuck!" she yelled, and he grinned. She'd warned him that she was a screamer. He sank all the way in, gritting his teeth against the onslaught of pleasure at being buried inside Rosalie.

"So fucking perfect," he growled, his grip tightening on her hips as he fucked her, slow and hard and deep, her pussy clenching around him. Hot and tight and the most glorious thing he'd ever felt. A part of him hoped he was leaving bruises on her so she'd remember him. So a week from now, she'd look down and remember the way he felt deep inside her.

Because Jack was sure as hell going to be remembering it. For a long time.

He slammed into her over and over again, his thrusts brutal and deep, pushing her up the bed. He slid a hand up her spine and into her hair, hauling her upright, his teeth bared against her neck as his hips kept moving. He couldn't have stopped if the building was on fire.

"This is how bad girls get fucked," he grated, his voice sounding like he'd swallowed a handful of gravel. "How they get punished. Until I fuck the bad right out of you." He bit at her shoulder. "Do you like being fucked like a bad girl? Taking all this cock in your wet pussy as punishment?"

"Yes!" she screamed, and he felt her flutter around him. Sweat slicked his chest, and he had a feeling neither of them was going to last much longer.

"Tell me what you like about it," he snarled, hips snapping against her.

"You inside me, fucking me so good. You. You, Jack," she breathed.

"Good girl," he whispered, and she clenched so hard around him he almost saw stars. He slid a hand between her legs and worked her clit with short, smooth strokes. "Come, Rosalie. Come all over my cock. I want to feel you explode."

She sucked in a sharp breath, whimpering, moaning, her head falling back against his shoulder. A shiver worked its way through her.

"Jack," she whispered, her voice shaky, almost unrecognizable. "Oh, fuck." He stroked her clit over and over, and then she shouted, "Oh, fuck! I'm coming! Jack!"

"Fucking Christ," he ground out as her pussy milked him almost to the point of pain. He gripped her hips harder and fucked her through her orgasm, his own barrelling down on him like a freight train. He rolled his hips, holding her in place as he came, long and hard, his cock buried deep inside her. "Rosalie," he moaned, releasing her hips and giving her ass another smack. "Fucking hell, Rosalie."

She pushed back against him, as though wanting him even deeper inside her. God, the way she'd screamed his name as she came…it was one of the sexiest things he'd ever heard in his life.

He blew out a long breath and she sagged against him, boneless.

"I'm never going to be good again," she said weakly, and he laughed, holding her against him. He kissed her shoulder and smoothed a hand over her hip as he carefully slid out of her. Rosalie instantly fell forward on the bed, spread eagle, face buried in the pillows. He laughed again.

"You good?"

She held a hand up high, flashing up a thumbs up. "So good," she said, her words muffled by the pillows. He chuckled and disappeared into the bathroom to take care of the condom, hissing slightly as he pulled it off. He was sensitive after how hard he'd just come. When he stepped back into the bedroom a moment later, Rosalie had flopped onto her back.

"You good?" she asked.

He sat down on the bed beside her and shrugged. "Mch. I'm okay."

Her heavy-lidded eyes flew open and she threw a pillow at him. "Ass."

"Ah, so she can dish it out, but she can't take it. I see how it is."

They locked eyes and both started laughing again, laughing so hard they had tears in their eyes.

And then they were kissing. Soft and unhurried. Sweet.

She broke the kiss, her forehead resting on his shoulder. Normally, this was the part of the evening where he'd say thank you, that he had a great time, that he hoped she enjoyed the rest of her trip, and that he should get going because he had work in the morning. But tonight, he didn't want to. He couldn't imagine walking out right now. Not with Rosalie all sex-drunk and sated cuddled into him.

But did she want him to stay? That wasn't a question he was used to weighing.

She peered up at him, her brow creased. Uncertainty flashed in her eyes. "I hope you're not expecting round two right away, because I need a minute."

He was unprepared for the relief that slammed into him, and he kissed her forehead. "Lucky for you, I'm closer to forty than thirty, and I, too, need a minute. Or twenty."

She grinned at him, and he could've sworn he saw relief in her eyes too.

Jack had never felt like this after sex before. Normally, once the main event was over, he experienced what he thought of as an emotional refractory period. He wanted to be alone, almost wanted to forget that the night had even happened. Which sounded cold and dickish, and maybe it was. But it was the truth. But with Rosalie, he felt sated, yes, but that need to withdraw, to distance himself from what he'd just done…it wasn't there.

So, he laid back on the bed and pulled Rosalie into his arms because it felt right. Natural. Unfamiliar and foreign, but good. Very, very good. She snuggled into him, inhaling deeply.

"You're good if I stay?" he asked, needing the reassurance.

"Yeah," she said, lifting her head to meet his eyes. "Definitely." She kissed a path across his pecs, nipping at his collarbone. "I'll be right back. I just need to use the bathroom."

He nodded and released her. He hadn't realized how tightly he'd been holding her. As though some subconscious part of him had been loath to let her go.

TEN

Rosalie stared at herself in the bathroom mirror, a wide grin stretching across her face. Her hair was an absolute disaster, a wild mess of tangles around her face. Her mascara was smeared, streaked down her cheeks. Her lips looked swollen, and she could see a faint bite mark emerging on her shoulder.

She looked well and truly fucked. Felt it too, a dull but almost pleasurable ache settling between her thighs. Not only had he fucked her hard and deep, but he'd done it with the biggest dick she'd ever seen in her life. Frankly, it was a miracle she could still walk.

And she wanted more.

Her grin spread.

She used the hairbrush Autumn—Jack's sister, which was sort of weird to think about, but, hey, small towns, right?—had given her, one of the makeup wipes to clean up her ruined mascara, and splashed some water on her face.

Stepping out of the bathroom, she swung by the mini-bar and snagged two bottles of water, tossing one onto the bed beside Jack, who looked absolutely, adorably wrecked. He'd pulled his underwear on, leaving the rest of his glorious body on display. Her eyes roved over his broad shoulders, his thick pecs, his arms that were roped with muscle, down to his abs. Next time, she wanted him on top, so she could see those abs in action as he moved inside her.

She let out a small whimper, and realized she was rubbing her thighs together.

Jack pushed a hand through his dishevelled hair, leaving it standing straight up in one spot, and then took the bottle of water with a grateful smile. He cracked it open and drained half of it in one go.

How was it possible for a man to be so charmingly adorable but also so...perfectly masculine, all at once?

"You know, I was a bit worried you might be down for the count when you ate it," she said, gesturing to the floor where he'd toppled over. He laughed without an ounce of embarrassment.

"Nah, it'd take more than that to keep me from you." He took another long pull on his water.

His eyes dragged over her, her nipples tingling in response. This was normally the part of a hook up where she kicked the guy out—politely, of course—but she wasn't going to kick Jack out.

She didn't want to dig into what that meant. Probably just some kind of residual oxytocin from the killer orgasm she'd had.

Pushing the thoughts away, she crossed the room and picked up Jack's discarded white T-shirt and tugged it on over her head. Oh God, it smelled good. She let the collar hang off of her nose for a second while she inhaled deeply, pulling his scent into her lungs.

She climbed onto the bed beside him, noticing that his eyes had gone molten when she'd put his shirt on.

It felt as though something tangled was sitting right in the center of her chest as they stared at each other, so she reached for her bottle of water and took a long sip.

"That was…" she started, then trailed off when she couldn't seem to find the right words.

He smirked, that dimple flashing. "Fucking incredible." She smiled, feeling lit up from within, and he reached for her, pulling her close. "Seriously," he said, tucking her against him and kissing the top of her head. "You were amazing. You kinda threw me with the bad girl stuff, but goddamn, that was fun."

"Yeah," she said, allowing herself the luxury of cuddling into him. "It was. Thanks for playing along."

"Yeah, you really twisted my arm," he said with a soft laugh, and she laid her head on his chest, sliding her arms around his waist. He was so warm and solid everywhere, all hard muscle, and smooth, hot skin. A sudden pang of sadness shot through her at the thought that after tonight, she'd never hold him like this again. Never feel his heart beating against her cheek, never smell the scent of his skin.

Oh my God, Rosalie. Get a fucking grip. This is what happens when you end a dry spell. Don't confuse hormones for actual feelings. You're smarter than that.

And she was. Rosalie didn't really date, but she enjoyed sex, which meant she'd had her share of hook ups and casual arrangements over the years. She didn't normally feel like this after sex, but she also didn't normally go so long without it.

Then again, most of the guys she'd hooked up with weren't nearly as hot as Jack, or as *big*.

"Are you sore?" he asked, as though he could read her mind. He trailed his fingers up and down her arm, leaving goosebumps in his wake.

"Only a little. Which is saying something for how wet I was, because you, my friend, are packing one seriously big dick."

And then Jack did something that threw her for a loop. A total upside down, heart flopping around helplessly in her chest loop.

He laughed, and he *blushed*.

It was endearing as hell. Adorable.

"Well, thank you. I'm glad you're not too sore."

"Is that an issue you've had in the past?" she asked, and he hesitated. She sat up, a playful smile curving her lips. "Don't tell me you were a virgin?" she teased. "I mean, I'm honored to be your first."

He laughed. "No. Most definitely not a virgin. I...don't usually talk about other women with..."

"Your current hook up?" she offered, since he seemed to be struggling with the language around what they were doing.

"Right." He frowned slightly. "And to answer your question, sometimes, yeah. It's been an issue."

"I'm not surprised. I mean, seriously, when you first pushed your pants down, I thought I was going to have to unhinge my jaw like a snake just to suck you."

He burst out laughing, the frown disappearing from his

gorgeous face, and in that moment, making him laugh when he'd seemed down felt like winning an award.

"There's an image," he said, pulling her against his chest again.

"So, do you date much, or...?" she asked. Oh God, why the hell had she asked that? It made it sound like she was fishing for something. It made it sound like what she'd said earlier, about not wanting promises or a boyfriend, was a bullshit line.

He cleared his throat softly. "No. Not really. I mostly just do...this."

"Hook ups and flings?"

"Yeah."

"Me too. I don't really date at all."

He tilted his head, looking down at her.

"Why not?" he asked.

She pursed her lips, then twisted them to the side, debating how much of herself she wanted to bare. She was normally a vault. Things went in—memories, experiences, emotions—and they did not come out again. But with Jack... there was a kindness to him, a warmth, that made her think *eh, what the hell?*

"Well...I just don't really believe in it. Love, happily ever afters, all of that. It's all just kind of..."

"Bullshit?" he offered, and she nodded.

"Yeah. My..." Her heart throbbed in her throat and she took a deep breath. "My dad was horrible to my mom. He took her for granted, cheated on her, and then eventually left, which almost destroyed her. He moved on, had a new family, did the same thing to them." She sighed, savoring the thump of Jack's heart against her cheek. "There's no such thing as happily ever after. People fall in and out of love all the time—love exists, but there's nothing lasting about it. And when it ends, the collateral damage it causes...it's better to just...not." She swallowed, her throat feeling thick and tight. "Besides, I travel a ton for work, so relationships just aren't in the cards," she added quickly, suddenly feeling vulnerable. "Which is fine."

"I'm sorry, Rosalie. You and your mom didn't deserve that," he said, his voice low and rough.

"What about you?" she said, very done with talking about herself. "Why don't you date?"

He hesitated, and then blew out a breath. "I...just don't really have time. Being the chief in a small town means I'm pretty much always on call, even when I'm technically not. It's consuming."

She nodded slowly. "I can see that." She frowned slightly, feeling a little off-kilter. She'd been expecting something more from his answer, and for some reason she had the feeling that he wasn't being completely forthcoming with her after she'd shared with him. But maybe that was just her own insecurity around letting people in making her feel weird and off-balance. "Did you always want to be a cop?" she asked, brushing the knot in her chest aside.

He laughed quietly. "Nah. When I was a kid, my big dream was to be a comic book artist."

"Aw, that's cute. So you liked drawing?"

He nodded. "My brother, Oliver, is the artistic one in the family—he paints and sculpts the most incredible things—but yeah, I liked drawing. Still do. I even keep a sketch book inside my cruiser. It's good stress relief."

"And what made you change your mind?"

He sighed. "Nine-eleven, honestly. I was fifteen when the towers went down, and I knew I needed to do something."

A silence fell over the room, and she snuggled into him, trying to pour comfort into him.

"Before that, I'd been feeling like maybe college wasn't for me. God, my mom cried and cried when I enlisted right after high school graduation."

"And your dad?"

"He was proud of me." She could tell what having his father's pride and approval at his heroic career choice meant to him.

"How long were you in?"

"Eight years."

"Wow. That's…a lot. You must've seen some shit."

He nodded slowly. "Two tours in Afghanistan, another two in Iraq. Definitely saw some shit. But I don't regret it."

"And when you were done, you came back here?" she asked, guiding them back to safer waters. She was realizing it was something she did a lot. Almost without thinking about it.

"Yeah. My family's here, the police department was hiring. It made sense."

"You're close with your family."

"I am. And I love it here. There's no where else I'd rather be."

"It's very pretty," she said, her eyes moving to the darkened window. Just then, a hard gust of wind rattled the window panes, shaking them in their frames.

"I'm really glad it snowed today," he said, weaving his fingers into her hair. Warmth blossomed across her chest as he tilted her face up for a kiss.

"Me too," she whispered just before his lips met hers, his kiss soft and gentle, but no less toe curling than any of the earlier ones. There was something about the perfection of Jack's mouth on hers that had her melting and unraveling, craving and needing. It felt like more than just a kiss.

"I don't even know your last name," he murmured against her mouth, tongue licking against her lower lip in a way that had her letting out a shuddering sigh.

"Crawford."

"Rosalie Crawford," he said, in a low, sweet voice just before kissing her again. She wound her arms around him, savoring the feel of being surrounded by him. After several minutes, the kiss gentled, and he kissed along her jaw, down her throat.

"I like you wearing my shirt," he said.

Butterflies exploded in her stomach, catching her completely off guard. She giggled. "Thanks. I like that it smells like you." She rolled her lips inward, as though that could stem the flow of things she shouldn't say.

"That's so hot," he growled, kissing her again. "I can't stop kissing you."

"Then don't. We've got all night, right?"

She'd meant it as a positive, but from the way he frowned and huffed out a breath, she had the distinct impression she'd said the wrong thing.

"Speaking of things we like..." he said, toying with her hair. "That lingerie you were wearing..." He blew out a low whistle. "Goddamn."

She smiled, her cheeks warming. "I have a thing for fancy lingerie." His eyebrow arched, and she nodded. "I have a whole collection."

"A whole collection I'll never get to see," he said, rolling her beneath him. "You're killing me here, Crawford."

A knot formed right in the center of her chest, a tangled snarl of emotion and lies she told herself and things she never let herself want. It sat there, cold and heavy, as Jack kissed her, slow and deep.

"Go easy on me, Shephard," she whispered. "I can't..." She shook her head, her eyes suddenly burning.

"I know. I know," he said softly, kissing her again. "It's okay."

Just then, her stomach rumbled loudly, reminding her that she'd never gotten around to eating dinner, and Jack pulled away with a quiet laugh.

"I got you," he said, sliding off of her. She tried to ignore the way she missed him already as soon as he left the bed, instead focusing on appreciating the hell out of his round, firm ass as he crossed the room to the mini bar. He opened it, emptied it, and returned to the bed, dropping everything in the middle. "Midnight snack buffet," he said, sweeping his hand over everything on the bed.

She laughed and then popped open the top of a mini can of Pringles, shoving two in her mouth at once. "Please," she said through a mouthful of crumbs. "Dig in."

He hesitated, surveying all the snacks. "It's..."

"What?"

"You're going to laugh at me."

"Maybe. Tell me anyway."

He laughed. "I don't really eat any of this stuff. I only have one cheat meal a week, and it's on Sundays with my family." He rubbed a hand over his abs, and she believed that Jack was not a man who ate junk food on the regular.

"How about if I guess which one of these is your favorite, you make an exception, just this once?"

His eyes sparkled, little lines fanning out around his eyes as he smiled. "Okay. Deal."

She surveyed the options in front of her, then tilted her head as she studied him, weighing the snacks against what she knew about Jack. She pushed all the salty snacks to one side.

"I'm going to go with sweet tooth," she said, tapping a finger against her lips. "And that's not just because I want all the chips for myself, which I do." She lined up the Snickers, Reese's Peanut Butter Cups, Skittles, and the little clear plastic boxes of candy with the logo of a local store on them. She looked up at Jack again, who was watching her with amusement, hands on his hips, and she pushed the chocolate bars aside. "I'm thinking candy over chocolate. Because when you eat sugar, you want the pure stuff. We're talking corn syrup and food dyes." She squinted and then picked up the box of gummy bears and handed it to him. He hesitated just for a second and then took it with a grin, dimple flashing, and popped it open.

"Did I get it right?" she asked excitedly. He tossed a couple in his mouth and nodded.

"Nailed it. These, or jelly beans are my weakness. My *only* weakness," he added, and they both laughed. "What's your favorite TV show?" he asked, picking up the remote and sitting down on the bed beside her, the mattress dipping slightly under his weight. "And I'm not talking the answer you say to impress people or look cool. I'm talking ultimate comfort watch, can quote every line show."

"Oh, that's easy. *Seinfeld.*"

"Shut up," he said in a perfect imitation of Elaine Benes. "That's mine, too."

"Really? Not what I would've guessed."

"What would you have guessed?" he asked, turning the TV on and navigating to Netflix.

"I don't know. Something grittier, like *Breaking Bad* or *Law and Order*."

"So she's good at guessing favorite candy, but terrible at guessing TV shows. Noted." He turned to look at her, and for a moment, their eyes caught and held. "Favorite episode?"

"'The Chinese Restaurant,' obviously. Yours?"

"It's a toss up between 'The Chicken Roaster,' and 'The Library,'" he said.

"Oooh, 'The Library' is a good one, too. Your call."

He grinned at her and then put "The Chinese Restaurant" on.

ELEVEN

Rosalie clutched her stomach, tears once again forming in her eyes. She couldn't remember the last time she'd belly laughed so many times in one night. She and Jack had spent the entire *Seinfeld* episode happily munching on treats—he'd even allowed himself a couple of jelly beans, the horror—and quoting lines at each other, both of them knowing the episode practically by heart. She'd polished off two mini cans of Pringles, along with the Skittles, and her stomach was no longer rumbling.

"Of course I'm not Cartwright!" they said in unison towards the end of the episode, both doubling over in laughter. "Seinfeld! Four!" After several seconds, their laughter died and their eyes met. Heat seemed to spark in the air, and Jack shoved the snacks onto the floor, hauling her into his lap so that she was straddling him.

It scared her, honestly, how right all of this felt. How easy and natural and effortless. It wasn't an awkward hook up. She wouldn't forget Jack's name a year from now. She wished they had more than just tonight.

Fucking terrifying.

Jack wove his hands through her hair, holding her close as he kissed her, his tongue sliding almost lazily against hers.

"Can I fuck you again?" he murmured against her lips. "Please?"

It was his last word that practically undid her, making a mess of her insides, and she nodded against him, the kiss growing hotter and needier. His hands slid under her shirt —*his* shirt—as the TV continued to play quietly in the background, and she wondered if he could feel the wild beat of her heart below her breast. His thumbs traced over her nipples, making her arch into him, making her bite at his lower lip. Slowly, completely unhurried, he lifted the shirt off over her head and then lowered his mouth to her breasts, licking and sucking. Rosalie moaned, her head falling back as she started to writhe against him, each pull of his mouth on her nipples shooting an arrow of pleasure right to her clit. She spread her legs wider, and his hand dipped between them.

"Christ, you're dripping," he said, a note of awe in his voice. And it was true. She was already wet and aching for him, wanting more.

"For you," she whispered, and she felt his cock jerk in his boxer briefs. His delicious, perfect cock. "Fuck me, Jack. Please. I need it. I need you," she moaned as he slowly spread open her pussy, tracing his fingers up and down all of her sensitive flesh.

"I love the way you say please like that," he said, his voice taking on that gruff tone that did funny things to her insides. He toyed with her clit as he leaned over the side of the bed, fishing another condom out of his pocket. "This is my last one," he said, and she didn't miss the note of regret in his voice.

"Then let's make it count," she said, kissing him as he slid two fingers against either side of her throbbing clit. She was so wet that she'd left a mark on his gray boxer briefs. She lifted her hips off of him just long enough for him to toss them aside, and they both moaned when she slid her ridiculously wet pussy against him, his skin hot against her.

He ripped open the condom and rolled it down his impressive length, but instead of pushing inside her like she'd been expecting, he kissed her again, palms sliding up and down her back, into her hair, down to her ass. Kissing her and kissing her until she was writhing in his lap. He chuckled and moved one of his hands between them again, petting and stroking her clit. He dropped his face to her neck, kissing and licking and sucking as he worked her with his fingers. She gasped and shook in his arms.

"So sweet and responsive," he murmured against her skin, fisting his cock and sliding it against her pussy, over and over, until they were both moaning. He teased his head through her slit, the wet sound filling the space between them. "And so fucking wet, my God."

"Jack," she moaned, lifting her hips and clinging to his shoulders.

"Sit on my cock, sweetheart," he said, his voice like sandpaper. "Take me deep."

Slowly, she sank down on him, savoring the burning stretch of his thick cock sliding inside her. Jack held her tight, his face a mask of ecstasy as she sank lower and lower, taking him inch by delicious inch. She kept moving until he was buried deep inside her, so deep she could feel him in her stomach.

And then his hands were in her hair again as he kissed her slow and deep, her pussy stretching around him. He flexed his hips upward, making them both groan.

"You're so hot and tight, Rosalie. How the fuck did I last before?"

She shook her head, words failing her. "You feel so good, Jack."

"God, what are you doing to me?" he asked, an almost dazed expression on his face.

Words failed her again, so she lifted her hips and rocked back down onto him. Jack groaned, and Rosalie gripped the headboard behind him, using it for leverage as she started to ride him.

"It's so fucking good," she said, her head thrown back, tension and heat already curling low in her belly.

"Damn right it is," he gritted out. "That's it, ride me, sweetheart. Fucking ride me."

She moaned at his filthy words, arousal and need spiraling through her, making her pussy spasm around him. He smacked her ass and then gripped her hips, urging her up and down. He pulled her up, looking down at his cock, which glistened in the low light. Glistened with her.

"Look at that," he said in a husky voice. "Fuck."

She sank back down onto him, and his fingers went to her clit, circling in firm, steady strokes, matching the rhythm of her hips. Heat and pleasure flared inside her, twisting her insides into something tight. Into something that was going to burst, and soon.

"I want to feel you come on my cock again," he said, and she nodded, her head thrown back as she rode him.

"I'm so damn full and your fingers...yeah, just like that." She gasped as he shoved his hips up, going deep, and Rosalie's arms started to shake, her control over her movements slipping as white hot pleasure flowed through her. Jack lowered his head and sucked one of her nipples into his mouth, biting at it.

"Goddamn, I wish I had more condoms," he said, sweat beading along his hairline. "I wish..." Just then she swiveled her hips, and his words died, melting into a groan. "Oh, God. Rosalie." He stroked her clit a little faster, but it was the broken way he said her name that had her tipping over the edge, her pussy clenching and fluttering around Jack's thick cock as she struggled to keep herself upright. She was nothing but a mass of pleasure, shaking in his lap as her orgasm rocked through her, stealing her breath, her thoughts. Everything. Narrowing her entire existence to this moment. To the feeling of Jack inside her, the scent of his skin, the sound of his deep groans and ragged breaths.

Rosalie managed to swivel her hips again, and she could tell the exact moment Jack lost it, his eyes heavy-lidded, his thrusts losing their finesse. He pumped up into her jaggedly twice more before falling back against the headboard, pulling Rosalie tight against his sweat slicked chest. She could feel the pulsing of his cock inside her, and she wished they had another condom, too.

He pressed his head to her shoulder, both of them gasping for air. Tears suddenly pricked at Rosalie's eyes, and she blinked frantically, trying to push them away.

What the hell was wrong with her?

Oxytocin overdose. That had to be it.

"You okay?" he asked, as though sensing something was up. When she didn't say anything for a second, he eased her back from him, slipping his fingers under her chin and forcing her to meet his eyes. Worry instantly flared in his. "Shit, Rosalie. Did I hurt you? Are you okay?"

"You didn't hurt me," she said, shame flooding her at the way her voice came out all wobbly and broken. "I'm fine. I... it was just an intense orgasm, I think. Really, I'm good. Better than good."

"Promise?" he asked, concern still etched on his handsome face.

"Promise."

She slid off of him, and he disappeared into the bathroom to dispose of the condom. He came back a minute later with more water, setting the bottles on the bedside table before pulling back the covers and gathering her into his arms.

Cuddling wasn't normally on the menu when Rosalie hooked up with someone, but with Jack...she wanted to. She really wanted to. So she let him gather her against him, snuggling into his solid warmth.

"Thanks, Jack."

"For what?" he asked, brushing a strand of hair out of her eyes.

"For the amazing, fun, mind-blowing sex. It's been a while for me, and I really needed this. And for being so cool."

He smiled softly at her, just a hint of that dimple showing. "Thanks for suggesting we do this in the first place." He stroked a hand up and down her back. "Are you tired?"

She stifled a yawn. "A little. But I...let's keep talking, okay?"

He nodded. "Okay." He grew quiet, his breaths slow and even as he smoothed a hand up and down her back, rubbing small circles between her shoulders.

"What are you thinking about?" she asked.

He hesitated, then said, "You."

She bit back a smile. "What about me?"

"The truth?"

"Of course. I always want the truth." And it was true. She did. Honesty was important to her. Maybe because she worked in an industry where people were often full of shit. Or maybe it was because of all the lies her father had told over the years.

"I was thinking that it kind of sucks you're going home tomorrow, because I'd like to do this again."

Fear trickled through her, but also something else. Something she didn't recognize and couldn't name. Fear, because she already liked him—a lot and that was danger-ous, unsafe territory for her. And the other thing, the warm, glowy thing, was probably from the great sex.

"It does kinda suck," she said when she realized she'd left his comment hanging too long. "But I'm glad we had tonight."

He nodded slowly, playing with a lock of her hair. "Yeah. At least we had tonight."

At five in the morning, Jack's watch buzzed softly on his wrist, and he carefully disentangled his arm from Rosalie, slipping out of the bed and tucking the covers around her. They'd talked for hours, finally drifting off to sleep a couple of hours ago. Despite his almost complete lack of sleep, he felt awake and alert. As though he knew how important it was to take in these last few moments with her.

Fuck.

When he'd decided to turn over a new leaf, feeling all heart-eyed over a woman he'd known for less than twenty-four hours hadn't been in the plans. But here he was, sated and relaxed with an ache in his chest, quietly gathering up his clothes. He slipped into the bathroom and quickly pulled on his clothes, trying to ignore the pit in his stomach. He didn't want to leave. He didn't want last night to be it. But he'd put out a feeler about seeing each other again, and she'd very clearly shut it down.

His stomach churned as he realized he'd probably just gotten a much-deserved taste of his own medicine. God, if he'd ever left women feeling the way he was right now, he was an asshole of colossal proportions. Huge.

Just more proof that one night hook ups weren't what he needed anymore. Hell, maybe they'd never been what he'd needed.

Dressed, he braced his hands on the counter and studied himself in the mirror. He was surprised to find he looked the same—dark circles under his eyes and in need of a shave, but otherwise unchanged—because he *felt* different. Something had changed in him last night. Maybe it was just a residual emotional hangover from learning about Norah's engagement.

No. That wasn't it, and he wasn't going to lie to himself. It was Rosalie. Not only had the sex been mind blowing, but he couldn't remember the last time he'd laughed so much. The last time he'd had so much *fun* with someone.

He wanted more.

He sighed and scrubbed a hand over his face. Rosalie had been upfront from the start, telling him she wanted to hook up, that she wasn't looking for promises or a boyfriend. Just some fun for the night. Despite the ache in his chest, he needed to respect that.

He blew out a breath and checked his watch. Shit, he needed to get home so he could grab a shower and shave because he was supposed to be on duty by six-thirty. Frankly, it was kind of amazing that his phone hadn't gone off last night, what with the bad weather. He pulled it out of his jeans pocket, and while the battery was almost dead, it was still on, and there were indeed no messages from dispatch.

Miracle of miracles.

He slipped his phone back in his pocket and stepped out of the bathroom, carefully and quietly pulling on his boots and shoving on his coat. He gingerly hung Rosalie's up, pausing to allow himself a brief inhale of her scarf. His stomach clenched, his chest tightening.

There was a soft rustling of sheets from behind him, and he turned, wondering if he'd woken her up. But Rosalie's eyes were still closed, her hair a mess on the pillow, one arm hanging off the side of the bed, her breathing slow and steady. God, she was beautiful. So fucking beautiful.

Before he could stop himself, he crossed the room and brushed her hair off her face, bending down to press a gentle kiss to her forehead. She stirred slightly, and he stood, backing away with his heart in his throat. Carefully, he tiptoed to the door and let himself out, making sure it was locked behind him.

He scrubbed a hand over his face again and then made himself walk down the hallway, his legs feeling heavy, like his boots were full of lead. Okay, maybe he *was* pretty freaking tired this morning. But damn, was it worth it. Snippets of their night together replayed through his mind, and he found himself grinning as he made his way down the stairs and into the lobby.

"Good morning, sunshine," came a familiar voice from the lounge, and he whirled. Well, fuck. Autumn stepped out of the shadows, a watering can in her hands, circles dark enough to rival Jack's under her eyes. He stopped, shoving his hands in his pockets. "Have a good night in room ten?"

Well, at least his town manwhore reputation would stay firmly in place as far as his family was concerned.

"Who says I was in room ten?" he said, pulling his beanie out of his pocket and shoving it on his head.

"Only room with a single woman," she answered easily. "Unless you were guest starring with one of the couples."

He chuckled. "My lips are sealed."

"She's interesting," said Autumn, setting the watering can down on the front desk and shuffling through some papers. "Rosalie, I mean. Did you know she works for Carrie Clark?" she asked, her tired eyes gleaming slightly.

"I do."

She laughed. "Right. You probably know all kinds of things about her now. As you should."

He did. He knew what her favorite TV show was, that she liked fancy lingerie, and that she was passionate about music. He knew she loved to travel, and that she was smart as hell. He knew what she sounded like when she came, how she tasted, how she felt.

They'd spent so much time talking after round two last night that he knew plenty about her. Like that she spoke conversational Spanish, loved yoga and Pilates, and that her favorite form of stress relief—other than sex—was video games. He knew she'd danced ballet as a kid, that she'd grown up in and around NYC, that she loved beer, and didn't know how to swim.

He knew her dad had left and broken her heart. He knew that she ran scared when it came to love and relationships because of it.

And still, it wasn't nearly enough. Fucking hell, but it wasn't.

Ignoring the pain shooting through his chest, he made a show of checking the weather through the front windows and then turned to Autumn. "You okay? Don't take this the wrong way, but you look tired."

For a second, she looked as though she was going to argue, but then her shoulders slumped. "I...I don't know if Hux is coming back."

Logan Huxley was a longtime family friend and the head chef at the hotel's restaurant. But back in the fall, he'd had some family stuff to take care of, and had been granted a leave of absence. Jack also suspected that Autumn had long been carrying a torch for the chef, who'd been best friends with their runaway brother, Finn, before he'd abandoned all of them.

"What do you mean?" asked Jack, stepping towards her. God, she looked so sad. So tired and distraught.

She bit her lip, worry slicing through Jack at how pale

Autumn looked, her normally pink cheeks a sallow gray. "You know about his dad, right?"

"I know he's some kind of biker asshole who lives on the other side of the country." Hux had spent a lot of time with the Shephards growing up because his own family hadn't been there for him, for a lot of complicated, heavy reasons.

She swallowed and nodded, shuffling through the same pile of papers again. "Yeah. Well, I guess his dad's in jail, and he might be going to prison. He owns a bar in Arizona, and he needs Hux to run it for him while all the legal stuff gets sorted out, otherwise his half-sister won't have any money, or something." She frowned, as though she wasn't fully buying Hux's story. "I don't know why he doesn't just tell his dad to...to..." Tears pooled in her eyes, and she wiped at them hastily. "I'm not crying for me. I'm crying for him. His family's always treated him like a burden, like an inconvenience. But the first sign of trouble and he's there for them, even though they were never there for him. Never." Her voice shook on the last syllable.

"Families are complicated," said Jack, trying to pull his little sister in for a hug, but she sidestepped him.

"No offense, but I don't want your sex hands on me."

He rolled his eyes. "I do wash my hands, you know."

She sighed, wrapping her arms around herself. "Sorry. I'm...tired."

"It's okay," he said. "I'm sorry that Hux might not be coming back for a while. That must be stressful. For the hotel," he added carefully. He didn't want to pry into Autumn's feelings for him. Clearly, there was something there, but until she made it his business, he was going to stay out of it.

She nodded, worrying her bottom lip between her teeth. "Yeah. It is. And I miss having him around. He's my friend, and I wish I could help him, you know?"

"You are helping," said Jack. "Keep talking to him. Be there for him. I'm sure he appreciates having someone safe to talk to about all of this."

She nodded again. "We were on the phone until like three in the morning."

"Maybe you should see if Adam can help out for a bit this afternoon so you can get some rest. I'm sure he wouldn't mind."

She tilted her head, considering. "Yeah, maybe."

He stepped forward and gave Autumn another hug. This time, she didn't resist. "You can't solve everyone else's problems, Autumn. Okay?"

"Yeah. Okay."

"I gotta go, I need to get ready for work. But I'll see you on Sunday, right?"

"Of course. Don't forget, you're on dessert duty. If you're taking requests, I'd kill for some cupcakes from You Little Tart," she said, referencing the local bakery.

"Noted." He pulled away, lifted his hand in a wave, and stepped out into the dark morning.

Rosalie stretched and rolled over in bed, sliding one hand across the rumpled sheets to find the other side of the bed empty and cold. Jack had told her that he had to leave early because he had to be at work by six-thirty, which was…she squinted at her watch. Which was over two hours ago. So, yeah. He was long gone. Which was fine. Ideal, even. No weird, awkward goodbyes to stumble through, no regrets. Just a perfect night, filled with amazing sex and great conversation with a super hot guy. She'd be greedy to ask for anything more. Greedy, and foolish.

She sat up in bed and stretched, her muscles a little sore. She checked her phone, knowing she needed to flip back into work mode, but there were no urgent texts or emails to claim her attention. So, she flung the sheets back and crossed to the window. A crystal blue sky greeted her, the sun shining brightly, not a cloud in sight. Fresh snow covered everything, the sun glinting off of it, making the world look bejeweled. Wrapping her arms around herself, she took several deep breaths. She knew she should get herself together, walk to where she'd left the car, and head back to the city.

And yet...she wanted to linger. Almost as though a part of her was clinging to the magic of last night.

She sighed and headed for the shower, feeling as though a tug of war was taking place inside her. On the one hand, she was relaxed and sated. Gloriously well-fucked. She'd had her share of one night stands, and last night with Jack had been the best. The absolute best. She felt grateful and happy that they'd met and had so much fun together.

She turned on the shower, running the brush through her hair and then twisting it up with an elastic she'd found in her purse as she waited for the water to warm up. On the other hand, she felt...sad. The sadness was an echo of what she'd felt last night, and the last thing she wanted to do was unpack it. Sadness was messy, and she knew if she prodded at it, it would be like trying to put toothpaste back in a tube. Once it was out, it was out, and you had to live with it. Better to leave it where it was. Safe and contained, and likely to fade as soon as she got back to normal life.

She tested the water and then stepped under the spray, the hot water glorious against her sore, tired muscles. Slowly, she lathered up the lavender-scented soap and washed away last night while memories of it flitted through her mind.

"God, he was so *hot*," she said out loud to herself, her stomach dipping and swirling as she remembered the feeling of Jack inside her, of his lips on her nipples, her clit, the way his muscles had flexed and bunched when she'd ridden him hard. She slipped the washcloth between her legs, gasping a little at the contact. She was sore and tender. But in the best possible way.

She worked the washcloth over her hips, noticing the tiny bruises emerging in a line, right where Jack had gripped her when he'd fucked her from behind. A smile pulled at her lips as she traced her fingers over them. A dirty little souvenir, just for her.

She finished washing and then lingered under the hot spray, letting last night replay again and again. And not just the filthy parts, although those were definitely on repeat in her brain, but all of it. The sound of Jack's laugh when he'd tripped over his jeans and practically face planted. The way he'd held her as she'd talked about her dad.

Oh, God. Blood rushed to her cheeks as she remembered the way she'd spilled her guts about her stupid family history. A lump formed in her throat as embarrassment rushed through her. Why had she told him that? She never talked about that shit, not with anyone. Now he was going to remember her as the chick with daddy issues.

Okay, it was definitely good that she was unlikely to see him again. Even if Carrie came back to shoot the video here, it would only be for a few days, tops. Even in a town this size, it had to be possible to avoid someone for three days. Right?

But then there was that weird tug in her chest again, because it wasn't true that she didn't want to see him again. Embarrassed as she was, she knew she'd jump at the chance to spend time with Jack. Which meant she already liked him too much.

"Girl," she said to herself, shaking her head as she turned the shower off. "You're a mess this morning."

She dried off, got dressed, and pulled her hair into a messy bun, giving herself a once over in the mirror before heading downstairs. She checked her phone again, noting a few emails she needed to deal with. Satisfied there was nothing urgent, she double checked that she had everything and then headed downstairs.

Autumn sat behind the front desk, and she smiled warmly at Rosalie. "How was your night?"

Rosalie was pretty sure she was imagining things, but she could've sworn there was a knowing glint in Autumn's eyes.

"It was great," she said, fishing in her bag for her wallet. "This place is amazing. Thank you so much for your hospitality." She paid for the room on her corporate Visa, tucking the receipt into her bag. "Thanks again," she said, turning towards the door.

"Wait!" said Autumn suddenly, casting aside the folder in her hand. "Do you want a ride to your car?"

"Oh," said Rosalie, stopping in her tracks. "Yeah, actually. That would be great." She was a little thrown by the offer, but happy to accept it all the same.

Autumn nodded, and then picked up the front desk phone. "Hey, it's me. I'm just going to give a guest a ride to her car. I'll be back in twenty minutes or so. Can I forward the phone to you?" She listened for a minute and then laughed. "Sure. Okay, thanks." She hung up, hit a few buttons on the phone, and then placed a "Staff will return shortly" sign on the front desk. "It's quiet today, so I don't think anyone will know I'm gone."

"Well, thank you for the ride. I appreciate it."

"I didn't think you'd want to trudge through the snow in

those boots," said Autumn, glancing down at Rosalie's feet. "Which are gorgeous, by the way."

"Oh, thank you. And you're right, I'm not exactly decked out for walking in the snow. I guess I should've planned better."

Autumn shrugged. "Sometimes the best things happen when things don't go to plan." Okay, she definitely knew *something* because that glint was back in her eyes again. "I hope your stay gave you the chance to fall in love with our little town. You know, really sell it to your boss."

Oh. Or maybe not. God, she was touchy this morning.

"Where is your car?" asked Autumn, pulling a set of keys out of her purse.

"City hall...um, Hemlock Square?"

Autumn nodded and stepped out from behind the desk. "No problem."

When they stepped outside, the air was fresh, clean and crisp, birds chirping happily from the snow-crusted branches. It felt like a completely different world than the one she'd experienced with Jack last night. When they'd walked from the pub to the hotel, it had felt like they'd been in their own personal snow globe, just the two of them, no one else in the world.

She followed Autumn to her car and got in the passenger's side. As soon as Autumn turned the car on, a Sabrina Carpenter song came on full blast. She quickly reached forward and turned down the music.

"Sorry. I guess I should be listening to Carrie Clark. Which I do. But this song makes me...think of someone," she said after a second, her cheeks going a little pink.

Rosalie smiled and shook her head. "This is a great song.

She actually opened for Carrie on her tour last year. She's really sweet." Rosalie reached forward and turned it back up, bopping her head in time with it. They let the song play, filling the air with lyrics about mixed signals and longing.

"It must be so interesting working in the music industry," said Autumn after a moment. "Do you like what you do?"

Rosalie nodded. "I...do," she said. "It's definitely interesting, and I love music in general." It was the most honest answer she could give without getting into details.

"It must be consuming, working for a big pop star like that," she said, coming to a stop at one of the few traffic lights in town.

"It can be, but I like to work. And I like the travel that comes with it." The hollowness she'd been feeling lately, though...not so much.

"Must make it hard to date, though," said Autumn, and something flickered in Rosalie's chest. It did make it hard to date, which was just fine with her.

Rosalie shrugged. "I'm sure running a hotel is like that, too," she said, deftly turning the subject away from herself. "You said that this song reminds you of someone?"

"Oh, you're good."

"Good?" Rosalie asked, eyebrows raised.

"You don't like to talk about your personal life." She pulled into the parking lot at Hemlock Square, right next to Rosalie's car, which was nothing but a lump of snow. She sighed. She didn't even know if there was a snow brush in the car. Great.

Autumn cut the ignition and stepped out of the car, then pulled a large brush out of her backseat.

"I'm just kind of a private person," Rosalie said, feeling

for some reason as though she owed the younger woman an explanation. Maybe because she'd been so nice to her that she didn't want to come off as prickly.

"I get that," she said, starting to slowly and thoroughly clean off Rosalie's car. "But there's being a private person and keeping stuff to yourself, and there's putting up walls to keep the world out. I don't know you very well, but I think you do the latter." She looked at Rosalie from across the car, an assessing, almost shrewd expression on her face. "And at first, the walls feel safe. Necessary. But eventually, if you're not careful, they start to feel like a prison."

Rosalie felt nailed to the spot, breath whooshing out of her lungs. Instantly, the urge to argue and deny rose up inside her, but she couldn't even get her mouth to form words. She'd never in her life been so casually and accurately assessed, especially by someone who barely knew her. Someone who happened to be the sister of the guy she'd spent the night hooking up with.

Autumn sighed, scraping at a bit of ice on Rosalie's windshield. "The guy that song reminds me of, that's what he does."

Ah. So this conversation was more projection than anything else. But still, Rosalie felt oddly exposed. Normally, Carrie was the only one who commented on Rosalie's lack of love life. She wasn't used to having strangers dissect her on a personal level.

"He...he's been through some stuff, and he's got walls. Thick ones," Autumn continued. "He doesn't let anyone get close because he doesn't want to get hurt, but all he's doing is hurting himself by..." She trailed off, swallowing thickly. "Sorry. I guess there's a lot on my mind this morning. I swear, I'm normally much more upbeat than this. And less rude. I'm...tired."

Rosalie's heart softened. There was an actual melting sensation in her chest, and she crossed in front of the car, taking the brush from Autumn. "Does this guy know you're hurting over this?"

Autumn shook her head, and it struck Rosalie how tired she looked. "No. He...I...no."

"Maybe he should."

"It's...complicated."

Rosalie studied Autumn, taking in the dark circles under her eyes, the worry etched across her pretty face, and she didn't know what to say. She wasn't an advice giver. But she also got the distinct impression that Autumn needed a friend.

"Listen, I don't know you, really, or this guy, but I think you have two options. Option one, you tell him how you feel. You wade into the mess, knowing it'll be messy and that you might get hurt, but at least you'll know the truth. Or, option two, you accept that it's not going to happen between the two of you, and you move on. You live your life, you lean on your friends, you stay busy, you date someone else."

"Option two sounds more like avoiding than moving on," said Autumn wryly, and Rosalie realized she was right. It was avoiding, because it was exactly what Rosalie would do if she was catching feelings for someone. "And trust me, I've tried to move on. It's been...a long time. And he's clueless, and I know it's unlikely to ever happen. I've dated other people, lived my life. Plus, he's one of my closest friends and I know if I say something, it'll make things weird, and more than anything he needs a friend right now." Rosalie brushed the last of the snow off the car and Autumn shot her a smile. "You probably think I'm a nut case."

"Not at all," said Rosalie quickly, wanting to reassure her. "I just wish I was better at giving advice."

"You're a good listener," said Autumn, tilting her head. "Thanks for letting me ramble about my problems."

"Of course," she said, grabbing her keys out of her purse. "Thanks for the ride, and the hospitality."

Autumn nodded, taking the snow brush back from Rosalie. "Of course. I hope we see you again." She hopped back in her car, slowly reversing and then turning out of the parking lot, driving off with a wave.

Rosalie unlocked her car and slipped inside, tossing her bag on the seat beside her. It felt like a lot longer than eighteen hours since she'd stepped out of the car and into the snow. Time could be so funny that way.

The engine purred to life, and once she'd punched Carrie's address into the GPS, intending to go straight to her place for the remainder of her working day, she pulled smoothly out onto the road, passing by the cute cafes and shops she'd never had the chance to visit. If they came back, maybe she'd have time to check them out.

Following the directions, she navigated her way out of town, passing by a large sign with a painted image of the falls proclaiming "Leaving Gossamer Falls – Come Back Soon!" Just then, the car shook strangely, making Rosalie grip the wheel tighter, her heart vaulting into her throat. A loud pop came from somewhere outside, and it suddenly felt as though the car was being jerked to the right.

"Oh, shit!" she said, easing her foot off of the gas pedal and doing her best to pull the car onto the shoulder. The car slid for a second, making her shriek. Finally, she came to a shuddering stop on the side of the road, her heart hammering in her ears. With a shaking hand, she cut the ignition, shuttering the car in silence.

Holy. Shit.

Pressing a hand to her chest, she took several deep breaths, trying to calm down her wildly beating heart, and then undid her seatbelt. Checking her mirrors before stepping out, she pushed open the door and circled around to the back of the car.

"Fuck," she said in an agonized tone when she saw that the rear passenger's side tire was completely flat. "Fuck, fuck, fuck." She paced anxiously back and forth in front of it, chewing on her bottom lip. She had absolutely no idea what to do. None. Did the car have a spare? No idea, and even if it did, she wouldn't have the first clue how to change it. She'd never owned a car in her life. She'd grown up in and around NYC, and hadn't even gotten her driver's license until she was in her early twenties.

She huffed out a frustrated sigh and got back in the car, fishing her phone out of her purse and hitting Trevor's name on her contacts list.

"Hey," he answered on the first ring. "You're not back yet."

"No, didn't you see my email? I got snowed in. I'm on my way back right now, but I've got a flat tire. What am I supposed to do?"

"Don't you know how to change a tire?" he asked, but she could hear the teasing lilt in his voice.

"No, I don't. It's one of the many ways my father failed

me," she deadpanned. Trevor and Carrie were the only people who knew about her messy family history.

And Jack. Jack knew too, now.

Trevor laughed. "Um. Huh. Let me see if we have triple A or something." She heard the gentle click of a keyboard in the background. "Also, Google says to stay in your car. Does that car even have a spare?"

"I don't know!" said Rosalie, leaning across the car and flipping open the glovebox. The driver's manual fell out and onto the floor, sliding under the seat. "Oh, for fuck's sake."

"So, from what I can see, no triple A, but there's a Nissan roadside assistance number you can call. It should be in the manual."

Rosalie laughed. "Can you please just look it up for me?"

"What am I, your slave?" He made an outraged tsk, but she heard the sound of more typing in the background. "Okay, ready?"

Just then, she caught a flash of something in her rearview mirror. A police SUV had just pulled in behind her, and her heart crashed against her ribs as her stomach swirled.

Calm down. It's probably not him.

Then again, he has a staff of four. It might be.

Oh God, do I even want it to be him?

Yes. I do.

"Hang on," she said, flipping down the sun visor and checking her appearance in the mirror because she was utterly ridiculous. "A cop just pulled up behind me. I'll call you back."

"I'm not bailing you out again," he said, laughing. "Be good."

Oh, if Trevor only knew.

Rosalie disconnected the call, her eyes still glued to her rearview mirror. Butterflies exploded through her entire body when Jack stepped out of the SUV, looking absolutely delicious in his uniform. A huge grin spread across her face, and before she could stop herself, she pushed open her door and stepped out.

It was utterly adorable the way his steps faltered when he saw her. "Rosalie?"

"Hey," she said, raising her hand in a little wave. Her legs practically vibrated with the urge to run and fling herself at Jack.

A smile spread across his face as he walked toward her with increasingly quick steps. "What...are you okay?" He pulled his aviator sunglasses off, blue eyes bouncing between her and her car.

She grimaced, gesturing at the car with a wave of her hand. "Flat tire."

He nodded, not taking his eyes off of her, smile still in place. Granted, she couldn't stop staring at him either, drinking in every single detail of his uniform, from the gold badge that proclaimed him the chief of police, to the bullet-proof vest laden with gear visible under his navy blue winter coat, to the way his round, muscular ass filled out his uniform pants nicely. Very nicely.

He unclipped the radio attached to his shoulder and spoke into it. "Hey Cheryl, it's Jack. I'm going to be off with a disabled vehicle on Foundry Bridge Road, about a mile south of the train station. Should be twenty, maybe thirty minutes."

The radio beeped. "Copy that, Chief. Radio in when you're clear." He blinked several times, staring at Rosalie as he stuck the radio back on his shoulder, and then nodded again. He slipped his sunglasses into a pocket on the front of his vest, and then clapped his hands together. "Let's see what we're working with here."

God, she couldn't stop staring at him. Couldn't stop staring and smiling. Couldn't stop the giddy rush rising up inside her at the sight of him again.

Danger signs flashed through her mind, alarm bells blaring, but for once, she didn't care. She wanted to curl around him like a cat, to stick to him like Velcro. Her mouth was dry, her muscles shaky, and for a second, she couldn't pinpoint why. But then it hit her, socking into her like a punch.

She was *relieved*.

He crouched down and examined the flat. "You got a spare?"

She grimaced again and shrugged. "I don't know."

She waited for him to judge her, but he just nodded again, a neutral expression on his face. "Pop the trunk, let's take a look."

She pulled the keys out of her pocket and pressed the button to unlock the trunk. He peered inside, giving her another chance to thoroughly ogle him, before she heard a soft click.

"Aha! Success." He lifted the trunk's floor panel up and pulled out a spare tire, a jack, and a wrench.

"Is it…" She lost her train of thoughts for a minute as she

watched him haul everything around to the side of the car. "Can I drive back to the city on that?"

He nodded. "You should be fine. This isn't just a donut, you've got a full spare. But you'll want to take it to a tire shop and get it looked at right away."

"I'll let Trevor know."

"Trevor?" he asked, and something inside her thrilled at the almost indiscernible—but still very much present—note of jealousy in his voice.

"The business manager."

"Right." He leaned the spare tire against the side of the car. "Can you put your hazards on? And the parking brake?"

"Oh. Right. Yes, I can do that."

As she hurried inside the car to do as he'd asked, her happiness warred with confusion, and was tinged with disappointment. He seemed happy to see her, but...she'd expected him to be flirtier. Then again, he was working. He was being professional. And she wasn't exactly being flirty either.

And just because they'd spent the night together didn't mean anything. She knew that. Hell, it was what she'd *wanted*. A meaningless hook up with a hot guy.

But it hadn't been meaningless, had it? And seeing Jack again was bringing that point home, as much as she didn't want to admit it.

Regret crashed into her as she remembered the way he'd subtly suggested seeing each other again, and she'd squashed it because she was scared. Maybe that was the cause of the hint of distance she was picking up on?

God, she was bad at this. All of it.

Jack retreated to his SUV, coming back a moment later

with traffic pylons, which he set up around her car, and some wedges he placed in front of the car's front tires. Shrugging out of his bulky coat, he tossed it on top of the roof of her car, and then got to work removing the hubcap.

"So…" she said, standing awkwardly to the side, feeling both utterly useless and grateful for his help. She shuffled a little closer to where Jack was working, gravel from the shoulder skittering beneath her boots. "You just happened to be driving by?" She didn't doubt it, she just couldn't quite believe her luck. Then again, Gossamer Falls was a small town. People were bound to cross paths.

"Yeah. Just doing my regular patrol route."

"Lucky me."

He chuckled and glanced up at her. "That's what I was going to say."

"Oh?"

He picked up the wrench and started working on loosening the nuts. His muscles strained visibly beneath his shirt as he put all of his weight on the wrench. "Christ, that's tight," he said, and heat pooled low in her belly at his words. His eyes snapped to hers, and she bit her lip because she knew they were both remembering the night before. He cleared his throat and returned his attention to the tire, working on loosening the nuts. Once he was satisfied, he slipped the jack under the car, cranking it until the flat tire was a good six inches off the ground.

"You seem like you've done this before," she said, partly because the silence was getting to her, and mostly because a sense of panic was starting to envelop her. She needed to say something, do something. She was happy to see him again, she wanted to see him a second time…and yet she couldn't find the words. Every time she opened her mouth to flirt or suggest something, the words turned to ash on her tongue, dissolving into nothing before they could materialize.

Because she was scared, but it wasn't a visceral, terror-inducing kind of fear. No, it was the kind that she'd lived with for so long, simmering just below the surface of her subconscious, that she didn't even realize it was there most of the time.

Jack unscrewed the lug nuts by hand, dropping them one by one into the hubcap he'd laid on the ground. "A few times, yeah."

"You said 'lucky me,'" she blurted, twisting her fingers together. She blew out a breath, tucked her hands in her pockets. The fidgeting wasn't helping. "What...I mean, I know what I meant, but did you..." She cringed inwardly at how awkward and insecure she sounded. Not at all like the confident "bad girl" she'd been last night.

He pulled the flat tire off easily, setting it down on its side. He shrugged, slowly mounting the spare tire on the lug bolts. "I meant, I didn't think I was going to run into you again. Sucks you've got a flat, but I can't say I'm not happy to see you again."

Everything inside her lit up, and she felt as though she were floating.

Jack set to work tightening bolts by hand, his thick fingers twisting them with quick, efficient movements. She found herself clenching her thighs. Why was watching Jack change a tire—in uniform—so hot?

"I can't say that, either," she admitted, her cheeks burning. She didn't even recognize herself right now. She wasn't a woman who got blushy and shy and awkward around men. The opposite, really.

What was Jack Shephard doing to her?

He grinned as he lowered the car a bit, then tightened the lug nuts with the wrench. He gave a satisfied nod, and then lowered the car completely, tightening the nuts even more.

"What *can* you say, Rosalie? You're not giving me much to go on here." He didn't look at her as he fitted the hubcap back on.

She sucked in a breath at his words, even though she knew he was right. She wasn't giving him anything.

"I had an amazing time with you last night and I'm glad we ran into each other again because I didn't like that we didn't even get to say goodbye," she said all in one go, shoving the words out of her mouth before they could die on her tongue. Fear curled through her as soon as they were out.

"Well, well, well." A cocky grin pulled at his lips. "And here I thought I was just another notch on your bedpost," he teased, and she bit her lip, blushing furiously.

He rose to his full height, brushing his hands off on his pants, and then moved closer, so close that she backed into the side of the car. She couldn't stop staring at his mouth, his face, his throat.

"Never just a notch," she said, her voice catching in her throat. Her pulse thrummed wildly as his gaze dropped to her mouth. He swallowed and then gave a tiny nod, as though he'd just decided something. Reaching into the front pocket of his vest, he pulled out a card.

"If you come back for that video shoot, give me a call.

Hell, even if you don't come back for the video shoot, give me a call anyway. The city's not that far."

She reached between them and took the card from him, running the tips of her fingers over the embossed letters that read "Chief Jack Shephard, Gossamer Falls Police," with his phone number and work email address below it.

"I know you're not looking for anything serious. I'm not either. But I'd be lying if I said I didn't want a repeat of last night. And I want you to text me when you get back to the city, otherwise I'm gonna worry."

"You'd be worried about me?" she asked quietly, running her fingers over the card again and then tucking it into her pocket. As she did, her fingers brushed against another piece of paper. Her fortune from last night. She'd almost thrown it away, but had slipped it into her pocket instead.

"Yeah, Rosalie. I would." His blue eyes dropped to her mouth again, and she shivered, but not from the chilly air.

Her throat tightened, a lump of emotion sitting right in the middle of it. No one ever worried about Rosalie. Her entire life, she'd been the one looking after others. It felt... nice, to know that someone cared enough about her to worry.

Jack swallowed thickly and started to lower his face to hers. Her toes curled in her boots in anticipation, but just then, the radio on his shoulder crackled to life again.

"Chief, are you still off with that disabled vehicle?" came a male voice on the other end. "I just picked up the Miller kid for shoplifting over at the gas station."

Jack sighed. Reaching behind her, he grabbed his coat off of the roof of the car and shrugged it on. Then he unclipped the radio. "Copy that, on my way."

"Duty calls," she said with a small smile.

"Yeah. I need to go. But seriously. Text me to let me know you got back safe, okay?"

She nodded. "I will."

"Good." And then his mouth was on hers, his lips warm and firm, the gentle slide of his tongue against hers making her sigh. Something inside her settled, and she looped her arms around his neck, kissing him back with slow sweeps of her tongue into his mouth. He tasted like mint and something sweet. Fruit, maybe.

He broke the kiss far sooner than she would've liked, his nose brushing against hers. "I'll see you, Rosalie." He gave her hip a squeeze.

"I'll see you, Jack."

She hopped back into her car and pulled out onto the road, putting Gossamer Falls in her rearview.

FOURTEEN

"Oh my God, she's alive," said Trevor as Rosalie stepped into Carrie's Tribecca penthouse about three hours later. She'd stopped by her apartment first to change and freshen up, and then headed over to Carrie's to get caught up on work.

"She is, although the car you gave me tried to kill me."

"Oh please, you probably drove over a nail or something. Don't be so dramatic," said Trevor, which was hilarious, because he was, without a doubt, the most dramatic person Rosalie knew.

She tossed him the keys. "The spare's still on there. Jack said that it needs to be checked out."

Trevor's perfectly groomed eyebrow climbed up his forehead so slowly it was almost comical. "Who's Jack?"

Her mind flashed back to their brief text exchange earlier.

ROSALIE:

Hey Jack, it's Rosalie. Back in the city, safe and sound.

JACK:

Sorry, who is this?

JACK:

Kidding.

ROSALIE:

Ha ha. He's got jokes

JACK:

How was the drive?

ROSALIE:

Smooth sailing, after the tire incident.

ROSALIE:

Well, until it fell off.

JACK:

Ha ha. She's got jokes

ROSALIE:

Just you wait, Shephard. I might knock your socks off

JACK:

Already did, Crawford

JACK:

Gotta get back to work, but let me know about the video shoot

ROSALIE:

I will.

Rosalie blushed, and shook her head, taking her time

hanging up her coat. "The chief of police who changed my tire."

"The chief of police changed your flat tire? Wow, they must really be desperate for Carrie to film the music video there."

She turned, rolling up the sleeves of her cashmere sweater. "I mean, yeah, they really want us to come. It wasn't desperate, more…eager. Very eager." The sound of tinkling piano keys reached her ears. "She's in the music room?"

Trevor's expression morphed, his lips forming a small O. "Oh, shit. You don't know yet."

"What?"

"Jordan broke up with her."

"Ah, shit."

Carrie had been dating NHL hockey player Jordan Newhouse for several months, and had fallen hard for him. Rosalie had always had a sinking feeling that this was where things were headed, given Jordan's obvious discomfort with Carrie's level of fame.

Rosalie headed into the kitchen, which was large and immaculate, with skylights in the slanted ceiling letting the sunshine pool on the floor. Despite its size, Carrie's penthouse was cozy and welcoming, with a lived in, unfussy quality to it that Rosalie had always found welcoming.

Quickly, she made two cups of tea and piled a plate high with cookies before heading into the conservatory. She knocked briefly before sticking her head through the door, which was slightly ajar.

"Carrie?"

The piano stopped, and she took in her boss and friend's

form, sitting slumped at the piano, wearing an oversized sweatshirt and a pair of black leggings, her blond hair in a messy ponytail.

She glanced over her shoulder, the sweatshirt slipping down. "Hey," she said, her famous voice raw and ragged.

"Trev told me about Jordan. I'm sorry." She crossed the room and set the plate of cookies on the Steinway, extending one of the mugs to her. Carrie took it with a small smile that didn't reach her gray eyes.

"Thanks." She blew steam away from the rim of the mug and then took a careful sip, wincing at how hot the tea was. Her eyes were rimmed in red, her face free of makeup.

"You doing okay?" asked Rosalie, grimacing internally at the asinine question. Of course, Carrie wasn't okay.

"I...I feel stupid. Like I should've seen it coming." She took another sip, winced again. "Isn't it wild that we can be with someone for months and have no clue as to their true feelings? And yet, knowing what I do now...it doesn't change how I felt. My feelings were still real, which makes all of this suck so much more." She picked up a cookie and bit half of it off. She shook her head and let out a bitter laugh, crumbs spilling from her mouth. "He was more worried that I was going to write songs about him than any pain he might've caused me." She cleared her throat and put on an exaggerated male voice. "Uh, you're not gonna write about me, right babe?" She laughed again. "Of course I'm going to fucking write about you! Hello, have you *met* me? It's kinda my thing." Carrie was known for her confessional songs, giving fans a peek into the ups and downs of her life. She displayed a kind of vulnerability that Rosalie couldn't even wrap her head around.

"I'm sorry. Maybe a puck will hit him in the face and knock his teeth out," said Rosalie with a little smile, and Carrie laughed again.

"You know what they say about karma." She sighed, shaking her head. "Anyway. The good thing is that it's making me want to write some new stuff for the first time in a while. Process my emotions, try to heal. I know the record company's been wanting to know when I might have the next album ready. So, maybe it'll be later this year."

Songwriting had always been cathartic for Carrie, and it was thrilling for Rosalie to have a front row seat to Carrie's process. Yeah, she was a pop princess, but she was also a gifted songwriter who had a knack for capturing her emotions in a way that was both memorable and relatable.

"They'll be happy to hear that," said Rosalie, taking her tea and sitting down on the cream-colored sofa across from the piano. "For now, we want to release a statement before Jordan's team does so that we can get ahead of whatever narrative he wants to spin. When you're ready, we'll do a bigger story with *People*."

Carrie nodded and turned back to the piano, picking out a melancholy progression of chords, her long, slender fingers moving effortlessly over the keys.

Rosalie pulled her phone out of her pocket and started drafting an official PR statement.

Carrie Clark and Jordan Newhouse have decided to end their relationship. Carrie thanks her fans for their love and understanding during this difficult time, and as always, for respecting her privacy. She wishes Jordan

*the best and will be focusing on her music as she
moves forward.*

As Rosalie distributed the statement to all of the standard outlets, answered emails, and took phone calls, Carrie continued to plunk away at the piano, sipping at her tea and eating cookies.

"Oh, by the way," she said after about half an hour of quiet companionship, swiveling on the piano bench to face Rosalie. "Those pictures and videos you sent of the town and the waterfall? It's perfect. I think we should shoot the music video there. Do you think we'll have any logistical issues?"

Excitement soared through Rosalie, and she did her best to school her features into a neutral expression. "No, not at all. They're very keen to have us come. I'll connect with the production company and the label and get things in motion."

"I was reading more about it. The legend and everything." She wiggled her eyebrows, her mood clearly improving. "It says that if you're kissed by the mist of the falls under the light of the full moon, your true love will be revealed to you before the next full moon." She sighed. "I mean, it doesn't get much more romantic than that, does it?" She tilted her head, studying Rosalie. "What is this?" she said, swooping her index finger in a circle.

"What?"

"This blushy, dreamy look on your face."

"I don't have a blushy, dreamy look."

"You definitely do," said Trevor, stepping into the room, laptop under one arm. Trevor sat down on the sofa beside her, crossing one leg over the other and then resting his chin on his closed fist. "Rosalie...who is Jack?"

"Jack? Who's Jack?" asked Carrie, looking interested as she picked up her discarded mug and curled her fingers around it.

"I told you, he's the chief of police in Gossamer Falls."

"Uh huh," said Trevor, batting his eyelashes at her. "And what else?"

Rosalie swallowed thickly. She wasn't going to get into details about her steamy hook up with Jack. Sharing wasn't her style, and she especially wasn't going to while Carrie was nursing a broken heart.

"Nothing else," she said, but even to her own ears, her voice didn't sound convincing. Not at all.

"Bullshit," said Trevor affectionately.

"Did you bang a hot cop?" asked Carrie, turning back to the piano and playing the opening chords of "Careless Whisper."

"I..." Carrie stopped playing and she and Trevor looked at her with amused expectation. "Did. Yes. I banged the hell out of him."

Trevor held his fist out for a fist bump. "That's my girl. Now, tell me everything and I won't punish you for holding out on me."

At the mention of the word punish, her night with Jack started playing through her brain like a movie. A very dirty, very sexy movie.

"We don't..." She said, shaking her head, cutting her eyes in Carrie's direction.

"Oh, please," she said. "I'm fine. Or, I will be. If there's one thing I know how to do, it's heal from shit. Don't deprive us of good gossip on my account."

"There's no gossip," said Rosalie, feeling self-conscious.

"I was stuck there for the night, we met at this cute little pub in town, we went back to my hotel and had a one night stand."

"And then he changed your flat tire this morning," added Trevor, eyebrows wiggling.

"He did." Rosalie took a sip of her tea. "I'd just gotten the flat and he happened to be on his patrol route."

"Is it still a meet cute if you've already banged?" asked Carrie, a mischievous grin pulling at her full lips.

Rosalie laughed, and so did Trevor.

"Are you going to see him again?" Carrie peered at Rosalie over the rim of her mug. "When we go back for the video shoot?"

Rosalie bit her lip, grinning down into her tea. "Maybe, yeah. He gave me his number after the flat tire thing, and he made it clear he wants to hang out again."

"Hang out," said Trevor, making exaggerated air quotes. "Meaning hook up."

"Netflix and chill," added Carrie.

"Pretty much," said Rosalie. "And...I think I'll take him up on it."

Carrie blinked slowly as she studied Rosalie. "Oh. Oh! You like this one!"

"Of course I like him. I don't bang guys I dislike."

"That's not what I mean. I mean like like."

"Playground crush like," added Trevor.

Rosalie felt heat flood her cheeks, and she stood, pacing to the floor to ceiling windows that looked out over the city. Everything was so cold and gray here compared to Gossamer Falls, with its cute shops, snow covered roofs, and beautiful waterfall. But here, there was no color. Just an endless sea of gray sky and gray buildings and gray streets filled with too many people.

She'd never felt like that while looking out at the city before. Huh.

"Do you like him?" asked Carrie softly. "I know you don't really do relationships, but maybe…"

Rosalie turned. "Maybe what?"

"Maybe it's time to rethink some of those long-held beliefs. I know you think they're protecting you, and maybe they are. But what if all they're doing is keeping good stuff out?"

Rosalie swallowed thickly, her legs suddenly heavy. She glanced back out the window, eyes roving over the city. She'd felt unmoored ever since getting back into town. Lost and adrift without a compass. Which was completely disorienting because she'd lived here her entire life.

"I think that's a lot easier said than done," she said after a moment, and Carrie laughed softly.

"No kidding. But nothing that's worth doing comes easy. The hard stuff is the good stuff."

"Amen," said Trevor, and they all laughed.

"I mean, he's not looking for anything serious either," said Rosalie, moving away from the chill of the window and back toward the couch. "So it's not like anything with Jack could go anywhere."

"Why isn't he?" asked Trevor.

"I don't know. I got the sense that there was something there, something heavy, but he didn't share and I didn't pry."

Carrie shrugged. "So…see him again when we go back for the video shoot and see where it goes, no labels, no expectations. Because you're clearly into him, so I think you owe yourself at least that much."

A thrill coursed through her at the thought of seeing Jack again, and she pulled out her phone, scrolling through their text messages again.

"Have you been texting him? Already?" Trevor asked, neck craned as he tried to read the texts.

"Yes, and honestly, I don't know why you're so interested in my love life."

"Because you don't have one, honey," said Trevor, but his tone was kind. "And I have never seen you blushing and excited over a guy. That means something."

"He just asked me to text him when I got back to the city to let him know I'd made it safe and sound. That's all." Trevor and Carrie exchanged a knowing look, and Rosalie darkened her phone screen. "What?"

"That is not one night stand behaviour," said Trevor, and Carrie nodded in agreement.

"Definitely not."

Rosalie's stomach dipped and swooped, and she felt like she was a high school girl who'd just found out the star quarterback liked her back. It was a giddy rush of excitement and nerves, tinged with a hint of disbelief.

"When is the next full moon?" asked Carrie suddenly.

"Um..." Rosalie looked it up on her phone. "In about three weeks."

"I want to film the video with the full moon in the background. I don't want a CGI moon like I know the production company's going to suggest. I want the real thing."

Rosalie grabbed her notebook and started jotting what Carrie was saying down.

"I want to showcase the legend of the falls, really use the scenery. Three weeks is perfect. We can get through pre-production and have everything ready to go." She turned her assessing gaze on Rosalie. "And that gives you three weeks to figure out how you feel about this guy."

FIFTEEN

Sunday night dinners at the Shephard house were a tradition, and one that Jack looked forward to. Unlike some people, he genuinely enjoyed spending time with his family, and considered himself lucky to have such a loving, close one. Sure, they had their differences and argued sometimes, but they always sorted it out. They'd always been a close bunch, and had grown even more so after their father, John Shephard, had passed away unexpectedly from a heart attack a couple of years ago.

"Are you excited?" Jack asked, glancing into the rearview mirror of his truck to where Chloe was sitting in the backseat, Nintendo Switch in her hands. She didn't look up.

"About what?" she asked after several seconds, frowning at the screen.

"Carrie Clark coming to town," he said, his own stomach giving a little jolt as he said the words. Rosalie had texted him yesterday to let him know that the music video shoot was a go, and they'd be back in a few weeks to film under the next full moon.

Jack had never been so excited for a full moon in his entire life.

"Oh," said Chloe, tongue pressed to the corner of her mouth as she jammed at the buttons. "Dammit!"

"Hey, hey, language," he said, frowning.

"Whatever."

"No, not whatever." He pulled up to the curb in front of his mom's house and put the truck in park. "I don't care what your friends are allowed to say, but I don't want to hear swear words coming out of your mouth."

"Dammit isn't a swear word. They say it on TV, and on the radio."

"It is in my book."

"Just because you're the chief of police doesn't mean you get to decide what's a swear word or not."

Jack reached into the back seat and gently took the Nintendo Switch out of her hands. "Chloe. What's going on with you?" She was a typical tween with her sullen, testy moments, but it wasn't like her to be openly rude.

She crossed her arms over her chest, looking out the window. "Nothing."

"Doesn't seem like nothing."

"I already talked to Mom, so it doesn't matter." Her chin quivered. "And you're a guy, so I can't..." The chin quiver got stronger.

Norah hadn't mentioned anything to him about any issues with Chloe, but maybe she hadn't realized that whatever it was was bothering her this much.

"I'm not a *guy*, I'm your dad. You can tell me anything, Chloe."

She huffed out a breath, eyes still trained out the

window. "Brayden Lewis called me sasquatch in gym class because of my hairy legs, and everyone laughed."

Oh, that little shit. Jack's gut clenched and he swallowed, hard, tempering his papa bear emotions.

"So I asked Mom if I could start shaving my legs, and she said I was too young. But I'm not!" Chloe insisted, whirling around to face Jack. Her cheeks were pink, her eyes bright with tears. "If I look like a sasquatch, I'm not!"

Jack sighed. Chloe was almost twelve. Her chest wasn't flat anymore, and she'd started getting the occasional pimple. God, how had she grown up so freaking fast?

He nodded slowly. "First of all, I'm sorry that happened to you. It sucks to feel like everyone's laughing at you, but—and I know this is small comfort—it'll pass. Second, I'll talk to your Mom and see what she says, okay? I'm not the expert, but maybe you're not too young."

She nodded, inhaling a shaky breath. "Okay. Thanks, Dad."

"And one more thing." Her eyes flicked to his. "Brayden Lewis is a goober. He's probably only picking on you so no one picks on him first. Middle school is a jungle. But it gets better."

The hint of a smile pulled at Chloe's lips, and it was the best part of Jack's day.

"He is a goober," she agreed.

"But don't call him that at school," said Jack, undoing his seatbelt. "Grab that box of cupcakes, would you?" Chloe nodded and undid her own, grabbing the box of mint chocolate cupcakes from You Little Tart. Jack studied her as they walked up the path to the house's front porch, which was neatly shoveled thanks to Beckett. She'd grown again, getting taller and taller, all gangly arms and awkward legs. Her hair was a dark blond, the same shade as his, and she had Norah's big brown eyes and freckles. His nose, her mouth. His stubbornness, her love of books and learning.

"I am excited," she said as they stepped into his mother's house, picking up their conversation from earlier. The smell of pot roast and garlic potatoes filled the air, and something inside Jack settled as they shrugged off their coats. This was the house he'd grown up in, where his mother and his sister Autumn still lived. It was home, in the purest, truest sense of the word. Home as a place, but also home as a feeling of safety and belonging. "Do you think I'll get to meet her?" she asked, toeing off her boots and placing them on the rack by the front door.

"I don't know, kiddo," he said. He hoped he'd be able to arrange something, maybe with Rosalie's help, but he didn't want to make any promises. "We'll see."

She nodded, and then took off into the house. "Aunt Autumn! Did you hear about Carrie Clark?"

Jack chuckled and took off his boots. The news that Carrie Clark was coming to Gossamer Falls to film her new music video had burst across the town that morning, and everyone was buzzing about it. In just a couple of short weeks, the mega superstar would be here.

Which meant Rosalie would be here. A small smile pulled at his lips as his blood heated. In the few days since she'd gone back to the city, he hadn't stopped thinking about her. Hell, he hadn't even tried to stop thinking about her because he didn't want to. He liked thinking about her. How pretty she was, how good she smelled. How amazing she'd felt pressed against him, all soft and warm. How much he'd laughed with her. How the hours he'd spent talking with her had felt like minutes.

He pulled his phone out of his back pocket and opened up their last string of text messages.

ROSALIE:

I have good news! We're coming to town to film the music video! Please don't say anything yet, though. We'll do an official announcement in a day or two when we've got all of our ducks in a row.

JACK:

So that means I get to see you again?

ROSALIE:

If you want, yes

JACK:

I very much want to see you again

ROSALIE:

Me too <3

ROSALIE:

I keep thinking about how much fun we had

JACK:

Meh, it was okay I guess

ROSALIE:

Ass

JACK:

Still can't take it I see. We'll have to work on that

ROSALIE:

Please. I can take anything you give me

JACK:

Challenge accepted

ROSALIE:

One request though

JACK:

Anything

ROSALIE:

Can we use real handcuffs next time?

JACK:

Only if you bring your sexiest lingerie

ROSALIE:

Deal

Jack grinned to himself and tucked the phone back in his pocket, his heart thrumming in his chest. He was counting down the seconds until he could see her again. And hell, that had to be progress, right? They'd hooked up and he wanted to see her again. Was excited to see her again. That had to count as growth of some kind.

He passed the living room on his right, a fire crackling merrily in the stone fireplace against the far wall. On the mantel above, there were several framed family photos, including one taken about a year before his dad had died. Stepping closer and letting the fire warm him, he picked it up off the mantel, examining it. His parents stood in the middle, arms looped around each other's waists, while Adam, Oliver, and Beckett stood beside their dad, and Finn, Autumn, and Jack stood beside their mom, with Chloe in front of Jack, his hands on her shoulders.

His eyes roved over the picture, taken almost four years

ago now. Chloe was so much younger, only about seven, reminding him again of how fast she was growing up. He looked at Finn, who he hadn't seen in years now—something that would've been unthinkable before grief did its work on all of them—smiling happily as the sun caught his dark brown hair. He looked at his father, feeling that familiar stab right in the middle of his chest. His hair had been white and thinning, but he'd still been strong and healthy, standing tall and proud surrounded by his family. Little had they known that he'd soon be gone, the victim of a sudden, massive heart attack. Not a day went by that he didn't miss him.

With a sigh, he set the picture back in its place and made his way into the noisy kitchen, which was filled with people and food and the soft jazz music his mother loved so much. The ache in his chest softened into something warm and sweet as he stood in the entrance to the kitchen, watching his family. All these people who he loved, and who loved him, unconditionally. Without question, without fail.

"Jack!" said his mother, setting down her salad tongs and wiping her hands on the kitchen towel tossed over her shoulder. She came over and gave him a hug, and he wrapped her in his arms. Her dark curls were shot through with gray, and gathered into a low ponytail. The top of her head barely grazed his chin as she gave him an affectionate squeeze. "Hi, baby," she said, pulling back and pinching his cheek.

"Hey, Mom," he said, and the expression on her face shifted as she studied him. But she didn't say anything, just patted his arm and returned to tossing the salad on the large island in the middle of the kitchen. In the far corner, Chloe was animatedly showing Beckett her new Nintendo Switch game while he nursed a beer and asked questions. Oliver, the family's resident chef, was crouched in front of the oven, peering inside. Jack crouched down beside him, the scents of melted cheddar and garlic making his stomach growl.

Oliver chuckled. "These are for everyone," he said, still peering at what Jack could now see were twice baked cheesy garlic potatoes.

"Not if I have anything to say about it," said Jack, clapping Oliver on the shoulder. "Smells amazing."

"You want a glass of wine, or some beer?" asked his brother Adam from the other side of the kitchen, where he had the fridge open.

"A beer, thanks," said Jack, crossing the space to where his brother was extending a bottle towards him. He took it and twisted the cap off. "So, how's the book going?"

Adam, the oldest Shephard brother, had been in charge of the Shephard Inn not that long ago, but everything had changed when Hazel Woodward, the famous author and now Adam's girlfriend, had come to Gossamer Falls looking for inspiration. They'd fallen in love, and were writing a book together, reviving Adam's once dashed hopes of being a published author. He'd written mysteries several years ago, but the trilogy had flopped, mostly because of his publisher's ineptitude and ridiculous expectations.

But now, thanks to Hazel, Adam had rediscovered his creative spark, and was madly in love. Honestly, Jack had never seen Adam so happy, so smitten, so light and carefree. And it had only increased after Hazel had permanently left New York City to Gossamer Falls a few months ago, moving into Adam's cabin on the edge of the Hudson Highlands.

Hazel appeared from around the corner, and Adam immediately slid his arm around her, tucking her against his side. Something in Jack's chest twisted at the casual, loving gesture. It wasn't jealousy. Not exactly. He was happy for Adam and Hazel. After all, he'd played a role in helping Adam get his head out of his ass when it was obvious to Jack how much he liked Hazel, and how perfect they were for each other.

"It's going pretty well, I think," said Adam, taking a sip of his wine. "We're probably about a month out from having a finished first draft."

"How is it, living with this guy?" Jack asked Hazel, half-joking. "Now that you've been here for a couple of months, is he driving you nuts, or what?"

"It's perfect," said Hazel simply, leaning her head against Adam's chest, a slightly dreamy look in her eyes.

Jack swallowed thickly. Had Norah ever had stars in her eyes for him like that?

Or maybe the better question was: had he ever had stars in his eyes for her?

Then again, maybe it wasn't fair to compare a couple in the thick of the honeymoon stage to over ten years of marriage.

"And you know why it's perfect?" said Autumn, breezing into the kitchen with a wine bottle in each hand. "Because I'm always right about these things." She set the wine down on the counter, and his mother Julie immediately scooped one of the bottles up and started opening it. "From the moment I met Hazel, I knew she and Adam were going to fall in love."

Jack arched an eyebrow at her. "Oh, really? You knew,

huh?"

"Yep. From the very start."

"I don't know that being right once constitutes *always* being right," he teased, grabbing a crouton from the salad on the counter and popping it into his mouth. Julie smacked at his hand with the salad tongs.

"It's not just once." She sent him a knowing look that pinned him in place. Was she talking about him?

"Oh, yeah?" asked Beckett, sauntering over. Chloe slid onto one of the stools lined up against the island, Switch in hand.

"Chloe, honey, let's turn the game off," said Jack, and she nodded.

"Lemme just get to a save point and then I'll put it away. I swear."

"Deal."

"Yeah," said Autumn, seamlessly picking up the thread of conversation. They were all used to talking around each other, in between other conversations. When you grew up in a family of eight, it was just the way things went.

"What else have you been right about?" asked Beckett. "Have I met my true love yet?"

"Nope. Not yet. But I have a feeling someone else here has."

Oliver's head whipped around so fast Jack was surprised he didn't hurt his neck. "Who?"

Autumn mimed twisting a key shut over her lips. "Time will reveal all. Besides, the falls haven't had a chance to work their magic on these two yet. But they will."

"Are you talking about yourself?" asked Adam. "Because I know you—"

"Nope!" said Autumn a little too loudly with forced brightness. "You'll all just have to be patient." She sent Jack another knowing look, and he couldn't name the emotion that washed over him. Was it hope? He didn't know. All he knew was that he had the sudden urge to hold his breath, that his stomach was full of odd flutters, and for the first time in a while, he had an overwhelming sense that everything was going to be fine. Better than fine, even.

For several moments, he stood completely still in the kitchen as his family moved around him, chatting and laughing. He wasn't normally one that put any stock in magic or the legend of the falls, but after watching Adam and Hazel fall hard and fast...And it's not like Autumn was psychic or something, although she did always seem to know things that she had no way of knowing...

Nah.

Impossible.

SIXTEEN

"Honey, are you alright?" asked Julie, laying a hand on Jack's arm. She was holding a glass of red wine and peering up at him with concern. "You have the strangest look on your face."

He rubbed at his chest and nodded slowly. "Yeah, Mom. I'm good."

Her eyebrows knit together, and she tipped her head in the direction of the living room. "Come sit with me for a minute."

He grabbed his beer from where he'd set it on the island and followed his mom into the living room, where the fire was crackling. Outside, light flakes had started to drift down from the darkened sky, swirling on the breeze before landing on the pile of snow on the front lawn.

Julie sat down on one of the loveseats, and Jack sat down next to her. "I just wanted to see how you're doing," she said, her voice low, her eyes full of worry. "You know, after Norah's engagement."

"Oh. Right." Truth be told, he'd been so caught up

thinking about Rosalie and how she was coming back that he hadn't spent much time dwelling on it. Which was probably for the best. "I'm happy for her. You know I think Ian's a great guy."

"I know that, but I'm asking how *you* are. You're allowed to have feelings about this, and any feelings you do have are completely valid."

"I...I don't know. I'm happy for her. But there's a bittersweetness to it. I thought she and I were going to grow old together, and this feels...very final. You know? I know we've been divorced for a while, and we're doing the best we can co-parenting, but she's in love with someone else and getting remarried, and it's...I don't know. Weird, I guess."

"That's understandable. But you two were so young when you got married. You're not the same people now as you were then. And I'm sorry that it didn't work out, and you know I'll always love Norah because she's Chloe's mom. But maybe this is a sign that there are bigger and better things out there for you, too."

He nodded slowly, letting his vision go fuzzy around the edges as he stared at the fire. What did it mean that everything seemed to make him think of Rosalie? The snow, the hotel, any mention of Carrie Clark, talk of meeting someone...He couldn't get her out of his head, and fuck, he didn't want to.

"Maybe there is," he said slowly. He took a sip of his beer, and his mom waited for him to continue. "I've been doing a lot of thinking lately. Some soul searching, with Norah getting engaged and...I just...maybe...I'm ready."

"Ready for what, honey?"

He met his mother's eyes. "To really put myself out there

again. Not just casual little flings—which, I hope you know, those clowns in the kitchen greatly exaggerate—but something…" His gaze drifted to the family photo on the mantel again. "Something real. And meaningful."

"I know they exaggerate, and you're also a grown man who can do what he pleases."

"Maybe what I've been doing isn't pleasing me anymore."

"And what would?"

"I want…what Adam and Hazel have," he said, the words falling out of his mouth before he could really examine them. But it wouldn't have mattered, because they were true. "I want to feel like that. To fall in love, head over heels, crazy in love."

He felt as though all the air had been sucked out of his lungs, a faint sense of panic clawing at him now that he'd said the words out loud. But ever since he'd spent the night with Rosalie, it was as though the broken pieces inside him had started rearranging themselves. Into what, he wasn't sure, but something different.

"If that's what you want, then that's my wish for you, too," said Julie softly. "That kind of love is special and rare. I had it with your father, and Adam certainly has it with Hazel."

"And with Norah…" Jack trailed off.

Julie hesitated, toying with the hem of her sweater before laying her hand on Jack's thigh. "Like I said, I will always love Norah. I think she's a lovely person, and a wonderful mother. But I don't think she was your once in a lifetime, soulmate type of love."

"You don't?" Jack asked, his eyebrows inching up his

forehead. He'd been starting to think the same thing himself, but he was surprised to hear it from his mother.

Julie shook her head. "No. But when you were eighteen, no one could talk you out of anything. Believe me, I tried when it came to joining the Army." She smiled sadly, the lines of her face softening. "I love you, Jack, but you're someone who needs to learn things on his own time, in his own way. Just like Finn."

"When he comes back, will you forgive him for leaving?" he asked.

"I like that you said 'when' and not 'if.' And yes, I'll forgive him. Of course I will." She squeezed his leg. "And he will come back, when he's ready. Just like you'll be willing to take a risk on love, when you're ready. And it sounds like maybe you are."

The corner of Jack's mouth pulled up in a smile. "Maybe I am."

Julie pulled him in for a hug, rubbing her hand up and down his back. "Then what's meant for you will find you. It always does." She stood and made her way back into the kitchen, leaving Jack alone with the popping fire and the swirling flakes outside, whirling even faster than the thoughts inside his brain.

"So," said Beckett, leaning against the open entryway to the living room, beer in hand. "How'd it go with, uh...the brunette. The one who has terrible taste in hockey teams."

"Rosalie." God, just saying her name made his heart beat a little faster.

"Yeah, Rosalie," said Beckett, nodding. He took a long swallow of his beer. "You two looked awfully cozy when you walked her back to the hotel."

Jack opened his mouth, and then closed it. "Did we?" he finally asked.

Beckett narrowed his eyes at him and then a Cheshire-like grin slowly spread across his face. "Oh, man. You're so fucked."

Jack's head snapped up at that. "What are you talking about?"

"One night and you caught feelings. Look at you. You're all moonfaced just talking about her."

Jack was going to deny it, but then decided there was no point. He was done running from the truth of his feelings, no matter how messy they might be. "I like her."

The simplicity of his statement seemed to catch Beckett off guard, and he pursed his lips. "So...you gonna see her again? I assume she's coming back for the music video thing."

"Yep. Plan to."

"You seem...different."

"I feel different."

"Damn. Must've been some night."

Jack stood and walked through the entryway, clapping Beckett on the shoulder as he passed. "You have no idea."

Beckett studied him for a moment, his expression morphing from teasing to something more serious. He knew that expression because it was one he'd often seen on his own face. It was the expression of a man who hid behind sex and humor, but deep down he was lonely. And damn if he knew what to do about it.

"You'll get there," he said quietly, giving his younger brother's shoulder a squeeze. "You're still figuring shit out."

Beckett just nodded, rubbing absently at his chest. "Yeah."

They made their way back into the kitchen, where Chloe was busy helping Autumn set the table while Julie pulled things out of the oven. These were the kind of moments Jack wanted to wrap himself up in. The sound of his family laughing and talking, the scent of delicious food wafting on the air, the snow falling outside, the familiarness of home. For him, this was what life was about. Family and shared moments, love and trust and safety. He glanced over to Adam and Hazel, whose heads were bowed close together as they peered at Adam's phone and whispered happily.

He wanted that. Someone to share all of this with. Hazel fit into their family like a missing puzzle piece, slotting in as though there'd always been a space for her. And there was space for more, Jack knew. Having grown up in such a big family, he knew that love only grew with each new family member.

Once everyone was seated, with Chloe on his left and Autumn on his right, dishes were passed around, and a contented silence filled the room. After several moments, Adam cleared his throat gently. "So, Hazel and I have a fun little announcement to share."

Every set of eyeballs went to them, and Autumn practically vibrated in her seat.

Hazel glanced over at Adam, who smiled warmly at her and nodded. "We're getting a puppy!"

Excited gasps and squeals erupted from around the table, and Adam pulled his phone out of his pocket. He turned it to face everyone, showing them the picture of an adorable tan and white puppy with blue eyes and a pink nose. "This is

Phoebe. She's a Nova Scotia Duck Tolling Retriever, and she's coming home with us in two weeks."

They passed the phone around, everyone cooing over the adorable picture.

"I can puppysit for you!" said Chloe, eyes lingering on the photo. Jack could see the longing in her eyes, but he worked too much to be a good parent for a dog, and Chloe only lived with him half the time, going back and forth between his place and Norah's from week to week. Adam and Hazel, however, who were writers and worked mostly from home, were perfect.

"Well, I can't wait to meet her," said Julie, handing Adam's phone back to him from across the table. "She looks so sweet. And she'll be good practice for you two."

"Practice?" asked Adam, one eyebrow arched.

"For the grandbabies you're going to give me." She winked at them, making her words playful and light, but Jack didn't miss the soft, loving look that passed between Adam and Hazel. Clearly they'd already talked about kids and it was something they wanted.

Jack couldn't argue with them about wanting kids. Even though his marriage had ultimately failed, Chloe was the best thing he'd ever done, hands down. Sometimes, he let himself daydream about having another baby. He knew it was unlikely, given his lifestyle, but the idea, the hope that maybe he'd be a father again someday was still there. Feeling a bit emotional, he slung his arm over Chloe's shoulders and pulled her close, kissing the top of her head.

"Ew. Why?" She pulled away and stuck her tongue out at him.

"Ew? *Ew?* I'll show you ew," he said, and tickled her ribs in exactly the right spot.

She squealed and squirmed until she finally gasped out, "Okay, okay, not ew. Not ew! I take it back!"

Later that night, Jack scrubbed a hand over his face and stifled a yawn. Chloe had gone to bed a couple of hours ago, and he was currently half asleep on the couch pretending to watch a talk show while he thought about Rosalie.

It was...nice. To have someone to think of. And he couldn't help but wonder if she thought about him, too.

He yawned again, turned off the TV, started the dishwasher, and headed up to bed. He'd bought the small two-bedroom house on Willow about a year after the divorce. It was close to the police station, close to the park, close to the water, close to the school...then again, in Gossamer Falls, just about everything was ten minutes away, at most. But still, it was the perfect place for him and Chloe, when she was here. He and Norah shared custody fifty-fifty, with Chloe alternating weeks between their houses. Granted, there was some flexibility with work schedules and things that came up, but Chloe's time was divided pretty evenly between the two homes.

He wondered if Norah and Ian would move, now that they were engaged. She was still in the house on Hickory they'd bought after he'd returned from the military. Maybe Ian wouldn't want to live in the house where his soon-to-be wife had lived with her first husband.

He pushed the thoughts aside with a sigh and turned off

the light in the hall. He brushed his teeth and changed into pajamas, sleep pulling at him. But the second his head hit the pillow, his eyes popped open, sleep slipping away. Sighing again, he turned on the light and grabbed his phone from the bedside table, scrolling.

After he'd exhausted Instagram and Reddit, he found himself opening his texting app, re-reading the few messages between him and Rosalie.

And he realized, despite spending the night with his family, that he felt very alone.

JACK:

> I know you're probably sleeping, but I just wanted to let you know that I've been thinking about you and I'm looking forward to seeing you again.

He sent the message before he could talk himself out of it. It wasn't flirty or funny, but it was real.

His heart picked up speed when his phone buzzed in his hand. He hadn't expected her to write back at all tonight, never mind so quickly.

ROSALIE:

> I'm not sleeping, and I've been thinking about you, too. I'm glad I'll get to see you again. You're up late. Working?

JACK:

No, not tonight. Just up late. You?

ROSALIE:

I was working up until a little while ago. I don't know if you heard, but Carrie and her boyfriend broke up, so I've had lots to do with keeping the press fed while protecting Carrie's privacy.

JACK:

Oh, shit. That sucks. She ok?

ROSALIE:

Not really, but she will be. She's a survivor, and eventually the news cycle will move on to the next story. Just have to ride it out.

JACK:

Break ups are never easy.

ROSALIE:

I wouldn't really know.

JACK:

You've never been through a break up?

ROSALIE:

Not really. I've had boyfriends, sure, but it was never anything serious. Things always just seemed to come to a natural end once the relationship had run its course.

JACK:

Maybe. Or maybe you've left a trail of broken hearts behind you.

ROSALIE:

Very doubtful.

He grinned. He hadn't seen Rosalie coming, but now that she'd slipped into his life, he had a feeling nothing would ever be the same. That regardless of what ended up unfolding between the two of them, he wouldn't be the same.

ROSALIE:

What about you? Are there a string of broken hearts in your wake?

JACK:

A few, but I've been single for a long time.

ROSALIE:

And before that?

JACK:

Before that I was married.

ROSALIE:

Oh. So you're divorced?

JACK:

Yeah. For a while now.

ROSALIE:

I'm sorry. That must've been hard.

JACK:

It was, but it was years ago, and we're friends now.

Guilt tugged at him. He felt bad for not mentioning Chloe, but he had a rule that he didn't discuss his daughter with women he was...Well, it didn't seem fair to put Rosalie in the same category as his other hookups, given how he felt about her. Given that he wanted to see her again, given that he was texting her when he should've been trying to sleep.

This thing with Rosalie, it felt right in a way he hadn't ever experienced before. Easy, and real, and obvious. At least, to him.

ROSALIE:

Does she still live in town?

JACK:

Yeah, she does. She just got engaged
recently, actually.

ROSALIE:

How do you feel about that?

JACK:

Mostly fine, I think. They've been together
for a while. Makes sense.

ROSALIE:

Good, I'm glad it's not difficult for you.

JACK:

It's not. It's more weird than difficult, but I'll
adjust.

ROSALIE:

I can imagine it would be weird, definitely.

ROSALIE:

I should probably go. I have an early Zoom
meeting with the video production
company to work out some key details
about the shoot. But text me again, okay?

ROSALIE:

I liked hearing from you.

JACK:

I will. Sleep well, Crawford.

ROSALIE:

Night, Shephard.

Jack set the phone down on the bedside table, turned off
the light, and fell asleep almost instantly.

SEVENTEEN

Rosalie dropped down onto her couch in her quiet living room in her quiet apartment that looked out over the city. It was after nine, and she'd been going since seven that morning. She was beat. Her brain felt like mush, and her body was tired. Her feet ached from her heels, and her jaw was sore from talking. It had been a productive day—her favorite kind—but a long one, too. Normally, Carrie was more involved in some of the business meetings, but with the breakup still fresh, she was taking a little needed time to herself. Rosalie didn't begrudge her that, but it did mean that there was even more work on her and Trevor's plates than usual.

She counted to three in her head and then forced herself up off the couch, padding into her bedroom so she could change into leggings and a worn sweatshirt. She pulled her hair up into a ponytail, washed her face, and then moved into the kitchen, where she pulled some soup out of the fridge, poured it into a bowl, and tossed it into the microwave. She scrolled on her phone as she waited, deliberately ignoring her emails and Slack notifications. She was done for the day. Totally done. All she had capacity for was a couple episodes of *Seinfeld*, maybe a chapter of her book. That was it.

At the thought of *Seinfeld*, Jack flitted to the top of her mind. Granted, he was never far from the top, always right there, beneath the surface. And it should've scared her, how much she liked him after such a short amount of time. Truth be told, it did, a little. But the excitement was bigger than the fear for once, as though it was swallowing it up, suffocating it. Snuffing it out like a candle deprived of oxygen.

The microwave beeped, and she took her soup back to the couch, setting it down on the coffee table to cool and putting on an episode of her favorite show.

ROSALIE:

Important question for you.

JACK:

Hit me.

ROSALIE:

Is a hot dog a sandwich?

JACK:

No way. A hot dog is a hot dog. It's its own thing. A taco isn't a sandwich. Therefore, a hot dog cannot be a sandwich.

ROSALIE:

But a taco doesn't have bread.

JACK:

A tortilla isn't a kind of bread?

ROSALIE:

Fair, but I still think a hot dog goes in the
sandwich category.

JACK:

Agree to disagree on that one. Or was this
just your way of getting me talking about
hot dogs and tacos?

JACK:

OMG is this a sext and I'm just really
dumb???

ROSALIE:

LOL no I truly didn't mean it as a sext.
Although I'd be open to that on a night I
have more brainpower.

JACK:

Long day?

ROSALIE:

Yeah. It was good, but very long and busy.
How was your day?

JACK:

I'm actually at work right now.

ROSALIE:

Oh, well, I don't want to bug you.

JACK:

You're not. I'm just at the station getting
caught up on some paperwork. This is a
very welcome distraction, trust me.

JACK:

But since we're talking about food, here's a
question for you. Best French Fry topping?

ROSALIE:

I know I'm an outlier with this one, but I like either ranch dressing or spicy/garlic mayo. I really don't like ketchup.

JACK:

Oh my God. She thinks a hot dog is a sandwich and doesn't eat ketchup. Next you're going to tell me you don't like pepperoni on your pizza.

ROSALIE:

Hey, let's not get crazy now. Nothing wrong with pepperoni.

JACK:

But?

ROSALIE:

But…I like veggie toppings better lol

JACK:

You're killing me here, Crawford.

ROSALIE:

Just being honest. Sorry if you can't take the authentic me.

JACK:

Yeah, you're a lot to handle.

ROSALIE:

Is that a sext?

JACK:

It would be if I wasn't at work.

JACK:

Peanut butter, or Nutella?

ROSALIE:

The answer is obviously Nutella.

JACK:

Finally, she gets one right.

ROSALIE:

You eat Nutella? I had to coax you into
eating gummy bears, if I remember
correctly.

JACK:

On occasion, yes. I do.

ROSALIE:

And what's that occasion? Halley's Comet
passing by the earth?

JACK:

LOL. And that's not a token LOL. I literally
laughed, out loud, alone in my office.

ROSALIE:

Do you like it? Being the chief?

JACK:

Most of the time. It's a lot of responsibility,
and I'm never really off duty, but I do like it.

ROSALIE:

You're a helper, aren't you? The military, the
police, the food bank. You care about
people and try to look after them.

JACK:

I do. It's easy to look at the state of the
world and feel a little bit hopeless. Helping
gives me hope. If I can make the world a
tiny bit better, then I've done my job.

ROSALIE:

That's really sweet. And admirable.

JACK:

When you come back to town, you should come check out the food bank.

ROSALIE:

I'd like that.

JACK:

My turn for a random question.

ROSALIE:

Shoot.

JACK:

Favorite fairy tale?

ROSALIE:

Oh, I wasn't expecting that. Hmm.

ROSALIE:

Are we talking classic fairy tales? Or, like Disney movies?

JACK:

Your choice.

ROSALIE:

I do like Disney.

JACK:

You do?

ROSALIE:

Queen of the basic bitches, remember?

JACK:

Right. Okay, so which one's your favorite? And why?

ROSALIE:

Oooh, we're getting deep. Okay, I'm going to say Beauty and the Beast. Because I love the setting, the music, the romance, the emotions. Belle is selfless in her love, both for her father, and eventually, for the Beast. And it teaches us that internal values, like kindness, are more important than looks or status.

JACK:

That is a very thoughtful answer. Did you see the live action version?

ROSALIE:

I did! And I really liked it.

JACK:

So did I.

ROSALIE:

You saw the live action Beauty and the Beast?

JACK:

Yep. I'm a man of many layers.

ROSALIE:

So I'm learning.

There was a pause in their messages, and Rosalie figured he'd returned to his paperwork. She picked up her soup and started eating, only half paying attention to the show on TV. But after several minutes, her phone buzzed again.

JACK:

Now that you've brought up sexting, I can't stop thinking about it. Are you free tomorrow night?

Adrenaline jolted through her. It had been a long time since she'd done anything like that. Then again, it had been a long time since she'd talked to a man long enough to get to the sexting stage of...whatever this was.

ROSALIE:

I will make sure I am.

JACK:

Perfect. I'll text you tomorrow, okay? I need to get back to work, but I'm really glad you texted me.

ROSALIE:

Enjoy your paperwork.

JACK:

I won't. But I'll be thinking about you, so it won't be so bad.

She bit her lip, staring down at her phone screen. A sense of panic took root and tried to bloom, right in the middle of her chest. Did she want Jack thinking of her, saying those things to her? And if she did, that was bad, right? It had to be.

And yet...she knew she wasn't going to stop. Jack Shephard was too swoonworthy to resist.

JACK:

I'm here, and I'm alone. Are we still on for tonight?

ROSALIE:

On like Donkey Kong.

ROSALIE:

Oh God

ROSALIE:

Can we pretend I didn't say that?

JACK:

No way. Adding it to the list of adorable things I like about you.

ROSALIE:

I'm…nervous.

JACK:

Am I about to take your sexting cherry?

ROSALIE:

No, but I haven't done this in a long time, and I don't like doing things when I'm not sure if I'll be good at them or not.

JACK:

Only one way to find out.

ROSALIE:

Right. You're right.

JACK:

Why don't you tell me about one of your fantasies? Something you've always wanted to do?

ROSALIE:

This is a judgment free zone, right?

JACK:

Obviously, yes. Your freak flag is safe with me.

ROSALIE:

I've always wanted to have sex in a public place. Like the stacks in a library or something.

JACK:

That's really hot. I can just picture you in a tiny little skirt, hair up in a bun, rocking the sexy librarian look. No panties.

ROSALIE:

Would you fuck me in a library, Jack?

JACK:

Fuck, yes I would.

ROSALIE:

Tell me what you'd do to me.

JACK:

I'd take you to a quiet aisle, find a shadowy corner and turn you around so that your ass is pressed against my hips. I'd trail my hands up the insides of your thighs, spreading them open, slowly taking the tiny skirt you're wearing with me, revealing your perfect ass. Are you wet?

ROSALIE:

I am now.

JACK:

I'd push your legs further apart and then slowly slide two fingers into your hot little pussy.

ROSALIE:

I gasp out a moan, and you put your hand over my mouth to keep us from getting caught.

JACK:

Are you fucking yourself with your fingers right now?

ROSALIE:

A toy

JACK:

Goddamn

ROSALIE:

What happens next in the library?

JACK:

You press back into me, riding my fingers. You're so wet and tight, squirming and needy. I could get you there, easily, with just my fingers, but I want to feel you come on my cock. So I pull my fingers out of your pussy and slide them into your mouth so you can lick them clean.

ROSALIE:

How are you so good at this?

JACK:

I have a dirty imagination, and you inspire me, Crawford.

ROSALIE:

Tell me what happens next.

JACK:

I kiss you so I can taste your pussy on your tongue, my other hand on your tits, massaging and rubbing as I pull you against me.

ROSALIE:

I'd start to beg you for your cock as I undo your zipper.

JACK:

And what would you say?

ROSALIE:

Please, Jack. Fuck me. Please, please fuck
me. I need your cock.

JACK:

I laugh and tease you, dragging the tip of
my cock through your wet slit over and
over. I bite along your neck, and this time,
when you beg, I slide inside you, deep.

ROSALIE:

I moan your name and then bite my lip
because I know that was loud. I can't help
it. You make me feel so fucking good.

JACK:

I'd tell you to hold on to the bookshelf in
front of you, and then I'd wrap your hair
around my fist, holding you exactly where I
want you.

ROSALIE:

oh god yes fuck me

JACK:

I love what a dirty girl you are, Rosalie. My
dirty girl. Don't you make a fucking sound
as you take this cock where anyone
could see.

ROSALIE:

You make me feel so full and tight.
Don't stop

JACK:

Oh shit, I think someone's coming. The
librarian, maybe. I hear footsteps, but I
don't stop fucking you.

ROSALIE:

I'm so close right now. I'm fucking myself
with a toy, wishing it was you

JACK:

Jesus fuck I'm close too

ROSALIE:

What happens next?

JACK:

I slide my hand between your legs and pet
your swollen clit, circling it and fucking you,
hard, hard, harder, fast and deep and you
start to come all over me, squeezing me,
milking me, and I fucking explode, Ropsalie

JACK:

*Rosalie

JACK:

I come inside you and you're boneless
against me. But someone's still coming, so
I pull out, zip my pants, and tug your skirt
back down. Can't hide the cum dripping
down the insides of your thighs though.

JACK:

You still there?

JACK:

Rosalie??

ROSALIE:

oh my fucking god I just came so hard

ROSALIE:

my neighbors probably heard me scream
your name and you're not even here

JACK:

goddamn, that's hot

ROSALIE:

Did you come?

JACK:

yeah

JACK:

The idea of my cum dripping down your thighs pushed me over.

JACK:

hang on

JACK:

Can I call you?

ROSALIE:

Sure

"Hi," Rosalie answered a moment later, and Jack grinned, reclined on his bed with one hand behind his head, his pants still open, a towel still covering the come on his bare stomach. She sounded breathless and almost shy.

"Hey," he said. "I was looking forward to this all day."

"Me too," she said, and he could hear the smile in her raspy voice.

"I really like your voice," he said, letting the random thought slip past his lips. In the aftermath of his orgasm, his brain-body connection wasn't the best. "It's sexy."

"Thank you. When I was younger, I was always self-conscious about it. I wanted to sound like a Disney princess, all sweet and feminine."

"Disney princess voices don't make me hard the way yours does."

She laughed, warmth flowing though him. She sighed, and then there was a pause, as though she was weighing what she wanted to say. "I'm...I'm glad we're coming back to Gossamer Falls. But even if we weren't..." Another pause. "I'd want to see you again."

Her words sank into him, and a smile stretched across his face. "I'd want to see you again, too." He knew that what she was giving him was a big deal for her. That she was opening up, trusting, letting him in—something she'd made clear she didn't do. So, he decided to give her a little honesty of his own. "I think about you every day, Rosalie. Every goddamn day."

She let out a shaky breath while he held his, waiting for her answer. "I'd tell you not to say that kind of stuff to me, but I like it too much."

His heart stopped, completely, then restarted at double time, pounding so fast that he had to sit up just to catch his breath.

"Yeah? What else shouldn't I say to you? That you're gorgeous? Smart as hell?"

She let out a happy little laugh. "Exactly. That's the stuff." She sighed. "You...live inside my brain, Jack. And I think I like it."

He chuckled. "Rosalie Crawford, do you...*like* like me?"

"Maybe. Pass me a note during homeroom so I can check yes, no, or maybe."

He laughed, and then changed the subject because he wanted to keep talking to her. "How's everything going with work?"

"Good. Busy getting everything coordinated for the shoot." There was something in her voice, in her tone, that made him frown.

"Work is good, but?" he prompted.

"But...I don't know. It's nothing to do with Carrie, but lately I feel restless."

"Restless how?"

"I find myself wondering if this is it? Is this what I do with the rest of my life? Put out press releases and manage someone else's life for them? I got into this because I have an MBA and I'm passionate about music, and it was a natural fit. But lately I just feel like...I don't actually contribute anything. Like, to the world, to society. It feels empty, sometimes." She made a frustrated sound. "God, that sounds so maudlin and sad. I don't mean it that way. It's just something that's been on my mind, and you asked, and you're easy to talk to. Sorry for the word vomit."

"Don't be sorry. The phone sex was fun, but...I like this, too. A lot."

"Talking about real shit."

"Yeah. Talking about real shit." That pang of guilt for not telling her about Chloe was back, stronger than before, sliding cold and sharp like a knife right between his ribs. "Speaking of real shit..."

"Ugh, hang on. I have another call." There was a pause. "It's work. I'd better take this. But I need to tell you something first."

"Yeah?"

She hesitated only briefly before saying, "Our texts are the best part of my day."

He smiled. "Mine, too."

"I gotta go, but talk soon?

"Of course."

They hung up, and Jack closed his eyes, envisioning Rosalie in Gossamer Falls, coming to Sunday dinners, slotting in effortlessly with his family.

He knew, then, that if he let himself, he could easily fall for her.

EIGHTEEN

T he sleek black limousine rolled smoothly along the highway, snowbanks and snow-covered pines whizzing by outside through the tinted windows. Rosalie sat on one of the long benches, facing the opposite windows, laptop open as she worked through some emails and other low priority work. On the other side of the limo, Trevor's face was illuminated by his own laptop screen, his fingers flying over the keys.

"You're such an aggressive typer," said Rosalie, grinning and shaking her head. "What did that keyboard ever do to you?"

"Nothing, and it never will because it knows who's the boss."

Carrie sat curled up in the corner of the limo, notebook open, gazing out the window as she twirled a pen between her fingers. Ever since the break up, she'd started working on some new music, mostly just poetry she could use as lyrics, but that was often how the songwriting process happened for her. Sometimes Rosalie wondered if she should try to write poetry or journal to process all of the things she didn't want to feel. To put them on paper, examine them, understand them. It would probably be healthier than pretending her emotions didn't exist, but then, if she did that, she'd have to feel them. All of them.

They passed by the cheerful "Welcome to Gossamer Falls" sign, and a little jolt of excitement shot through Rosalie. It felt a little surreal to be back here, even though she'd always known there was a good chance they'd wind up filming the music video at the falls. Surreal, and...good. Comforting, and welcoming. As though she belonged here. And she realized that it was because a part of her—a large part—*wanted* to belong in Gossamer Falls.

Carrie set her notebook down, peering out the window. "Oh, wow. This is even cuter than you described," she said, taking in the cozy shops and cafes as the limo wound its way up Main Street. The pedestrians on the sidewalk all stopped to gawp at the limousine as it passed.

This time, Rosalie would make sure she had the chance to properly explore the town. She'd missed out last time because of the snow, and hadn't gotten to visit the adorable boutique she'd seen, or the coffee shop, or the book store.

Trevor closed his laptop and looked out the window. "My God, it's like *Gilmore Girls* had a baby with Hallmark and it threw up everywhere." He let out a shudder.

Rosalie and Carrie both laughed. "Spoken like a city boy, through and through."

Rosalie's excitement grew as they continued up Main Street, her heart doing a little skip and a flop in her chest as they passed Hemlock Square and the municipal building that housed the police station. She craned her neck as they drove past, wondering if she'd get a glimpse of Jack.

"Looking for your lo-vah?" teased Trevor, eyebrows wiggling. He held his wrists out in front of him. "Take me, officer. I've been a bad, bad girl."

Rosalie threw a crumpled up receipt that had fallen out of her bag at him. "I have no idea why I tell you anything."

"Because you love me, and you don't have any other friends." He smiled at her, not unkindly, but something about his remark hit home, and she swallowed thickly, sitting back in her seat. It was true. Beyond Carrie and Trevor, she didn't really have any friends. And she'd always told herself it was because she was too busy with work. But was that the whole of it? Or was it because making friends meant letting people in, something she avoided at all costs?

"These houses are all so cute and cozy," said Carrie. She had a pensive look on her face as she tapped her pen against her lips. "Hmm. I wonder."

"You wonder what?" asked Rosalie, but before Carrie could answer, they'd pulled up under the Shephard Inn's porte cochere. Carrie's security team emerged from the black SUV that had proceeded the limousine, coming around the side of the limo and opening the door for them.

It was a brilliantly sunny day, the bright sunshine winking off of the snow, making it glitter and sparkle. The air was fresh and clean, and birds chirped merrily from the trees. Rosalie noticed several bird feeders hanging from the trees to the side of the hotel, flashes of bright red, soft yellow, and pale blue standing out against the white backdrop of snow.

Autumn stepped out of the hotel's front doors, accompanied by a tall, broad-shouldered man and several employees wearing long-sleeved gray polo shirts embroidered with the hotel's logo.

"Welcome," said Autumn warmly, introducing herself to Trevor, Carrie, and the security team. "I'm Autumn Shephard, the manager. We've got the entire hotel booked out for your team, so please, if there's anything at all that you need, just let me know."

"Adam Shephard, assistant manager," said the man, shaking hands with Rosalie, Trevor and Carrie's head of security. "As Autumn said, if there's anything we can do to make your stay more comfortable, please let us know."

The staff members started unloading the bags as Carrie stretched and looked around. "This place is amazing. When was it built?"

"1850," said Autumn. "It originally belonged to Robert Parker, whose family ran the foundry in town. The foundry closed at the turn of the century, and the family's wealth dried up. The house fell into disrepair, and it was vacant for several years between the two world wars until our grandparents bought it and turned it into a hotel in the late 1940s."

"Fascinating," said Carrie. She stepped past the security guards, looking around. She smiled at Autumn, a conspiratorial grin meant to win friends. "And I hear that it's haunted?"

"We have two friendly resident spirits," said Autumn easily, although her cheeks were pink and her eyes were glittering. It was a starstruck look Rosalie saw often on those meeting Carrie for the first time. "I'm sure they won't bother you, and can I just say, we are absolutely *thrilled* to have you staying with us."

"Well, after the pictures and videos that Rosalie sent, I knew this was the perfect place for the video shoot. Maybe even more."

"More?" asked Adam, but Carrie had already walked inside the hotel. Rosalie stared after her as staff continued to unload bags. All of the equipment for the shoot had been sent directly to the falls in a large trailer, which would be unloaded by members from the video shoot team. It had taken a lot of coordination, but they'd made it work. They always did.

"Hi," said Rosalie, lifting her hand in a wave as she greeted Autumn.

"Hi!" said Autumn back, completely ignoring the wave and pulling Rosalie in for a hug. Oh, well, then. Rosalie wasn't usually a hugger, but in this instance she didn't mind. "It's so good to see you again!"

"You too," said Rosalie, and she found that she meant it. Sure, Autumn was a little offbeat, and wore her heart on her sleeve—the complete emotional opposite of Rosalie—but she couldn't deny that she liked her. Her earnest honesty and easy warmth were appealing.

There was a flurry of activity as Adam and Autumn passed out room keys, and then led their group on a short tour of the hotel, showing them the lounge, with the restaurant beyond, the sun room, and how to access the grounds. They also passed out maps of the town with information about the Hudson Highlands and Gossamer Falls.

"Everyone, take thirty minutes to get settled, and then meet back out front," said Rosalie. "We'll head to the falls to get set up and rehearse for tomorrow."

Everyone dispersed, tromping up the stairs to check out

their rooms, but Rosalie hung back, wanting a chance to catch up with Autumn.

"How are you doing?" she asked, leaning against the front desk as Autumn slotted papers into a neat pile of folders. "Last time we talked, you had some heavy stuff going on."

Autumn smiled warmly at her. "You're so sweet to ask. I'm doing better, I think. I haven't picked door number one—telling him how I feel—or door number two—trying to move on. But I think I've accepted that this is just the way things need to be right now. We talk a lot, and he's still dealing with some family stuff. But he's opening up to me, and I'm just trying to be a good friend, which is what I think he needs most right now."

Rosalie nodded. "I know we don't know each other very well, but you strike me as someone who is highly capable of being a good friend."

Autumn ducked her head and smiled, clearly pleased with the compliment. "So...any plans while you're in town?" she asked, a hint of something in her voice. "Maybe to see a certain police chief?"

Rosalie laughed. "Ah. So you *did* know about me and your um...and Jack."

Autumn tilted her head and shrugged. "Not much gets past me. And I ran into him when he was on his way out early in the morning after the storm. I'm not Albert Einstein, but I can put two and two together pretty easily."

"Did he say anything?"

"He didn't kiss and tell, if that's what you're asking," said Autumn with a grin. "But he's been in a *very* good mood for the past couple of days, and if I was a betting woman, I'd put money on the fact that his mood has everything to do with you being in town. Which means you *are* going to see each other again."

Rosalie didn't have a name for the emotion that washed over her, leaving her breathless and her skin tingling. It was anticipation laced with hope, weighed down with a drop or two of fear.

"We've been texting," she admitted. "And yeah, we're planning to see each other. I don't...I mean, I can't..."

Autumn laid a hand on Rosalie's arm, the warmth of her touch seeping into Rosalie's bones. "Just take it one moment at a time. It's like that cheesy saying: yesterday's history, and tomorrow's a mystery, which makes today a gift; that's why it's called the present. Just have fun and see where it goes."

Rosalie nodded, feeling a little bit better. "I'm going to go freshen up before we head out to the falls." She glanced down at the room key in her hand, noting that it was a different room than the one she'd been in last time.

As she mounted the stairs, she fished her phone out of her pocket.

ROSALIE:

I'm here! Are we still meeting up later tonight?

Jack's reply came almost instantly, as though he'd been waiting for her text.

JACK:

Absolutely. Nine? I'd offer to take you out to dinner, but I don't get off work until seven, which really means eight, most likely.

ROSALIE:

Won't you be hungry?

JACK:

We can order food. I'm not depriving myself
of time with you to eat.

Rosalie stumbled on the top step, almost dropping her phone as her heart trampolined in her chest.

ROSALIE:

That's one of my favorite things that anyone
has ever said to me.

ROSALIE:

Pick a color.

JACK:

For what?

ROSALIE:

You said you wanted to see more of my
lingerie collection. So. Pick a color.

JACK:

Red.

She grinned, thinking of the lacy red bra with tiny white flowers and matching thong she'd packed. The thong was one of her favorites, with its little heart shape cut out right over her mound.

ROSALIE:

Done. See you at nine.

Jack slipped his phone back into his pocket and adjusted his sunglasses. Rosalie was here, back in Gossamer Falls. Just a few hours, and she'd be in his arms again, moaning his name, making him laugh. Making him want things he'd given up on long ago.

God, just knowing that she was here, in his town, made him feel antsy, and he unclipped the radio from his shoulder.

"Anything on the board, Cheryl?" he asked, drumming the fingers of his free hand on the wheel of his SUV.

"No, sir. I won't jinx us by using the 'q' word, but nothing right now."

"I'm going to head out to the falls and meet with the security team for the music video shoot, just make sure they have everything they need." He'd spoken with them on the phone earlier in the week, and he was going to be working with them during the actual shoot, but he wasn't scheduled to go out there this afternoon. But he knew that Rosalie would likely be there, which meant it was the only place he wanted to be right now.

"Sure thing, Chief."

"Radio me if you need me for anything."

"Will do. Enjoy the sunshine."

He clipped the radio back to his shoulder and put the cruiser in drive, heading in the direction of the falls. The sun shone brightly, glinting off of the snow on the side of the road, lifting his mood even more. He'd only made it a block before his phone rang, and when he saw Norah's name flash on the display, he answered it through the SUV's BlueTooth connection.

"Hey, Norah," he said, turning down Main Street. "What's up?"

"Hey. I'm stuck at a work thing, and I won't be able to get Chloe to her piano lesson. She's going to be at the hotel with Autumn after school, hoping for a glimpse of Carrie Clark. Could you pick her up there and take her to her lesson?"

"Sure, no problem," he said easily. "Does she have her music folder with her?"

"Shit. No. I'll text Ian and see if he can leave it in the mailbox on the front porch. Would you mind picking it up?"

"Not at all. I'll swing by and get it before picking up Chloe for her piano lesson. Will you be back in time to get her at 5:30? I'm working until seven, but if you're not back, I could pick her up at 5:30 and take her to my mom's for dinner." Technically, this was Norah's week with Chloe, but they always did their best to help each other out when life happened, and to leave Chloe's schedule and routine as uninterrupted as possible.

"I should be back, but I'll text you if that changes. Thanks, Jack. I really appreciate it."

"Not a problem."

When he pulled into the busy parking lot near the falls, he pulled out his phone to text his sister.

JACK:

Chloe's going to be with you after school at the hotel, right?

AUTUMN:

Yep.

JACK:

Okay. Norah's stuck at work, so I'll pick her up for her piano lesson around 4:15.

He shut off the SUV and stepped out into the sunshine, taking a deep breath of crisp, clean air. The rushing sound of the falls greeted him, still audible over the voices of the video production team, who were busy hauling gear down the stairs that led to the mouth of the falls.

He made his way down the stairs, eyes scanning back and forth as he took in the scene before him. Two small tents were set up on either side of the falls, and a trailer was positioned off to the side, near the stairs. Everywhere he looked, there were lighting rigs, coils of thick, black cable, and expensive looking cameras. Beneath the tents were several director-style chairs, and security guards stood at all of the entry points to the basin of the falls, where the shoot would take place.

He approached one of the security guards, who took in his badge and uniform and nodded at him, stepping aside to let him pass. A large plexiglass platform had been constructed not far from the base of the falls, and atop it was an antique looking piano painted with intricate snowflakes. Jack's brain jolted slightly when he realized that Carrie Clark herself was sitting in front of it, bundled up in a black parka and matching beanie while she chatted with a woman who Jack was pretty sure was the director.

"How did you get past security?" came a raspy female voice from his left, and he whirled, a grin spreading across his face when he spotted Rosalie several feet away, an iPad in her gloved hands. Her hair was down and tumbling over her shoulders, and she was wearing the same camel coat she'd been wearing the night of the snow storm. She rolled her lips inward as his heart spun in circles at the sight of her. It took every single ounce of control he had not to scoop her up into his arms and kiss the living daylights out of her right there. But, they were both working, and the last thing he wanted to do was cause a scene or embarrass her.

He tapped the badge pinned to his chest. "Chief of police, remember?"

She moved closer and pushed her sunglasses up onto her head. "How could I forget?" Her eyes roved over him, seeming to drink him in.

"Oh my God, is this him? The hot cop you banged?" said a man as he walked up to Rosalie. Her cheeks went bright red, and truth be told, Jack felt his own cheeks heating a little too.

"Uh…" said Rosalie, looking very much like a deer caught in a pair of headlights.

"Trevor Klein," said the man, extending his hand to Jack, who shook it. "I work with Rosalie." He swept his eyes over Jack in a very appraising, assessing gaze, and then turned to Rosalie. "Okay, yeah. I get it. I definitely get it." He winked at Jack and then spun around with a dramatic little flourish, returning to whatever it was he'd been doing before.

"I…" She opened and closed her mouth. "I only told Trevor and Carrie. They're my friends, and when I got back, they could tell…" She swallowed, blinking rapidly.

Jack moved closer, gently sweeping her hair off her shoulder. "Could tell that you'd been well and thoroughly fucked?" he said, his voice low enough that no one would hear them. She laughed on a shaky exhale.

"Uh, yeah." She swallowed again, her gaze flitting between his eyes and his mouth. It was as though an electrical current was arcing through the air between them. "It's…it's really good to see you again."

He nodded, his hands tingling with the urge to pull her against him, to show her how much he'd missed her. "It's really good to see you, too, Rosalie."

Their eyes locked and a beat passed between them, heavy with anticipation and meaning.

"Now that you're here, I'd love to show you around the town when you have time," he said. "If you feel like it, maybe we could have dinner with my family. We get together every Sunday."

Her face lit up, and she smiled, wide and bright. "I'd really like that."

Just then, a gorgeously ethereal song started playing over the sound system, with tinkling piano chords and lyrics about being seen and loved for exactly who you are.

"This is the song?" he asked, and Rosalie nodded.

"Yeah. Carrie really likes the legend of the falls, and the song is sort of about finding that person, the one who fits you like an old sweatshirt."

"An old sweatshirt?" he asked, his eyebrows raising. "That's not the most romantic image, is it?"

Rosalie shrugged, looking over at the falls, where Carrie was laughing with the director as she positioned herself on top of the piano, stretching out and singing along with her song.

"A lot of her songs are about how love and life happen in the small, quiet moments. The mundane, the everyday… that's where the magic is. Going grocery shopping together for the first time, dancing around under Christmas lights, finding that person who feels like home and comfort."

"Like an old sweatshirt," he said, nodding slowly.

"Yeah. Exactly."

"That sounds nice, actually."

"It wasn't like that with you and your ex?" she asked, and he could tell that she wanted to know more about that whole situation. Fresh guilt ate at him that he hadn't told her about Chloe yet. Tonight. He'd tell her all about Chloe tonight.

"No. We got married really young, before I was deployed, and by the time I'd finished my service, we'd grown apart." Just then, his radio crackled to life.

"Chief, are you available? We have a call about some teenage shoplifters over at the grocery store."

"Yeah, I'm on my way, Cheryl."

"Copy that."

Rosalie grinned at him. "Quite the hotbed of crime you have here."

He laughed. "I don't mind the small town pace. After being shot at in the desert for years, it's nice to have low stakes problems, you know?"

Her smile slowly faded, and she nodded. "Right. Of course."

He leaned in close. "You can ask me anything you want tonight, okay? Anything."

Her smile returned. "Yeah?"

"Yeah."

"Nine," she said, taking a step back.

"Nine," he echoed, winking at her and then bounding up the steps. He was counting down the seconds, and he had a feeling Rosalie was, too.

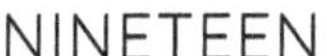

With the rehearsal nearly finished, Rosalie had decided to head back to the hotel. It was still afternoon, and she wanted the chance to get caught up or even ahead on some work before her night with Jack. She grinned as she stepped back into the hotel, the familiar lush carpeting and intricately detailed wallpaper both a thrill and a comfort.

"Hey," said Autumn as she stepped out of the lounge. "Would you like some hot chocolate? There's a fresh batch just out of the kitchen, made from scratch."

"Yes, please! That sounds amazing," said Rosalie.

"Why don't you go have a seat in the sun room and I'll bring it out to you?" said Autumn, and Rosalie nodded, shrugging out of her coat as she walked down the hallway, taking in the beamed ceiling and the plethora of framed photos on the walls. The last time she'd stayed here, she hadn't spent any time in the sun room. She'd only walked through it in the dark with Jack, and as she stepped in, her eyes darted to the bookshelf that hid the door to the secret alcove. Her stomach fluttered with butterflies as she remembered kissing him in that secret spot, and everything that kiss had led to.

There were a few other occupants in the sun room today, other members of Carrie's team taking a break to enjoy the way the sunshine was glinting off of the pristine field visible through the large windows. A young girl, maybe eleven or twelve years old, sat at one of the small tables, a notebook and a math textbook open in front of her. She frowned in concentration as she read the problem.

"Here you go," said Autumn, stepping into the sun room with two mugs of hot chocolate on a tray. She handed one to Rosalie and then set the other one down beside the girl.

"Thanks," said the girl, setting her pencil down and pulling the mug towards her.

"Rosalie, this is my niece, Chloe," said Autumn, laying a hand on the girl's slender shoulder. "Chloe, this is Miss Crawford."

Chloe looked up at Rosalie, her eyes wide. "Are you...do you work for Carrie Clark?" she asked, a little breathlessly. Rosalie clocked a couple of friendship bracelets on her wrist, and she grinned.

"I do. Are you a fan?"

Chloe swallowed and nodded rapidly. "Yes." The word left her lips at lightning speed. She glanced over at Autumn, and Autumn winked at her niece. Rosalie wondered which one of her sibling's kids Chloe was. She knew the Shephards were a big family, but she didn't know much about them beyond some names and occupations.

"Chloe is one of the biggest Carrie Clark fans I know," said Autumn.

"I know every song by heart." Chloe's cheeks were pink. "I just love her," she said, her voice dropping to an almost reverent whisper.

Rosalie glanced at Autumn and grinned. She had a feeling that she was being set up, and she didn't mind one bit. Autumn had been warm and kind to her from the start, and she was more than happy to be able to return some of that kindness to her.

"You know, if you wanted to come to the daytime portion of the video shoot tomorrow, I could definitely arrange that. Maybe you and your Aunt Autumn could come together?"

Chloe's eyes went wide as planets and she whipped around to Autumn, almost knocking over her hot chocolate. "Ohmygodcanwe?" she blurted out, all of the words running together in her excitement.

Autumn smiled, wide and bright. "As long as your dad says it's okay, sure. I'll ask Uncle Adam to come in tomorrow afternoon and we'll go."

"Oh my God!" said Chloe. She turned to Rosalie. "Thank you. Thank you so much. Can I...can I bring a bracelet to give her?"

Rosalie nodded. "Sure. And I'll make sure you get a photo together, okay?"

Chloe's face lit up, and in that moment, Rosalie could see the Shephard features in her face. The hair, the nose, the shape of her jaw. "Thank you," she said again, her fingers toying with the friendship bracelet on her wrist.

"It's no problem," said Rosalie, shooting Autumn a smile.

Chloe's focus moved to something behind Autumn and Rosalie, and she started gathering up her homework. "There's my dad," she said. "I have a piano lesson. I…I play some of Carrie's songs, when my teacher lets me," she added, shoving her books into her backpack, which was adorned with Carrie Clark-themed buttons and enamel pins.

Rosalie turned, her curiosity pulling at her as she again wondered which Shephard sibling was this sweet girl's dad.

She felt as if the floor had disappeared from under her when she spotted Jack walking straight towards them. His steps faltered as he spotted Rosalie, and she saw his easy smile fade, saw the way he pulled a breath into his lungs.

Jack had a kid. And he hadn't said a word about it to her.

Because Rosalie was an idiot who'd completely misread the situation between them. Because he'd told her that he didn't do relationships, wasn't looking for anything beyond sex, and she'd let herself catch feelings for him anyway.

Oh, God.

"Hey, kiddo. You ready to go?" he asked, his gaze darting back and forth between Chloe and Rosalie, who was frozen to the spot as humiliation washed over her. Jack had a kid, and he hadn't told her because it wasn't like that between them.

This was why she didn't do relationships. Why she didn't put herself out there. She didn't need this horrible feeling churning away in the middle of her chest, making her ache, making her wish the ground would swallow her up.

"Yep. We have to go to Mom's though, because I need my music folder."

"Already got it." Jack ruffled Chloe's hair and then took her backpack for her, still glancing repeatedly at Rosalie.

Was that guilt written across his handsome face? Or just the look of a man who kept his life compartmentalized and who was less than thrilled that two very separate parts were mingling?

"I invited Chloe and Autumn to come to the video shoot tomorrow afternoon," said Rosalie, her voice a little too loud. Why was it so hot in here? It was like an oven.

"I'm going to meet Carrie Clark!" said Chloe excitedly, clutching at her dad's arm. "Isn't that amazing?"

Jack's blue eyes sparkled as he smiled at his daughter. "That is. Did you·say thank you?"

"She did," said Rosalie quickly. She couldn't stop staring at Jack and his daughter. He had a kid. Probably from his marriage. And he clearly wasn't an absentee father, either. He was here, taking her to piano lessons, radiating warmth.

He hadn't wanted Rosalie to know. She couldn't seem to move past that thought. How many times had they talked or texted over the past couple of weeks? And he'd never...She swallowed, her skin burning, her stomach full of rocks.

She felt like the world's biggest idiot. She felt...confused. And sad. Disappointed, and embarrassed. She sipped her hot chocolate, not tasting it as she watched Jack shoulder his daughter's backpack for her.

"Enjoy your piano lesson," she said to Chloe, her heart feeling bruised. "And I'll see you and your aunt tomorrow." She caught Jack's eyes and then looked away. "See you." Her hot chocolate in hand, she grabbed her coat and headed out of the sun room, making a beeline for the stairs. She reached her room and shut herself inside, her heart pounding, and she was grateful that she was in a different room than before.

She didn't need the memories of her night with Jack right now.

She hung her coat up and then sank down on the bed, which was soft and plush, offering her a small bit of comfort. Really, it was fine. Jack hadn't done anything wrong. He was allowed to set whatever boundaries around his child that he saw fit. And he clearly didn't want Rosalie within those boundaries.

It was fine. He was fine. She was fine. Or, she would be, once she got over the embarrassment she felt at so obviously misinterpreting...well, everything.

She stood from the bed and pulled her phone out of her coat pocket. She didn't let herself re-read all of the old texts between her and Jack. Honestly, she'd be better off deleting them.

ROSALIE:

I'm really sorry, but I have a lot of work to
do tonight.

She watched her phone screen as three dots appeared, then disappeared, then reappeared, then disappeared. A minute passed, and then another. Finally, three dots and a message.

JACK:

No problem. Rain check?

ROSALIE:

Maybe? It turns out I'm going to be pretty
swamped.

JACK:

Everything okay?

All good.

He didn't reply this time, and Rosalie laid back on the bed, letting the weight of everything she was feeling pin her down.

All Rosalie wanted was to get out of her head about the whole Jack having a kid situation. She didn't want to think about it anymore. She didn't want to think about what it meant about how he felt—or didn't feel—about her, about how she'd opened up to him like an idiot and he hadn't even told her that he had a daughter. She tried working, answering emails, making phone calls. But her heart wasn't in it, something she'd been dealing with more and more lately. It wasn't that she didn't like working for Carrie. It just felt...meaningless, sometimes. Which sounded shitty, and she wasn't ungrateful for the job she had, but sometimes she wondered if she'd be happier, more fulfilled doing something else. She had no idea what, though.

When work failed to distract her from her churning thoughts, she ran a bath and grabbed a book, using a red-tipped match from the little matchbook to light a couple of the candles. And while the book, a historical romance with dukes and duchesses and balls and making out in carriages, was good, it didn't absorb her the way she needed it to. Maybe because she kept picturing herself as the heroine, and Jack as the duke. Not exactly helping her with her goal of not thinking about Jack.

Out of the tub, she dried off and pulled on a pair of matching cozy sweats and twisted her damp hair into a messy bun on top of her head. Sitting on the bed, she let her gaze drift out the window, where the setting sun was painting everything in hues of pumpkin and lavender. It was a moment of peace in what had been a surprisingly turbulent afternoon.

And still. She couldn't seem to shut her brain off. She ordered room service, not wanting to go down to the restaurant and see anyone, and ate it sitting on her bed, watching an old vampire movie she'd found on one of the streaming services.

But nothing worked, and finally, once she'd eaten and the sun had disappeared, leaving behind a velvet sky painted with gently twinkling stars, she gave up on handling her swirling thoughts alone. She slipped her shoes on, poked her head out of the door, and then padded down the hallway toward the hotel's biggest suite, located at the very back of the sprawling mansion. She waved at Chris, one of Carrie's main bodyguards, who nodded at her from his position in the hallway, and then knocked on Carrie's door. It opened a second later, Carrie's tall, willowy frame appearing in the doorway. Her blond curls were pulled back in a loose braid, and she was wearing a pair of pajamas with cats all over them.

"Hey," she said, frowning slightly. "I thought you had plans with your hot cop tonight. What happened? Did he have to work?"

Rosalie shook her head, and to her absolute horror, she felt her throat thicken and her eyes start to sting. No. *No.* She was *not* going to cry over this.

"Oh, shit," said Carrie softly. "You'd better come in." Rosalie stepped inside, and Carrie shut the door behind them, sealing them away in her gorgeous suite. The wood floors gleamed beneath her feet, strewn with colorful, plush area rugs. The living area had a plaid-upholstered sectional that faced a massive stone fireplace with floor-to-ceiling windows on either side. The bedroom door was ajar, giving Rosalie a glimpse of a king-sized four-poster bed complete with embroidered curtains. An antique-looking chandelier hung from the ceiling in the living room, which stretched beyond the fireplace and to the back of the space, where there were two enormous bookshelves laden with books, a desk facing another window, and a set of armchairs. A massive gift basket sat on the desk, and without waiting or asking, Carrie crossed the space and ripped open the cellophane, pulling out boxes of chocolates, fancy pretzels, and a bottle of red wine.

"I was looking for an excuse to dig into this, so I'm glad you came by," she said. She dipped into the bedroom and returned with two wine glasses. They settled onto the sectional sofa, facing the softly crackling fire. "So...what's going on?" she asked, effortlessly opening the bottle of wine and pouring them each a glass. Rosalie took the one Carrie offered to her, curling into the sofa and tucking her legs beneath her.

"He...has a kid."

Saying it out loud didn't make it feel any less surreal.

"And?" Carrie asked, one eyebrow arched. She sipped at her wine. "He's a single guy in his late thirties. He's bound to have a past."

"I know. It's not the fact that he has a kid that bothers me. It's that he didn't tell me."

"Oh. Huh. Yeah…that's…not great," said Carrie, her nose wrinkling.

"And I…told him stuff. About my family, about my childhood, really personal stuff that I don't really talk about with anyone because I thought we…"

Carrie blew out a breath. "You thought you were, like, dating. And this has you feeling like he sees things differently."

She nodded. "Pretty much. I feel like an idiot. I'm usually so good at not letting myself get caught up in situations like this."

"You felt a connection, and you let him see parts of you you don't normally share. That doesn't make you an idiot. It makes you brave."

Rosalie sighed and sipped her wine, letting her gaze go soft as she stared at the undulating flames. "Why didn't he tell me?"

Carrie shrugged. "You'll have to ask him. Maybe he had a good reason. Maybe he just never found the right time. Or, maybe you guys aren't on the same page. You won't know for sure unless you ask."

"I know. I'm…" She shook her head. "I don't do this, you know? Dating, relationships, putting myself out there. I don't know what I'm doing. I don't know how to do this."

"Babe, no one does. We all just kind of fumble our way along, hoping to find someone who'll see the real us and not run screaming in the other direction."

Rosalie laughed softly despite her low mood. "I haven't even been hoping for that. I've been perfectly content to just have my fun and not worry about connections or vulnerability or any of that shit."

"Perfectly content? Really?"

"What?"

Carrie shrugged lazily. "Actively avoiding something isn't exactly content. Contentment has an ease to it. An acceptance. There's a peace that comes with contentment. You... well, you survive. You have your fun, run at the first sign of emotion, and tell yourself you're not lonely."

"Wow. I feel naked right now."

"It's my job to observe the human condition and write songs about it."

"And that's what you'd write about me?"

Carrie stared into the fire. "She's been lonely places, comforting herself with lonely faces, telling herself the outside is where she's happy." She shrugged. "Something like that."

Rosalie's skin tingled uncomfortably. "How do you do it?" she asked quietly, sipping her wine. "How do you keep putting yourself out there after having your heart broken?"

"Because I know that I'm the one responsible for nurturing my heart. I love myself, and take care of myself, and it gives me a resilience that sees me through times like this. I process what I feel through writing songs, or in my journal." She met Rosalie's eyes from the other side of the sectional. "I let myself feel it all." She shifted, taking a long sip of her wine. "What have you done to nurture your heart recently, Rosalie? When was the last time you let yourself feel your feelings?"

"I...I don't know. That's...I don't know."

Carrie stood and retreated into the bedroom, returning a

minute later with a jade green notebook. It was crisp and new, unused. "Here. Start here. Write it all down. All of it. As often as you need."

Rosalie took the notebook, feeling the weight of it between her fingers. She flipped it open, the possibility of the blank pages igniting something in her.

"Once you get it all out, you'll have clarity about how you feel, and what you want to do from there."

"What would you do, if you were me?"

Carrie tilted her head, considering. "Well, it seems like you're into Mr. Chief of police. So, I'd want to know why he didn't tell me about his kid. I'd give him a chance to explain and try to listen with an open heart. The worst thing you could do would be to assume you know why and what it means without actually hearing him out."

"And if he tells me that...it's just a sex thing?"

Carrie shrugged. "Then you have a choice. You can accept that and have some fun, or you can decide that's not what you want, and move on with your eyes open."

Rosalie shivered despite the warmth of the fire. "Like it's just that easy."

"I never said it was easy. It's fucking hard."

Rosalie laughed.

"It is!" said Carrie. "But if you keep your heart locked away in this airless cage, eventually it's going to shrivel up and die. The only way it'll survive is to let it breathe."

"Take it out of the cage," she whispered, and Carrie nodded.

"I know the cage feels safe, but it's not. It's slowly killing you. Because, Rosalie, I can tell. You're not happy. You're lonely, and you bury yourself in work to compensate. Sure, you have flings and hookups, but sex, even great sex, is not the same as having that person. The one who gives you butterflies and makes you laugh. Love is the purest form of joy, and it's worth the risk."

Rosalie nodded, sipping her wine and letting Carrie's words sink in. She was right. Now, she just needed to find the courage to find out where she stood with Jack.

TWENTY

The next day, Jack's eyes were gritty with lack of sleep. He'd tossed and turned all night, unable to get the image of Rosalie's face, pale and lined with hurt, out of his mind. After she'd canceled on him, he'd written at least thirty different text messages to her, trying to explain, but he'd deleted every single one of them. Whatever words he managed to put down, they weren't enough. Not in the face of the pain he'd caused her. He'd been able to read it all in her drawn brows, her hunched shoulders, the set of her mouth. She'd been open and vulnerable with him, something that didn't come easily to her, and he hadn't done the same. He hadn't shared one of the most important parts of his life with her, and she'd been blindsided by it.

She'd pulled away, protecting herself. He knew, because it was exactly what he would've done if the situation were reversed. He also knew that he wanted to fix this. He just needed to find the right words. Needed to do...something. God, he was bad at this. Norah was the only serious relationship he'd ever really had, and they'd gotten married because it was practical and logical, not because they'd been madly, passionately in love.

He scrubbed a hand over his face.

Holy shit.

Holy shit.

He'd never been madly, passionately in love with Norah, had he? He'd thought he had been because he'd cared about her, because he loved her as Chloe's mother. Which meant that his reaction to her engagement was more about him and what was lacking in his life than Norah and any feelings he may have had for her. Because with Rosalie...he didn't even know what he and Rosalie were to each other, but the idea that he'd hurt her was burning his gut, had made it impossible to sleep last night.

The realization jolted through him as he walked down Main Street, approaching the intersection with Chestnut. The early afternoon sky was cloudy with the promise of snow, which would probably be perfect for the music video shoot. One of his officers was there this afternoon, while Jack would be there tonight while he was on duty, acting as a point person for the shoot's security team.

Maybe his opening, when he saw her later, could be to say thank you for letting Chloe meet her favorite celebrity, which had happened earlier that day when Chloe had visited the set and had the best day of her life, according to the texts he'd gotten from Autumn and Norah. Carrie had taken pictures with her, given her a guitar pick and a friendship bracelet, and had been kind and engaging with her young fan. Yeah, he could say thank you for that, which would naturally segue into talking about Chloe, which would lead to an apology...

Yeah. That might work. If she was there. If she was receptive.

He'd recognized her brush off for what it was, but he hadn't called her out on it. He'd let her push him away in the moment because he'd known that she was hurting. But he wasn't going to let that distance fester between them. Not indefinitely.

Cold wind whipped around him, rattling the bare branches in the trees lining the street. Canvas banners hung from the lampposts advertising the town's upcoming Winter Festival, flapping as a gust of wind stole Jack's breath. He tucked the bottom half of his face into his scarf, hunching his shoulders against the cold. He hoped Rosalie had a warmer coat than the camel one she usually wore, because wind like this would go right through it.

He reached his destination, pulling open the heavy wooden door, a bell chiming softly above him as he stepped into the small shop. The walls were lined with wood cabinets with glass doors, the jewelry inside twinkling under the soft lighting. A memory slammed into Jack as the door whooshed shut behind him, of coming here with every single penny he had to his name to buy Norah a ring. Being fresh out of high school, he hadn't had much money, but he'd managed to find something, a small emerald, that he'd always intended as a placeholder for a bigger, better ring. He never had replaced it. He wondered if Norah even still had it. He found that it didn't matter much to him, either way.

He spotted Adam by the long counter at the back of the store, arms braced on the glass as he chatted with the jeweler, a guy they'd gone to high school with named Liam, who ran the shop with his sister Grace.

"Hey," he said, coming to a stop beside his brother, jamming his hands in his pockets. Snow started to swirl down in fat, fluffy flakes, visible through the window at Liam's back.

"Hey," said Adam, not lifting his eyes from the row of diamond rings glinting on a navy blue velvet tray in front of him. "Thanks for coming. I wanted someone else's opinion before deciding."

"He's been agonizing over these four for over a week now," said Liam with a little smile. "Maybe you can nudge him towards a decision."

"Uh, sure," said Jack, stepping closer to the counter. "Wait. Adam." He shook his head, feeling as though he were watching a movie and he'd skipped a very crucial scene. "Are you proposing to Hazel?"

Adam nodded, eyes still fixed on the rings. "Yeah. Don't know when yet. But I'm not going to be able to wait much longer. Her divorce is final, so she's free and clear."

Jack blew out a low whistle. "Wow. I knew you two were serious, but I guess I didn't realize just how serious."

Adam finally looked at his brother, and something inside Jack softened at how freaking happy Adam looked. He'd spent most of his adult life waiting and hoping to find the one. Finally, Hazel had come along. "She's it for me, Jack. I've known it since we first started dating."

Jack smiled, clapping his brother on the shoulder. "Then I'm happy for you. Still not sure why I'm here, though."

"Because you've done this before, and I thought you might have some insight."

"I'm surprised you didn't ask Autumn. She seems like the obvious choice."

"Oh, she came with me a couple of days ago. And then I brought Oli by yesterday. But I want your opinion."

Jack's gaze met Liam's. "Oh, so when you said agonizing, you were serious."

Liam grinned. "As a heart attack."

Jack pulled his hands out of his pockets and rubbed them together. "Okay, then. Let's do this. Show me what the options are."

Adam held up the first ring. "Okay, so option one. Rose gold, pear cut diamond with a diamond encrusted band."

Jack studied it for a moment. "It's beautiful, but...I don't know if it really says Hazel to me, you know?"

"Do you mind if I ask you for some advice? Personal advice, about when you got engaged? I understand if you don't want to talk about it or revisit that."

Jack shrugged. Everything with Norah was so long ago that he was over it, and had been for a long time. "Shoot."

"When you picked out Norah's ring," said Adam, carefully setting the ring back down on the velvet tray, "how did you know you'd found the right one?"

Jack shrugged. "I was mostly focused on what I could afford. I didn't have much money, so it was about getting the most bang for my buck, so to speak. Although I did go with an emerald because green was always her favorite color." He sighed as he thought back. God, they'd just been kids. Wide-eyed, clueless kids. He didn't feel at all like the same person that he'd been then.

Adam nodded, his brows drawn together. "Budget isn't a huge issue. I just...I need to get it right."

Jack faced Adam, leaning his elbow on the counter. "You think she's going to say no if you buy the wrong ring? Dude.

Adam. My God, have you seen how she looks at you? You could propose with a ring made out of pipe cleaners and she'd say yes."

Some of the tension went out of Adam's shoulders then, and he let out a long breath. "I'm just…"

"A very large, very anxious man?"

Adam actually cracked a smile at that. "Just help me pick a ring, okay?"

The second ring was very classic and traditional, with a large solitaire diamond on a band of yellow gold.

"This one?" Adam asked, holding it up.

Jack shook his head. "It's too…basic, I guess. That could be anyone's engagement ring." He flicked his gaze to Liam. "No offense."

He tilted his head. "None taken. One person's basic is another's perfection." Jack was reminded of how Rosalie had identified herself as Queen of the Basic Bitches, and he bit back a smile.

The third ring was made out of white gold, and featured a large, round solitaire on top of an intricately criss-crossing band dotted with pave diamonds.

"I like this one better than the other two. It's more interesting. More unique," Jack said.

"And what about this one?" Adam asked, picking up the final ring.

"That's obviously the one," Jack said casually, still leaning on the counter. "That's much more Hazel than any of these others."

Adam frowned slightly. "It's my favorite, too, but it's not a diamond. I don't want her to be disappointed."

"The center stone is a pear-cut aquamarine," said Liam,

cutting in. "Flanked with a round moonstone on each side, surrounded by small diamonds on a delicate white gold band. It's a very unique item. We're hoping to get more in from this particular designer."

"Why do you like this one?" asked Jack. Adam held the ring between his fingers, gazing at it.

"Because the blue reminds me of the falls, and the moonstone reminds me of the legend that brought us together and changed our lives. This ring feels like our story."

"Then I think you have your answer."

"This is the one Autumn picked, too." Adam stared at the ring.

Jack gently plucked it from between his fingers and handed it to Liam with a little flourish. "He'll take it."

TWENTY-ONE

Sometimes Rosalie didn't understand where Carrie got her energy. How she had the patience and focus to go through the same motions, listen to the same song, repeat shots and poses over and over and over again, but she did, and she did it all with a grace and professionalism that not many others in the industry had.

The shoot was going well, and they'd been blessed with an overcast day, which made for excellent lighting, and naturally falling snowflakes. They'd likely have to be enhanced in post production, but the natural beauty around them was so stunning that the editors would have an easy time achieving the ethereal vibe they were going for.

The sun was setting, and the earlier clouds had cleared, painting the sky in hues of orange and soft purple as it sank behind the falls. And while Rosalie appreciated the beautiful sunset—when had she ever taken the time to appreciate a sunset in New York, she wondered—it meant that her long, busy day wasn't over yet. The moon was full tonight, and if possible, Carrie wanted the real thing in the music video.

They were all gathered in a large tent, eating the catered dinner provided to them by a local restaurant, while Carrie reviewed that afternoon's footage with the director and the assistant director. She was smiling, looking pleased with how everything was going. Rosalie always loved watching her in action. Yes, she was a popstar, but she was also savvy as hell when it came to her marketing, and branding. She was truly the most creative person Rosalie had ever met.

Rosalie munched on her red pepper and grilled chicken quesadilla as she fought the urge to check her phone for the twentieth time since they'd started their dinner break. She hadn't heard from Jack since she'd blown him off, and she hadn't texted him because...well, she was a chicken, in all honesty. Besides, what needed to be discussed had to be in person. Texting wouldn't get them anywhere.

Carrie sauntered over, her plate full with a mango avocado salad, roasted cauliflower bites, and a chicken and broccoli pasta that smelled amazing. "Any word from hot cop?" she asked, plunking down beside Rosalie and lifting a forkful of food to her mouth.

Rosalie shook her head. "No, but I haven't texted him yet, either. I will, though. I know we need to talk." She set her plate down and rubbed her sweaty palms over her jeans.

For a moment, they sat in peaceful companionship, the drumming rush of the falls outside like a soothing white noise. At first, Rosalie had been a bit taken aback at the constant pounding of the water, but now she found she liked it. There was something grounding about it, something almost hypnotic. She'd never thought of herself as a nature lover, but spending time near the beautiful waterfall, on the edge of a forest covered in snow-dusted pines, was making her think otherwise.

A lot of things in Gossamer Falls were making her question what she thought she knew about herself.

"Hey, do you think during the night shoot portion, you could take some behind the scenes footage on your phone?" asked Carrie, chewing thoughtfully. "Oh my God, this is good. We have to go to this restaurant tomorrow."

"Sure. You want some sneak peek, teaser type clips for social media?"

She nodded. "Yeah. Instagram, TikTok. It'll be a casual drop that this is the next single, and the video's coming soon."

"Perfect. I'll try to get a bunch of different angles and shots and clips, and then we can edit together the best ones. Do you want me to drop something on social media now, like a tiny clue about what's happening?"

"That's a great idea. Maybe post a picture of the falls or the moon with a lyric from the song and the looking eyes emoji?"

"Perfect. See, you don't even need me." Rosalie was joking, but something jolted in her chest when she said the words out loud. A sudden cool gust of air whipped through the tent, ruffling her hair, kissing her cheeks. And Rosalie could've sworn she heard a single whispered word echoing through the air.

Stay.

She and Carrie slowly turned toward each other. "Um…"

Carrie frowned slightly, her perfectly groomed brows knitting together. "Did you hear something?"

Rosalie hesitated before nodding briefly. "Yeah. Did you?"

Carrie nodded. "I did. And, um, actually...I've been thinking about staying here to work on some music, maybe for a couple of weeks, and I could've sworn I heard a voice say 'stay.'"

"You're thinking of staying here?"

"Yeah. I talked to Autumn earlier, and she said the suite's mine for as long as I want it. There's just something about this place that's got my creative juices flowing."

"This place is special," Rosalie agreed quietly. "I can't explain it."

"Not everything in life needs an explanation."

"Fair enough."

"Are you dying to get back to the city?"

Rosalie shook her head. "No. I never would've thought of myself as a small town girlie, but...I like it here. It's cozy and peaceful and beautiful."

"It is."

They finished their meals and chatted some more about the town, about the songs Carrie was working on, about other work-related things. The sun disappeared completely, and portable stand lights flickered to life.

When Rosalie stepped out of the craft services tent, she wrapped her coat around herself and took a deep breath of fresh, crisp winter air. And then all of the air whooshed out of her lungs at the sight before her.

The moon hung above the falls, luminous and full, casting an almost otherworldly glow on everything it touched. The setting had been beautiful before, but now, kissed by moon beams, it was transformed. Gray was now silver, black was now a velvety navy, and the falls themselves...well, she could see why they were called Gossamer Falls.

Rosalie stared at the thundering water, the pounding of it filling her ears and her heart. Transfixed, she moved closer, stepping carefully over the rocks. She let out a soft laugh as ice cold mist landed on her face, and a sense of peace and belonging unlike anything she'd ever experienced came over her. She looked up at the moon, struck by its beauty and wondering how on Earth she'd never taken the time to appreciate it before. The sound of the rushing water enveloped her like a hug, and it was as though the rest of the world had dropped away.

A rush of surprisingly warm, sweet hair gusted past, and she heard another whispering voice, this one louder than the one she'd heard in the tent.

Make your wish
Find your love

"I am losing my mind," she said out loud, blinking rapidly. A shiver worked its way down her spine, and she turned around, feeling the weight of someone's eyes on her. But there was no one there. Crew members had started setting up for that night's portion of the shoot, but no one was paying any attention to her.

The whisper returned, more insistent this time.

Stay
Make your wish
Find your love
Around the corner

A chill shot through her that had nothing to do with the cold. Around the corner? But that couldn't be the same…

"Yep, definitely losing my mind," she said, her voice far less certain than it had been a minute ago. She inhaled a steadying breath and closed her eyes, and all she saw was Jack's handsome face. And so, she opened her mouth and whispered, "I wish for Jack."

She opened her eyes and immediately glanced around, hoping no one was watching her make an absolute fool of herself. God, this place must've really been getting to her if she was making wishes for men who she wasn't even sure wanted her for anything beyond a good time.

A gust of air swirled around her, warmer than anything she'd felt in days, and her eyes stung with unshed tears. Tears of hope, of longing, of loneliness, of fear. Of desperately wanting to belong to someone but being shackled to her past. Everything she'd held onto about her dad leaving, about relationships, about love and trust and vulnerability was no longer the shield she'd once needed. Now it was like an anchor around her neck, dragging her down into a dark, lonely place.

A current of electricity ran up her spine, and she turned. Jack stood about twenty feet away, watching her with an unreadable expression on his face. Their eyes met, and she felt her entire world shift on its axis, reorienting itself around him. It was unlike anything she'd ever experienced in her thirty-four years. He lifted his hand in a tentative wave, and when she did the same, a smile spread slowly across his face.

She started to move closer to him, but was intercepted by the assistant director with questions about the shots Rosalie was planning to get for social media. They needed to figure out where to position her so that she wouldn't be in the primary shot, but she could still get some good footage to use to tease the new single and video. When the conversation was over, she looked for Jack, but he was deep in conversation with Carrie's head of security.

As though he could feel her eyes on him, he turned. And while he was still listening to the security guard, his attention was focused solely on her. The conversation ended, and he mouthed three words to her from across the distance.

Can we talk?

Hope soared to life inside her as she nodded. Obviously, they needed to talk. He hadn't told her about his daughter, but as Carrie had pointed out, she needed to hear him out and give him a chance to explain.

His daughter. That...was scary. Chloe seemed sweet and smart, and it wasn't *her* that made Rosalie break out into a cold sweat. It was the idea that Jack had a kid, and that was serious. That if they got involved, Rosalie would play some kind of role in Chloe's life, and she didn't know if she was up for that. If she was good enough or brave enough or strong enough to not only dive into a serious relationship, but one that involved a kid.

With the dinner break over, the director summoned everyone back to the set and started setting up for the next shot, which featured Carrie in a gorgeous white dress with a flower crown on her head, sitting at her antique, snowflake-bedecked piano. The falls were behind her, and the full moon was above. It was an absolutely breathtaking set up, and Rosalie knew that this music video was going to be a fan favorite, no doubt about it.

Slowly, she started to move around with her phone out, sticking to the areas approved by the assistant director, and once again, she had a flash of disappointment that this was what she was doing with her life. Taking videos that literally anyone could take to promote a video that was going to be a success with or without her. She wasn't making a difference anymore. Carrie didn't really even need her. She didn't have anything special to offer, and there were times—like right now, where she was basically just a social media person—where she felt her skills were going to waste.

The thought left a bitter taste in her mouth, and she shook her head, trying to break free of it. She could figure out how she felt about her job after the shoot. Right now, whether she was excited about it or not, she had a job to do.

She moved closer to where Carrie was playing the piano, her upper body swaying in time to the music. The moonlight glinted off of her hair, her dress, the mist in the air shimmering like silver. It was the fairy frost that Indy had mentioned, and it looked absolutely beautiful. She inched closer, raising her phone, trying to find the best angle to frame the shot.

There was an ominous cracking sound from beneath her feet, and she realized that she'd stepped off of the rocks and out onto the frozen creek. The ice groaned, and panic shot through her. Heart in her throat, she moved to step back towards the rocks. She wasn't supposed to be standing on the creek.

Before she found her footing on the rocks, the thin ice gave way with a snap, and she was swallowed up by the icy water.

"Rosalie!" Jack's hoarse cry echoed off of the rocks. His body was in motion before her head disappeared beneath the freezing water. She couldn't swim; she'd told him that the night they'd met. She couldn't swim, and she'd fallen into the creek. "Rosalie!" he screamed again, his legs eating up the distance to where she'd fallen in. People scurried out of his way as he scanned the space for something to use to pull her out. He spotted a length of thick, heavy cable, not plugged into anything and coiled by the base of a camera. He snagged it as he ran, skidding to a stop on the rocks.

"Grab the end of this cable," he called out to the EMTs and security guards who were racing over. "We've gotta pull her out." Several men came running, each taking up a length of the thick coil.

Rosalie's head appeared above the water as she sputtered and shivered.

"Kick your legs," said Jack, kneeling down on the rocks. He wanted to get closer to her, but if he stepped onto the ice, he was likely to fall in too, and that wouldn't help anything. "You're going to be okay, Rosalie. I've got you."

The shoot had stopped around him, everyone gaping at where Rosalie had fallen into the freezing water. Rosalie kicked her legs, her eyes wide and panicked as she barely managed to keep her face above water.

"So...cold..." she chattered between gasping breaths. "Can't...move."

"I've got you," he repeated. Lying on his stomach on the rocks, he extended the end of the thick cable towards her. "Hold on to this. We're going to pull you out."

"I...can't. My fingers...not working..." For a brief, horrifying second, she sank beneath the water again, and Jack reached forward, plunging his arm into the frigid water and grabbing her shoulder. He pulled until she was able to get her head above the surface again, and she sucked in a gasping breath.

"Stay with me, sweetheart," he said, pushing the end of the cable into her frozen hands. "Just hold this as tight as you can. On the count of three, we're going to pull, and you're going to kick as hard as you can, okay?"

"Oh-okay," she said. Her lips were turning blue, her eyes huge and terrified. "I've...I've got it."

"One, two, three!" he called out, and he pulled as hard as he could, anchored by the security guards behind him. Rosalie kicked, her upper body emerging from the water. "That's it, keep pulling!" he yelled. The muscles in his arms screamed in protest, but he didn't care. All that mattered was getting Rosalie out of the freezing water. "Roll onto the ice," he said, giving one last pull as they hauled her out. She did, and he scrambled to his feet, racing over to her. He stood at the edge of the ice and slipped his arms under her, lifting her to his chest. He started walking away from the water immediately, getting them to safer ground.

Around them, people clapped and cheered that Rosalie was safe, but Jack knew that she wasn't out of the woods yet. The risk of hypothermia in a situation like this was very, very real. The mist of the falls fell on him as he set her down and started peeling her soaked coat off of her. The moon highlighted her pale skin and her shivering form, and despite the terrifying thing that had just happened, Jack felt a sense of peace come over him, unlike anything he'd ever experienced before. Peace, and purpose, and a bone-deep knowing that Rosalie was it for him. He'd never felt anything even close to this with Norah, but with Rosalie...somehow, he already knew that she was everything.

If he hadn't fucked it up before they'd even began by not telling her about Chloe.

The EMTs crowded around, but Jack waved them off. "I've got her," he said. If anyone was going to take care of Rosalie, it was going to be him.

"Let's take her into the tent," said Carrie, and Jack had been so focused on Rosalie that he hadn't even noticed her approaching. "She needs to get warm."

Again, one of the EMTs approached, but Jack tightened his grip on Rosalie and let out a low sound, almost like a growl. "I said, I've got her."

He tucked Rosalie's shivering form against him, following Carrie to a white tent set up off to the side. The inside was warm with electric heat.

"I need to get her out of these wet clothes," said Jack. He tucked a wet tendril of hair behind Rosalie's ear. "We need to get her dry and then I'm going to take her to get warmed up."

Carrie nodded. "Here, Rosalie, you can change into these." She extended a sweatshirt and a pair of fleece-lined leggings to her. "Let me go find a towel." She dashed out of the tent, and Jack started methodically stripping Rosalie, needing to get the soaked, icy fabric off of her skin.

"You...saved...me," she said through clattering teeth. She was shivering violently now. Gently, he pulled her soaked sweater off over her head, letting it fall to the floor beside them.

"My heart stopped when I saw you go through that ice." He rubbed his hands over her bare arms, and just then, Carrie returned with two fluffy towels.

"Here," she said. "Do what you need to do. Make sure she's okay." She handed Jack the towels.

"Thanks."

"You're welcome. Oh, and once she's feeling better, make sure you talk. Because she really likes you, but you kinda messed up not telling her about your kid. I'm sure you can sort it out," she added with a cheeky smile, and then disappeared through the tent's flap, leaving them both in silence.

Well, damn. He'd just gotten a mild dressing down from one of the most famous people in the world. Today was just full of surprises.

Jack worked the towel over Rosalie's skin, then removed her wet bra and added it to the pile of clothing. When she was dry, he helped her pull on the sweatshirt, and then knelt down in front of her, helping her with her wet boots. He tossed them aside, one by one, and then peeled her wet socks off. Finally, he reached for the button on her jeans, and she helped him work them down over her hips, the fabric clinging to her skin. He tossed them aside and then her panties, working the towel over her hips, her legs, her feet, drying her thoroughly. Her shivering had lessened to the occasional tremor.

"She's right," he murmured, helping her slide the leggings up her legs. "I did mess up."

"Yeah. You did. And she's also right that I really like you."

"Will you let me take you to my house to get warm? You can have a hot shower, I'll make you some tea, and we can talk?"

She nodded, her arms wrapped around herself. "Yeah. You...thank you. For saving me."

He stood, cradling her cheek in his palm and pulling her against him. She sighed and melted into him. "I'll save you over and over and over again, Rosalie. Whatever you need, whenever you need, if you'll let me." He wanted to tell her that he'd happily spend forever taking care of her, but thought she'd had enough of a fright for the day, what with falling through the ice. No need to terrify the woman with the intensity of his feelings for her.

She snuggled into him. "I've never had someone to look after me. It feels...nice."

He held her tighter. "Good. Come on, let's get you to my cruiser."

"Aren't you supposed to be on duty?" she asked, her eyebrows lifting as he once again sank to his knees in front of her and started helping her into the pair of sneakers Carrie had found. They were too big for Rosalie, but they'd do for now.

"This is more important," he said, standing and shrugging out of his police jacket. He held it out for her, and she slid her arms into it, wrapping it around herself. He could've sworn she inhaled deeply, as though she were smelling it. But it might've been a sigh or a shiver. He pulled his police beanie off his head, and moved behind Rosalie, where he wound her hair up on top of her head, and then slipped the beanie on over top, keeping her wet hair contained and away from her skin.

"Won't you be cold?" she asked with a little shiver.

"Sweetheart, I didn't fall into icy water. I'll be fine." He tucked her hand in his and started leading her out of the tent.

"Jack?" she asked, and he stopped. She swallowed thickly, her eyes huge. "Is this...real?" Her voice was barely a whisper, and while her question was vague, he knew exactly what she was talking about. The falls, the magic, the connection between them that only seemed to grow, like a fire burning hotter and hotter, brighter and more beautiful.

He pulled her against him again and brushed his lips over hers. "Feels real to me."

Her face was tight with emotion. "Me too."

He kissed her again, soft and sweet, her lips cold against his. "Come on. Let's get you home."

TWENTY-THREE

Rosalie felt wired and jittery as Jack pulled his police SUV into the driveway of a dark green A-frame not far from the falls on Willow Avenue. Pine trees lined the driveway, separating it from its neighbors, and a neat row of shrubs stood on either side of the walkway that led to the front door. Jack parked the truck and jogged around to her side, opening the door and helping her down. The worst of the chill had passed, but she still felt too cold. Her thoughts were scattered, and it felt as though her heart kept beating irregularly in her chest.

She wasn't sure if it was from her plunge into the icy water of the creek, or something else. Something to do with Jack and whatever magic was happening between them.

He led her inside the house, which was quiet and dark.

"Chloe's at her mom's this week," he said, answering her unspoken question. "We have shared custody, and she trades off weeks."

She nodded as she followed him into the entryway, letting him take back his heavy police jacket and slipping off her shoes. The small entryway opened onto a living room with soaring windows, a large, soft-looking gray sectional, and a beautiful stone fireplace.

"I'd like you to go take a hot shower. It's the fastest way to warm up," he said. The stairs were off to the side, acting as a divider of sorts between the open living room and kitchen spaces. "My bedroom's on the right, and there's an ensuite in there. Take your time, use whatever you need. Okay?"

She nodded, her eyes still roving over the space. Framed family photos sat on top of the mantle. Jack with his siblings, Jack with who she assumed were his parents, Jack and Chloe, Chloe as a baby, Chloe as a little girl with pigtails on a pink bicycle. Something in her chest opened up at the sight of those photos, and she realized after a moment that the pain crawling through her was grief. Grief over her father leaving, over feeling as though she hadn't been worthy of his love. He'd moved on, made a new family, and hadn't looked back. He hadn't loved her the way Jack clearly loved Chloe.

She walked up the stairs, the muscles in her legs stiff and sore from kicking so hard under the cold water, and she paused on the landing. To the right, she could see into Jack's bedroom. To the left, there was an open door leading to Chloe's. The landing itself was another living space, with more soaring windows, a beamed ceiling and an area that clearly belonged to Chloe, with a large keyboard, a desk with a pink chair, a large bookcase, and two huge white beanbag chairs.

Unbidden, she found herself crossing the space to lean on the door jamb and peer into Chloe's room. The floors throughout the house were hardwood, and Chloe's room was no exception, but a large pink and blue area rug covered most of the floor. A double bed sat in the middle of the space, covered in a white duvet with large pink polka dots and a couple of feathery throw pillows. A rattan swing hung from the ceiling in the corner, surrounded by dangling fairy lights. The far wall was windowless and taken up entirely with Carrie Clark posters. Rosalie's lips twitched in a grin. Knowing what a superfan Chloe was, she was glad she'd been able to arrange for the meet and greet. A girly chandelier hung from the slanted ceiling, and a table sat tucked into the other corner, laden with various crafting supplies.

With a sigh, Rosalie padded into Jack's bedroom, which was more sparsely decorated than Chloe's, but no less cozy. A fluffy gray rug covered the hardwood, and a king-sized bed sat in the middle of the space. The wall behind it was covered in aged, gray pine, while the far wall was nothing but windows that looked out onto all those pines. A gray and white duvet sat rumpled on the unmade bed, the only untidy thing she'd spotted in the whole house. A nightstand sat beside the bed, with another family photo—this one of a much younger, shirtless Jack holding a newborn baby Chloe, a heart-twisting grin on his face—and a small stack of books. She eyed the titles on the spines. One was a health and fitness book, which made her smile, the second was a non-fiction book about World War II, and the last was a book about parenting through puberty.

Oh, poor Jack. She pressed her fingers to her lips, a smile twitching there.

The bathroom was a long, narrow room, with a large, walk-in shower at the far end. She reached in and turned it on, pulling her borrowed clothes off as she waited for the water to heat up.

She took her time in the shower, standing under the soothing spray until she was able to forget just how cold she'd been. The icy water had taken her breath away, had been like needles on her skin. It wasn't something she ever wanted to experience again.

Once she was warm, she stepped out of the shower, dried off, and instead of putting on her borrowed clothes again, slipped on Jack's blue robe, which hung from a hook on the back of the door. It was soft and worn, and it smelled like him, so she wrapped it around herself and buried her nose inside it, inhaling deeply. A hint of pine, something fresh and clean and crisp. She realized that it reminded her of smelling snow with Indy that first day in town. Jack smelled like snow falling.

Quite honestly, he smelled like home.

She made her way back down the stairs in the robe, her hair wet and unbrushed. She saw Jack in the kitchen, his back to her as he poured two cups of steaming hot tea. A fire now crackled in the fireplace, spreading a glowing warmth through the space.

"I owe you an apology," he said simply, and she sat down on the couch. His eyes flared as he spotted her in his robe, but then he swallowed thickly and brought the two mugs of tea over to the living room, handing one to her. She sipped tentatively, the hot liquid warming her from the inside.

"Yes, I think you do," she said, cradling the mug in her hands.

"I'm sorry I didn't tell you about Chloe. I should've. And I meant to. You didn't deserve to be blindsided with it."

"I was pretty shocked, given how much I'd opened up to you, that you hadn't done the same. It made me feel like..."

She trailed off and took another sip of her tea. "We weren't on the same page. About this. Us."

"I know. When you told me you had to work after meeting Chloe, I knew I'd fucked up."

"I'm sorry that I canceled our plans instead of talking to you. I panicked. I was stunned, honestly."

"It's okay. I get it." He took her free hand, sliding his much larger fingers through hers. "I should've told you. I'm sorry that I didn't."

"Why didn't you?"

He stared into the crackling fire. "I have a rule that I don't discuss Chloe with...with..." He trailed off, and she arched an eyebrow.

"Your hookups?"

He grimaced slightly and then nodded. "Yeah. But then, when it became clear that you were more than that, I wanted to tell you. I just never found the time or the words. It's a lame excuse, I know."

"Were you scared that I'd reject you if I knew you had a kid?"

He tilted his head. "Yeah. Partly. Especially because of everything you'd said about your dad leaving...I didn't want you to think I was like him."

Her heart squeezed in her chest. "I don't think that. Every situation is different, and you're clearly very involved with your daughter's life." She sighed, sipping her tea. "I get it, but you still should've told me."

"I know. I'm sorry, Rosalie. I promise, I won't keep anything from you again. I'm...not good at this stuff," he said quietly, his thumb tracing over the back of her knuckles. "Dating, relationships. I don't know what I'm doing."

She laughed softly. "And I do?"

"Maybe we could figure it out, together? If that's something you want."

An invisible weight lifted from Rosalie's chest, and she felt that same sense of peace she'd felt at the falls. A peace based on hope and connection and knowing that she was exactly where she was supposed to be.

"It is. I do want that, Jack."

A small smile tugged at his lips, hope written across his features. "I really am sorry, Rosalie."

"You're forgiven."

Two small words, said freely and honestly, that made her feel as though everything was going to be okay in the end. She set her tea down and shivered slightly at the loss of the warmth.

"Come here," said Jack, sitting back in the corner of the sectional and tugging her towards him. He settled her with her back to his chest, his arms around her. "When you fell in that water, I couldn't even breathe." His grip tightened on her, and she leaned back against him, absorbing his words, his warmth.

"Thank you for saving my life. For changing my tire. For walking me back to the hotel through the snow. No one's ever cared for me that way before. It's why it's so easy to forgive you for not telling me about your daughter. Because I know you're a good man. I know that you care about me. You're not like him," she finished in a whisper, and she wasn't sure if the words were for Jack, or for herself.

Jack buried his face in her neck and inhaled. She moaned softly, and he kissed a path down her neck, to her shoulder, pulling the robe open slightly. "And I never will be," he said, kissing her neck, her jaw.

"God, you are so forgiven," she said, her voice shaky. "But I think I could use a little more apologizing." She tilted her head, giving him more skin to taste and tease with his mouth.

"Oh yeah?" he asked, one hand dropping to the belt of her robe—his robe—and letting it fall open. Instantly, his hands were on her breasts, rough and strong and warm as he cupped them. The lust that flowed through her was strong, but the relief—relief that everything was okay, that he wanted this too, that he was finally touching her again—was even stronger. She arched her back as he pinched at her hard nipples.

"Can we go upstairs?" she asked.

Instead of answering, he scooped her into his arms and stood, making Rosalie laugh and loop her arms around his neck. She nuzzled into him as he walked toward the stairs, kissing his neck, his stubbled jaw. He set her carefully on his messy, unmade bed, then pushed the robe all the way open.

"Rosalie Crawford, you are the most beautiful creature I've ever laid eyes on."

"I need to see you," she said, more desperate for him by the second. "Please, Jack."

Kneeling in front of her on the bed, he pulled his shirt off over his head, then dropped his hands to his pants, flicking open the button and undoing the zipper. In record time, he was naked, and Rosalie slid a hand up his hard stomach, his skin warm beneath her fingers.

"Pretty fast when you don't have boots to trip over," she said, and they both laughed, warmth and happiness passing between them. When the laughter faded, he eased himself down on top of her, his thick, hard cock like a brand against her thigh.

"Fuck, I've been thinking about this for days. Weeks."

"Me, too," she admitted, wrapping her legs around his waist. She slid her fingers into the thick hair at the nape of his neck, holding him close. "I would lie awake at night, thinking about you, wondering if you were thinking about me. Wondering if you wanted more."

He pressed his forehead to hers. "I thought about you constantly, Rosalie. I wanted more from the moment I walked out of that hotel room."

Her heart soared in her chest as Jack kissed her, slowly and thoroughly, as though they had all the time in the world.

Because they did. She could see it, stretching out in front of them, a glimmering golden road filled with hope and possibilities.

"Ah, shit," he said, breaking the kiss. His forehead was still pressed to hers, and she could feel his heart pounding.

"What?"

"I don't have any condoms. I bought more and put them in my work bag because I thought I was heading over after I was done with my shift. The bag's in my locker at work. Fuck."

He eased back, but Rosalie tightened her grip on him. "Do we need one? I'm on the pill."

"I'm good, if that's what you're asking. And I haven't gone bare with anyone since the divorce."

"I just want you, then, Jack. Nothing between us."

His cock jerked against her thigh. She kissed his neck, his jaw, his shoulders, holding him close.

"Rosalie," he groaned, sliding down her body, kissing a path across her collarbones, over her breasts and down her stomach. He kissed her thighs, her calves, all the way down to her ankles. It was an apology and a promise, all wrapped up in one. By the time he kissed his way back up to her pussy, she was aching and wet, desperate for him. But she knew that tonight wouldn't be playful and dirty like that first time. There would be time for playful and dirty in the future. Tonight was about them. About taking a chance and trusting that the other person would catch you.

He gently parted her pussy lips with his thumbs and swept his tongue over her clit. She moaned, fisting her hands in the sheets. He did it over and over again, just that slow, achingly gentle movement. He traced a circle around it, kissed it, sucked it gently.

"You taste even sweeter than I remember," he said, sliding one finger inside her and curling it up, stroking slowly. "So fucking good."

"Oh, God," she moaned, her hips writhing as the pressure mounted inside her. If he kept this up, she was going to come very, very soon.

"Play with your tits," he said, his voice going a little rougher around the edges. "Show me how you pull on your sweet little nipples."

She did as she was told, lifting her hands to her breasts and rolling her nipples between her fingers, making her back arch off the mattress.

"Good girl," he murmured, still kissing and licking gently. "Such a good fucking girl for me."

"Jack," she whispered, playing with her nipples, pushing her throbbing pussy against his mouth. "Please."

"Please what?"

"I'm so close. Please. I need to come."

He chuckled against her, but added a second finger and sucked her clit into his mouth, working it with his tongue.

"Oh, fuck!" she screamed when the orgasm tore through her. Her vision faded at the edges for a second, the pleasure so intense that it left her light-headed. Before the last of the throbs had subsided, she was reaching for him, urging him up her body, the frantic need to feel him inside her again consuming her.

He kissed her, letting her taste herself on his mouth as he settled between her thighs. Moonlight streamed through his windows, bathing his skin in a silver glow, highlighting the planes of his face, the dips and valleys of his muscled torso. She'd never seen a more beautiful man in her entire life.

"Rosalie," he murmured, rocking gently against her. "Tell me you're sure, sweetheart."

She wrapped her legs and arms around him, holding him close. "I'm so sure. I need you. Please."

He pushed inside her slowly, just a little at first, and then more and more with each measured, deliberate stroke. Outside, a sudden wind whipped through the trees, knocking the branches together and rattling the windowpanes.

"You take me so fucking well," he said, his voice hoarse, his eyes bright. "So goddamn perfect."

He pulled out and thrust in once more, this time burying himself to the hilt and making her gasp, making her toes curl. His eyes were closed as though he were fighting for control, and Rosalie stroked her hands up and down his muscled back.

"Watching you fall into that water was my own personal hell," he said, thrusting gently. "And this, right here, in this bed with you, is my own personal heaven. Nothing has ever felt as good as you do right now, sweetheart."

She inhaled, drawing the scent of him into her lungs, feeling drunk on Jack. On his scent, on the feel of him inside her, on the way he cared for her.

"Jack," she whispered, her throat tight with emotion. "Yes. Oh God, yes."

He started to move a little faster, stroking in and out of her, over and over again, heat building between her thighs. He let out a low, masculine groan, swiveling his hips.

"Being bare inside you feels so fucking good. You're so hot and smooth. So fucking perfect."

She moaned and slid her hands down his back to his muscled ass, gripping it and urging him deeper inside her. He let out a strangled groan and kissed her, hard and deep, tongues and lips clashing as he started to fuck her harder.

"There's nothing between us," she whispered. "No secrets. No condoms. Nothing."

"Nothing," he repeated, his hips thrusting forward.

Something inside Rosalie started to unspool, and it wasn't just her impending orgasm.

"Don't hold back. I want you to come inside me. Fill me up."

"Fuck, Rosalie," he ground out, sweat dotting his hairline. "You have no idea what your dirty mouth does to me."

"You like when I tell you how much I love your cock?" She let out a shuddery moan as he fucked her harder and deeper. "When I tell you that I played with my clit every single day thinking about how much I wanted you again?"

He let out a low, growling sound, his thrusts getting rougher.

"That's it, fuck," she panted out, her voice high and breathless. "Fuck me with that thick, hard cock I can't get enough of."

"Oh my fucking God," he groaned, his hips snapping forward now, the base of his cock rubbing against her clit so perfectly that with another thrust, she was coming again, her pussy convulsing and fluttering around his cock as she clung to him. She screamed his name, her fingers biting into his biceps as she hung on against the onslaught of pleasure.

"Rosalie, fuck. Gonna come inside you. Fill that pretty pussy with my come."

"Yes," she hissed, arching her hips up to meet his. "Yes, Jack."

He groaned, a long, loud, deliciously masculine sound, and she felt his cock pulse and throb as he emptied himself inside her.

The night that Rosalie fell into the frozen creek was both one of the most terrifying and best nights of Jack's life. After they'd cleared the air about his not telling her about Chloe, and after they'd made love, they'd laid in Jack's bed for hours, cuddling and kissing and talking. He'd told her all about Chloe, about his divorce. He'd talked about his tours in Iraq and Afghanistan. She'd told him more about her family, about places she'd traveled, about her growing restlessness in her career.

He'd held her all night, and they'd made love again in the morning, slow and sweet as he'd rocked into her from behind, trailing kisses across her neck, her shoulders. She'd come around him with a soft cry, milking his cock in a way he was already addicted to. He'd wanted nothing more than to spend the day in bed with her, but they both had to work. He'd dropped her off at the hotel, and she'd hesitated getting out of the car.

"Jack?"

"Yeah?"

"What, um, what are we doing?"

He'd grinned at her. "I'm not the expert, but I think it's called dating."

She'd returned his smile and kissed him before hopping out of the SUV, and as she walked inside the hotel, Jack had felt as though a piece of his heart was walking away with her.

The next several days passed by in a blur. One of Jack's deputies was off with the flu, so he'd had to work extra hours to fill in. Rosalie had been busy too, finishing up the video shoot and arranging for Carrie to stay in Gossamer Falls for the next couple of weeks to work on music. Whatever had convinced the superstar to stay in Gossamer Falls, Jack was grateful because it gave him more time with Rosalie.

He met Norah for coffee to congratulate her in person on her engagement to Ian, and to let her know that he was seeing someone, too, and that he planned to introduce her to Chloe as his girlfriend that coming weekend. She'd given him her blessing, and told him she was glad to see that he was finally moving on and getting serious with someone.

Now, it was Saturday, and it was Jack's morning to volunteer at the food bank. As usual, Chloe was going to come with him—she usually put her headphones in and worked in the back filling hampers—while Jack handed out the hampers, talked with people, and when things slowed down, made phone calls to try to raise more money for the food bank. But this time was different, because this morning, Rosalie was coming, too.

Ever since he'd told her about his volunteer work with the food bank, she'd been interested, often asking him questions about how it was run. So, he wanted her to come and see for herself what they were doing. Making sure everyone in the community had access to good food was something that mattered to Jack.

Maybe it would matter to Rosalie, too. Maybe Gossamer Falls could become her home. He hadn't told her about the thoughts swirling through his mind, mostly because now that they were dating, he didn't want to send her running in the other direction. They were already moving fast, what with her meeting Chloe, seeing each other pretty much daily, even if it was just for a quick coffee when they had time, and he didn't want to give her any reason to pull the plug and run back to the city. Truth be told, he wanted her to stay here, in Gossamer Falls, with him. He wanted to ask her to stay.

But it was too soon. For now, he'd wait and see how things unfolded, wait and see what she wanted to do. He could be patient, for her. For a little while, at least.

"Do, um, you have any questions?" asked Jack, glancing at Chloe in the rear-view mirror.

"About what?"

"Me and Rosalie, dating. I've never...done the girlfriend thing before."

Chloe shrugged. "I dunno. I've met her already and she seems nice. Normal. What would I have questions about?"

"I don't know, Chloe. I'm just trying to..." He shoved a hand through his hair. "This is a first for us. I just want it to go well."

"Because you really like her." It wasn't a question, but an observation.

"Well, yeah. I do."

"That's good, right?"

"I think so."

"Then why are you being weird?"

"I don't know. Am I?"

"Yesssssss," said Chloe with an exaggerated eye roll. "It's not a big deal. Rosalie is your girlfriend. She's coming to the food bank this morning. I like her, Dad. I've already met her. It's all chill."

"It's chill, is it?" Nothing made him feel older than Chloe using slang he didn't fully understand. He'd bookmarked Urban Dictionary in his phone just to keep up.

"Yeah. It's because of Rosalie that I met Carrie Clark. She's cool."

Jack nodded, deciding to leave it at that. He was in foreign territory here, and he'd just have to do his best to figure it out as he went.

He pulled his truck under the porte cochere of the hotel, and then hopped out of the driver's seat. Rosalie was already waiting in the lobby, and she bounded out the front doors with a little wave when she spotted him. She looked beautiful, as always, even with her hair up in a ponytail, and wearing a sweatshirt and skinny jeans under her coat. He loved seeing her put together, but he liked casual Rosalie the best of all because she was real, and he knew how few people saw the real her.

"Hey," she said, wrapping her arms around him for a hug and planting a chaste kiss on his cheek. "Long time no see."

He laughed, because he'd seen her last night while Chloe had been at the movies with her friends. They'd gone for a walk in the snow, then had sex in the shower, then snuggled in bed watching *Seinfeld* before he'd had to leave to pick up Chloe.

"I feel like I get to see a new side of you today," she said, her eyes flicking between him and the truck, where Chloe sat behind the tinted windows. "Jack in full dad mode."

"Being Chloe's dad is a huge part of my life," he agreed, nodding. "Hanging out with the three of us together is a big step. Are you nervous?"

"Oh yeah. I barely slept last night, replaying the same questions over and over in my mind," she said quietly. "What if she doesn't like me? What if Norah doesn't like me? What if I screw this whole thing up?" She was talking faster and faster, and Jack slipped a hand under her chin.

"Hey, hey. Slow down. She already likes you. You arranged for her to meet Carrie, so she already thinks you're the shit. Plus, she's eleven. The only people she truly likes are her friends. You're not going to screw anything up." He tucked a loose strand of hair behind her ear. "The fact that this obviously matters so much to you makes me want to kiss the shit out of you right now."

She laughed. "It does matter to me. Because you matter to me, and therefore so does getting to know your daughter, as nervous as I might be."

He kissed her forehead and then opened the passenger's side door for her. She climbed in and immediately turned to Chloe.

"Hey, Chloe," she said. "I brought you something."

Chloe's eyebrows rose. "You did?"

"Yeah." Rosalie reached into her bag and pulled out a pretty frame that accommodated several pictures. "The ones with you and Carrie. I thought you might want a keepsake."

Chloe's eyes widened and she took the frame with a small gasp. "Oh, this is so cool. Thank you!"

"You're welcome," said Rosalie, and as Jack buckled up his seatbelt, he could see a hint of relief in the set of Rosalie's shoulders. His heart beat happily in his chest. He didn't have any expectations that they'd become best friends overnight, but he knew that Rosalie fit with him, and that with time, she'd fit with Chloe, too. If he was honest, he'd known it since the first night he'd met her. And since the night at the falls, it had been undeniable.

Maybe the legend was true, he mused as he drove, getting on the highway to drive to the next town over where the food bank was located. He'd been kissed by the mist of the falls under the light of the full moon, and he felt as though his true love had been revealed to him. The fact that he was meant to be with Rosalie was obvious to him.

God, if this was how Adam felt about Hazel, he could see why he was ring shopping only a few months in. It had been less than a month since he'd first met Rosalie, and now he couldn't picture his life without her.

They arrived at the food bank about ten minutes later, Rosalie and Chloe chatting about all things Carrie Clark for most of the drive. He pulled into the parking lot, his heart constricting at the families already lined up outside the door.

They headed inside through the back door, Chloe moving to her usual station in the back while she said hello to the other volunteers. Jack laced his fingers through Rosalie's and gave her a short tour, showing her where the food was stored, the small office used for management, and the front, which was set up like a storefront, with a counter where people who'd pre-registered for a hamper could pick one up.

"I like that this looks more like a grocery store instead of a typical food pantry," said Rosalie, her lips pursed thoughtfully. "I think it destigmatizes the food scarcity more and more people are experiencing."

"I couldn't agree more," said a woman from behind them, and they both turned.

"Rosalie, this is Barbara Peters. She runs the food bank."

Rosalie held out her hand. "Hi Barbara," she said easily. "I'm Rosalie Crawford, Jack's girlfriend."

"Welcome," she said warmly. "We're always happy to have more volunteers. I'm the only paid employee here, and I don't know what I'd do without volunteers like Jack, who take on so much."

Jack felt the tips of his ears go hot, and he ducked his head. "Just doing my part," he said.

"It's a shame you've already got a job, because it's going to be hard to find someone to take over when I retire in the spring."

"You're retiring?" asked Jack, his eyebrows raising.

Barbara nodded. "I'm ready. But first I need to make sure I'm leaving this place in good hands. If you know anyone looking for a job in the nonprofit sector that doesn't pay well and comes with a fair bit of stress, let me know," she said with a little laugh. "I'll let you get to it. I'm going to open the doors in five minutes."

For the next two hours, they were non-stop busy handing out hampers, restocking shelves, and answering questions from customers. Even though she'd never been here before, Rosalie was in her element, her natural warmth and ease with people shining through. She was radiant as she restocked a display of apples, gorgeous as she helped an elderly woman decide between canned tuna and salmon, beautiful as she laughed at something Barbara said. Jack felt proud that she was his.

That was how he thought of her now. His Rosalie.

With the initial rush over, Rosalie leaned on the counter. "Do you mind if I go talk to Barbara? I have some questions for her."

"Oh yeah?" he asked, one eyebrow arched. "You wanna move to Gossamer Falls and take over for Barbara at the food bank?" He was half-kidding, but his heart doubled its tempo as the words left his mouth, because, damn, did he want that. He was probably getting ahead of himself, but he didn't have to try to hard to picture a life with Rosalie in Gossamer Falls.

Her eyes slammed into his. "Yeah. Maybe." He could hear the question in her voice, and he grinned.

"You'd better go talk to her, then."

"And after, can we take Chloe for hot chocolate?"

"You don't need to bribe her," he said teasingly. "She likes you."

"I'm not trying to bribe her. I want hot chocolate, and figured she might, too. I've heard Deja Brew makes a delicious one."

"They do," he said, glowing from within at how easily she was including his daughter and fitting in with the town.

She shrugged. "Besides. I'd like to get to know her more. I don't want to push things, but...I do want to try, if that makes sense."

"It does, and it means a lot to me."

She smiled softly. "She's part of your life." She said it easily, and Jack felt his chest expanding with all of the emotions crashing through him.

He gave her a quick kiss on the cheek and then returned to his administrative work, sorting through the forms submitted by new users. In the background, he could over-hear Rosalie asking Barbara questions about corporate part-nerships, community engagement, donor cultivation, awareness campaigns, and more.

Fuck, she was smart, and it was hot as hell. And the fact that she was thinking about a future, here in Gossamer Falls...could a heart explode? Because Jack felt like his might.

Every winter, the citizens of Gossamer Falls—along with those of several neighboring towns scattered along the banks of the Hudson River—looked forward to the town's Winter Festival. It was a celebration held during the last week of February, meant to bring light and cheer to what could often be a long, cold winter. By the end of February, most people were sick of snow and cold, with spring still a month away—at least.

Attending the festival was a Shephard family tradition, and the only time Jack had missed it was when he'd been deployed. It was one of his favorite events in the town, and this year he was even more excited about it because he got to share it with Rosalie.

It had been nearly a week since their morning at the food bank, and she hadn't mentioned staying again. Maybe it had been a little throwaway comment said in the moment that didn't really mean anything. He'd been too scared to ask her, terrified she'd confirm that she hadn't meant it. But since she'd said it, all Jack could do was picture Rosalie in

Gossamer Falls. She could take Barbara's job at the food bank. There were a couple of places for rent in town, and she could make her own little home here. When she was ready, she could move in with him, as long as Chloe gave her thumbs up.

They could get married, maybe add to their family with a baby or two...

Fuck. Now he was really getting ahead of himself. He didn't even know if Rosalie wanted kids.

He couldn't help himself. The past week had been absolute bliss. They'd gone for coffee at Deja Brew and talked for hours about everything and nothing, laughing and flirting until Sienna, the coffee shop's owner, had had to shoo them out at closing time. After which they'd parked his truck by the river and Rosalie had given him the absolute hottest blow job of his life.

They'd spent an afternoon browsing the little shops downtown, exploring the bookstore, the antique store, and the clothing boutique he'd seen her eyeing. They'd left without buying anything, but he'd gone back and bought the emerald green knit scarf she'd tried on that had made her gorgeous brown eyes look like melted chocolate. He'd given it to her the following night, when she'd come over to watch the Rangers game. She'd especially enjoyed it when he'd tied her up with it afterward.

They'd had a movie night with Chloe, eating popcorn and losing themselves in Harry Potter. The next day, Rosalie had taken Chloe with her to have lunch with Carrie, officially cementing her as the coolest person ever—besides Carrie, of course—in Chloe's books. And Rosalie, despite her lack of experience with kids, seemed to genuinely enjoy spending time with Chloe and getting to know her. Jack admired the slow, easygoing approach she was taking with Chloe, letting things unfold naturally over time without pressure or expectations. It was the right call. Then again, given how good Rosalie was with people, he shouldn't have been surprised.

And over and over, Jack wondered: what if every day could be like this?

"Hey, where did you go?" asked Rosalie, slipping her hand in his as they crunched through the snow.

"Just thinking," he answered, giving her hand a squeeze.

"About?"

He stopped and pulled her against him, giving her a sweet, chaste kiss. It wasn't the kind of kiss he wanted to give her, but Chloe was nearby, so he needed to keep things PG. "You. Us. How happy you make me."

She grinned, a wide smile spreading across her face. "You make me happy, too. I didn't think this kind of thing was real, you know? I feel like I'm living in an R-rated Hallmark movie."

Jack laughed. "It could be like this every day," he said quietly.

She swallowed thickly, tucking the bottom half of her face into the scarf he'd bought her. "I know."

"Dad, I'm going to go find my friends, okay?" called Chloe from several feet away.

"Okay," he said. "Be safe and have fun."

"I will!" she shouted and scampered off down the path that led to the festival, cheeks pink with excitement.

The festival was held in the town park, called Mary's Park after Mary Elizabeth Axton, the woman who had written the original Gossamer Falls legend. It sat on the edge of the river, and in the summer, it was a prime place to stroll, eat ice cream, and watch the water. There was a playground and small splash pad for kids, and lots of trees with shaded benches. In the winter, the town created an outdoor ice rink on the grassy field.

The path from the parking lot to the park was lit with softly glowing torches, and over the crunch of their boots in the snow, Jack could hear music, laughter, and people talking. With Rosalie's hand in his, they rounded the bend, and she gasped.

"Oh, wow," she breathed, her eyes bright as she took it all in.

On one side of the park was a winter market, with vendors housed under small white tents lit with fairy lights, selling things like loose leaf tea, candles, knit mittens and scarves, and handmade décor. The ice rink sat in the center of the park, lit up with twinkling lights, pop music playing as people skated in a circle around the oval rink. The hill on the other side of the park had been transformed into a tube ride, people shrieking with laughter as they slid down the snow-covered hill. To the side of the hill was an outdoor food court, with a massive bonfire in the middle, sending sparks up into the night sky. Even from where he stood, Jack could smell the hot chocolate and mulled apple cider. Chloe was already at the s'mores station with her friends, and several people were walking around with gooey cinnamon rolls in little paper bags.

The main feature, however, was the towering white Ferris wheel right by the water, flanked with a small midway with traditional carnival games. It glowed in the night, a welcoming beacon for the festival.

"This looks amazing," said Rosalie, her eyes roving over everything. "I can see why everyone in town's been talking about it all week."

"Come on," he said, moving them through the crowd and toward the ice rink. "Let's go skating."

She paused, her feet skidding to a stop on the snow packed path. "Oh. Um. Uh…I don't have skates."

"It's okay. We can rent them."

"I…" She swallowed and her eyebrows inched up her head. "Don't laugh at me, but I've never skated in my life before."

"Never?"

She shook her head. "Never. Like, never ever."

He grinned. "Well, in that case, I'm delighted to be your first."

She laughed. "You gonna take care of me?" she asked in a mock innocent voice that had blood flowing to his cock. Jesus Christ, she was perfect. Perfect in every single way.

He pressed a kiss to her temple. "You know I will. Just hang on to me and you'll be fine."

"I'm going to fall on my ass."

"Maybe. I'll kiss it better for you if you do."

"Well, in that case," she said, her feet once again moving in the direction of the ice rink. Jack laughed, falling into step beside her.

He rented a pair of skates for each of them, and once they'd stowed their boots in one of the little cubbies and he'd helped her with her skates, he quickly laced his own up. Then, he helped her step tentatively onto the ice.

She let out a small shriek as her feet immediately slid out from beneath her. He caught her around her waist before she could fall.

"It takes a little time to get your balance," he said, helping her get upright again, her skates sliding beneath her. She clung to him, laughing. Once she was steady, he turned to face her, taking her hands in his. "Bend your knees," he said, and then started skating slowly backward, pulling her with him.

"Ahh!" she said, her eyes going wide as she almost lost her balance. But this time, she regained it quickly, her grip on his hands tightening. "Oh God, we're moving."

"We are. Try picking up your feet a tiny bit to get a feel for the skates, the ice."

She did, wobbling as he held onto her, still moving them in a slow circle around the outer loop of the ice surface.

"Faster?" he asked, and she nodded.

"Okay, yeah. A little...shit!" Her feet went out from under her and she landed on her ass. Laughter burst out of her, and he helped her up, his hands lingering around her waist.

"You're doing great," he said.

"Yeah?"

"Yeah. You've never been on skates before. You're doing awesome."

He took her hands and started skating backwards again, going a little bit faster than before. She started to pick up her feet a little, making uncertain strokes with her skates. After a couple of laps, she seemed to have found her balance.

He skated around beside her, taking her hand in his. She

wobbled and flailed her arms, but then moved forward, hanging onto him.

"Am I doing it?" she asked, pushing forward with small strokes. "Am I skating?"

"Yeah, sweetheart. You're doing it."

She looked over at him with a wide smile on her face, her eyes bright. A small laugh bubbled up out of her, her face lit up with joy. And it was in that moment that Jack knew that he was totally, completely, irreversibly in love with Rosalie Crawford.

Rosalie felt as if she were floating on a cloud. Her legs were sore from skating, and her face was nearly numb from whipping down the hill on a tube several times, but now that she had an apple cider and a warm sugar cookie bigger than her palm to munch on, she didn't mind so much. She stood with Jack near the bonfire, soaking up the warmth, letting it seep into her bones. There was something both cozy and invigorating about getting cold on purpose and then warming up. It made her want to do it again and again.

The festival flowed around her, music playing from the ice rink, people laughing and talking. They'd stopped to chat with Beckett, who was working at the Pour Decisions booth near the fire, doling out hot chocolate and apple cider and flirting with every single woman that walked by. He'd even jokingly tried to flirt with Rosalie until Jack had given him a murderous look and he'd backed off.

Chloe and her friends ran by and waved, on their way for another slide down the hill, and a man Rosalie recognized as

Jack's older brother Adam approached the fire, his arm over the shoulders of a very pretty woman in her late thirties.

"Hey," said Jack, tipping his chin at his brother. "I think you two have met, at the hotel?" he asked, his eyes bouncing back and forth between Rosalie and Adam. "This is my older brother Adam, and his girlfriend Hazel."

"You're the ones writing a book together," said Rosalie, and they both grinned. "Rosalie. Nice to formally meet you."

They shook hands and fell into easy conversation, talking about the festival, the town, Adam and Hazel's book, the new puppy they'd just adopted. Something in Rosalie's chest twisted at the way they looked at each other, love and joy radiating outward, but not in an over the top, gushing way. In an easy, natural way, as though they couldn't do anything else but love each other.

"How much longer are you staying in town?" asked Hazel, sipping at the hot chocolate Adam had just delivered to her.

"Oh, well. Um. I'm not entirely sure, to be honest. It's sort of up to Carrie and how much longer she decides to stay, I guess." She frowned. She had the feeling as though parts of herself were very much out of alignment, rubbing against each other in a jarring way instead of fitting neatly together.

Jack rubbed a hand in circles on her back. "Even still, the city's not that far," he said. "If you go back."

Relief that he was willing to keep seeing her even if she went back to the city gathered in her belly, soothing her. But she could hear the question in his voice. Did she have to go back? Did she want to go back?

What if she stayed?

What if everything she'd ever needed, everything she'd

ever wanted, even while refusing to believe it could happen, was right here in Gossamer Falls with Jack?

Something was expanding in her chest. Something that made it hard to breathe or think. Something that made her see her future in a very different light.

"Hey guys," said a masculine voice from behind them, and they all turned. An extremely handsome man was making his way towards them, the firelight catching on his light brown curls and long eyelashes, the shadows emphasizing the slight cleft in his chin and his full lips.

"Indy!" said Rosalie as the woman from the tourist office appeared just behind the handsome man.

"Rosalie!" she said, bounding forward and giving her a brief hug. "What do you think of our little festival?" She loved Indy's pride and enthusiasm for the town. She hadn't fully understood it that first day she'd arrived in Gossamer Falls, but she got it now. This place was special.

Magical, even.

"It's amazing. I think I've been doing winter wrong for my entire life."

Everyone laughed, and then Jack slid an arm over her shoulders. "Rosalie, this is my younger brother Oliver. And you know Indy."

As if she could read the question in Rosalie's mind, Indy said, "Oliver and I have been best friends since kindergarten."

"Wow. Since kindergarten?" she asked. She couldn't imagine being friends with someone for so long, for so much of her life. Then again, she'd changed schools so often that she hadn't had the chance to make those lasting connections.

But maybe it wasn't too late to put down roots, to make a life, to have real friends. To do something meaningful. For so long she'd thought that she had to do something big and special for her life to have meaning. To be the best, to make the most money, to work the hardest. To align herself with celebrities and fame. But now, she was realizing that while money and success were nice, they could also be a little empty. Thinking about the past couple of weeks here in Gossamer Falls, her heart felt more full than it ever had in her life. A quiet, cozy life filled with love and happiness and comfort wasn't small or insignificant. It had meaning, too, maybe even deeper than what she'd been chasing.

"Yep," said Oliver, rocking back on his heels. "One of the other boys in class was picking on me because I'd accidentally spilled juice on myself and it looked like I'd had an accident. Indy came over and rubbed his face in the sandbox until he promised to leave me alone. We've been friends ever since."

Rosalie laughed, and Indy shrugged. "What can I say? Kid deserved it. Oli was a sweetheart then, and he's a sweetheart now." Rosalie saw something flicker in Indy's eyes, a wistfulness, a longing, and she wondered if there was more to the story there.

"Hey, who wants to come browse the market with me?" said Autumn, appearing from the other side of the fire. An older woman was by her side, her graying curls spilling from under a bright red knit hat. "Mom and I want to look before the best stuff is gone."

"I'll go with you," said Hazel, finishing her hot chocolate and tossing the cup in the nearby garbage can.

"Rosalie, you should come with us," said Autumn, her

eyes twinkling in the firelight. There was something unnerving about the way Autumn looked at people, almost as though she could see right to the core of them.

"Oh, this is Rosalie!" said the older woman, and she moved forward, her hand extended. "I'm Julie Shephard, Jack's mom. And his," she said, pointing to Adam. "And his," she added, pointing to Oliver. "And obviously hers," she finished with a laugh, tipping her head in Autumn's direction.

Jack gave Rosalie a squeeze, and she shook his mother's hand. "It's so nice to meet you," she said.

"Likewise. Chloe has just been gushing about you."

Rosalie blushed, her heart feeling full. Truth be told, she adored Chloe, too. She was smart and hilarious, fun and caring.

"I've been enjoying getting to know her," she said, grinning from ear to ear. "She's a wonderful girl."

She glanced over at Jack, and she swore she saw him blinking back tears.

And she knew. She loved him. She loved Jack, and she could easily love his daughter, and she loved Gossamer Falls.

She didn't want to go back to the city.

She wanted to stay.

Rosalie walked along the market stalls with Autumn, Hazel, and Julie, barely taking in the displays of goods for sale as her mind spun and reeled with the realization that had slammed into her by the bonfire.

She didn't want to go back to the city. And, as much as it pained her to admit it, she didn't want to keep working for Carrie. It wasn't that she didn't like Carrie. But the job wasn't fulfilling anymore. It wasn't what she wanted.

Everything she wanted was right here. Jack, the town, his family. Maybe she could take over for Barbara at the food bank. Just the idea of it had her heart soaring.

"Oooh, look," said Hazel. "I didn't know Fiona was going to be here."

"Who's Fiona?" asked Rosalie.

"Fiona Crawley runs the Mystic Muse," said Autumn. "They sell all kinds of goodies, like crystals, tarot cards, incense. Very fun and witchy," she said with a little grin. Then her eyes went wide. "If she's offering readings, you should get one."

"Readings?"

"Have you ever had your tarot cards read?" asked Hazel. Rosalie shook her head. "I wasn't into that stuff at all before I moved here, but...having my cards read by Fiona kinda changed my life. In a very good way. It opened my eyes to what my heart truly wanted, and let me have faith that even though big changes can be scary, everything will work out in the end."

Rosalie's eyebrows went up. Given that she was currently contemplating some big changes, a little reassurance didn't sound so bad.

The women approached Fiona's tent, where she had a gorgeous display of candles, dried herbs, crystal jewellery, books, and tarot cards.

"Hello ladies," she trilled, adjusting her black scarf and then her thick glasses. A mass of blond and white curls puffed out from under her knit hat. "It's so nice to see—" She cut off midsentence as her luminous eyes landed on Rosalie. "Ah, yes. I knew someone new was coming. Yes, hmm. Welcome."

"Thank you," said Rosalie, a touch of uncertainty creeping in.

"Fiona, this is Rosalie," said Hazel.

"Would you like a reading, dear?" Fiona asked kindly. "I can see that you've already been to the falls, yes, but you... you need certainty. Reassurance. And what is that?" She leaned forward, peering through her glasses. "You've got a smudge..." She lifted her hand and for a moment, Rosalie thought she was going to wipe some bit of food or dirt off of her face. But instead, her hand hovered in the air, just to

Rosalie's right. "Ah, yes. Doubt. I see it now. Come. Let's see what the cards have to say, shall we?"

"We'll leave you to it," said Autumn with a wink, and the other women sauntered away, leaving Rosalie alone with Fiona.

"What do I do? I've never..." She shook her head.

Fiona gestured for Rosalie to have a seat in a folding chair on one side of a small round table. Fiona pulled a deck of worn cards out of her pocket and sat down opposite Rosalie.

"One of the biggest misconceptions about the cards is that they tell the future. They do not. They can only reveal what is already true, or what is on the path to becoming true, given current circumstances."

"I see," said Rosalie, intrigued despite her skepticism. After all, she'd been someone who didn't believe in love and relationships just a few short weeks ago, but now she felt differently. Maybe it was time to open her mind to even more.

"I'm going to pull three cards, each representing your past, present and future." She shuffled the deck with the practiced ease of someone who'd done it thousands of times. Then she laid out three cards face down on the little table. "The past," she said, flipping over the first card. "This card represents the energies and events in your past that are still affecting you. It can tell us what you need to release, or learn from." She peered at the card she'd flipped over. "The Moon. A major arcana card, meaning this shaped you deeply in the past. The Moon often represents fear and anxiety." She pursed her lips, gazing at Rosalie. "You had a very stressful childhood that shaped who you are today. Lots of adult anxieties put on a young girl, and you project those fears and anxieties onto the present. The Moon often indicates painful memories and emotional distress; this is what you need to release, I believe. This is where you heal, by letting go of these emotions. Feel them, acknowledge them, and release them so that they no longer have power over you."

Rosalie had gone very still, her heartbeat whooshing in her ears. She felt pinned in place, stunned even, by how accurate that was.

"My father left when I was a kid, and it destroyed my mom, so in a way, I lost both parents."

Fiona smiled sympathetically. "How very unfair for you, my dear. No wonder those fears and anxieties are still with you today. But this card is telling you that they no longer serve you. It's time to release them."

Rosalie nodded as Fiona flipped over the second card. "The present. This card represents the energies around you right now, opportunities and challenges. "Ah. The Four of Wands." She smiled. "This card represents celebration and joy. Harmony, and most importantly..." She looked up and met Rosalie's eyes. "A homecoming."

Rosalie's eyes went wide as her heart doubled its tempo. "A homecoming?"

"The current energy around you is one of happiness and relaxation. Joy, even. Because you've found where you belong. You've found a way of living that aligns with who you are, deep down inside. You have much in your life to celebrate, and this is indeed a very special time."

"And this is the present? Right now?"

"Yes. Perhaps where you are right now is where you belong? This could also indicate that the changes you've been contemplating are indeed the right ones."

Rosalie shivered, but not from the cold.

"The final card represents the future. This is the outcome of the present, the direction things are moving in. It can also show us what we truly want, even if we don't want to acknowledge it." She flipped it over. "Ah. Yes. A happy ending, my dear. The Ace of Cups represents love, new beginnings, and compassion." Fiona smiled softly, her eyes gliding over the cards. "You've had a difficult go of it. A childhood filled with fear and anxiety. But where you are now is where you're meant to be. You've found where you belong, and that's a cause for celebration. If you fully release that fear and anxiety, a new beginning filled with love is just around the corner."

Her last three words landed on Rosalie like boulders slamming into her stomach.

"I...I used a fortune telling machine. In Pour Decisions," she said, the words spilling out of her as she stared at the cards. "It told me love was just around the corner."

"Because it is. Open your heart to what's in front of you and let love in. You won't regret it. The Ace is an invitation to take what's being offered to you, whether it's a new relationship, a new career opportunity, a new way of living that will bring you love and happiness beyond what you thought possible. All you have to do is say yes."

Rosalie sucked in a shuddering breath. "Thank you. This was...surprisingly helpful."

Fiona grinned and then winked at her. "The cards usually are. Now, a little gift before you go." She stood and then rummaged around in a small drawer at the back of her tent and then held up a small stone, a rich, dark green flecked with vibrant spots of red. She pressed it into Rosalie's gloved hand. "Bloodstone, for the courage to say yes to all that's in front of you." She leaned a bit closer. "It's all yours for the taking if you're brave enough to say yes."

Rosalie closed her fingers around the small stone and then tucked it into her pocket. "Thank you. This was...really meaningful. How much do I owe you?"

Fiona waved her hand away. "On the house. Consider it a welcome home present."

Rosalie blinked, her eyes burning with tears. "Thank you."

"Of course. Come by the shop any time once you're settled," she said with a knowing smile.

"I will. Thank you again."

Rosalie stood and stepped out of the tent, feeling like a new person. Gone was the anxious girl who didn't believe in happy endings, who kept everyone at arm's length because she was scared.

And in her place was a woman, ready to claim what was being offered to her.

Jack met up with Rosalie in front of the Ferris wheel a little while later, a wide grin stretching across his face when he spotted her from several feet away. She looked radiant as she moved through the crowd, her face lit up with happiness. His heart flopped over on itself in his chest, and he held out a hand to her as she approached.

"How was shopping?" he asked, and she smiled, her eyes soft and bright. God, she was beautiful. So damn beautiful.

And smart and lovely and warm and funny and amazingly dirty in bed.

"Good. I didn't buy anything, but I had fun browsing." She was still smiling, her eyes moving over his face. "I kinda just wanted to get back to you."

He slung his arm over her shoulder. "I know the feeling." He'd hung out by the fire with his brothers, then had hit the midway with Chloe, where he'd won her a blue stuffed gorilla.

They lined up for the Ferris wheel, snuggled together for warmth, her head resting on his chest.

"Well, don't you two look cozy," came a female voice, and they both turned. Jack grinned.

"Hey, Norah," he said. "Ian." He nodded at his ex's fiancé. "This is Rosalie," he said, tipping his head in her direction. "Rosalie, this is Norah, Chloe's mom, and her fiancé Ian."

Rosalie smiled, big and warm, and held out her hand. "Hi. It's so nice to meet you."

"Likewise," said Norah, smiling with genuine warmth. "How are you enjoying the festival?"

They chatted for a few minutes, until Jack and Rosalie reached the front of the line.

"Oh, Jack," said Norah as she and Ian started to move away. "Can you take Chloe for two nights next week? I'm going to the city for a work conference, and Ian's not sure of his schedule."

"Of course. No problem."

She smiled and patted his shoulder in a friendly gesture. "Thanks. I owe you one."

"No worries. Have fun," he said as he and Rosalie moved onto the platform.

"You too," she said. "I'll see you around. Nice meeting you Rosalie!" she called out, and then Jack and Rosalie slid onto a padded bench in one of the little gondolas.

"She seems nice," said Rosalie, and he could tell she meant it.

"She is."

"I like that you have a good relationship with her."

"We're not together anymore, and haven't been for a long time, but she's Chloe's mom, and I do consider her a friend. Just because we broke up doesn't mean she's a bad person. Sometimes things just don't work out." The Ferris wheel started to turn, moving forward with a lurch, and Rosalie leaned into him. "Maybe because there's something else out there for us."

She sighed and snuggled into him, and as the Ferris wheel rose into the winter sky, small, soft snowflakes started to fall.

"After the past few weeks, I don't think I'm ever going to look at snow the same way again," she said, holding out her hand and watching a few flakes melt on her glove.

"There's a magic to it, isn't there?" he asked, his heart beating hard and fast in his chest.

"Definitely."

"Rosalie, I—" he started at the same time as she said, "Jack, I think—" She smiled and shook her head. "You first."

The wheel turned with a soft groan, and snowflakes melted against his overly warm skin. The festival was a blur of lights below them, the river a black ribbon stretching out into the night. "I don't want you to go back to the city," he said quietly, the honest, vulnerable words spilling out of his mouth. "I want you to stay. Here, with me. I know we haven't talked about the future, but I—"

Rosalie cut him off with a long, sweet kiss, her gloved palms against his cheeks. "I want to stay," she whispered against his mouth. "I don't want to go back to the city. I want to stay right here, with you, and Chloe and your family. I want a life here." She kissed him again, hotter and deeper this time, but unhurried. Jack's heart raced in his chest as he held her, his entire body practically vibrating with hope and happiness. "I know we haven't talked about the future," she said, staring into his eyes as if she could see to the very core of him. Maybe she could, because she was giving him everything he'd been wanting for the past few weeks. "But I know I want one with you."

He laughed, joy bubbling out of him, and then kissed her again, snow falling around them, sticking to their coats, to her hair.

"Thought you didn't believe in fairy tales and happily ever after, Crawford," he said, nipping at her bottom lip.

"I didn't. But then I met you, and now I know better."

He sucked in a shuddery breath. "I am so fucking in love with you, Rosalie. I think I started falling the minute I laid eyes on you in the pub."

She let out a small laugh, blinking back tears. "I love you, Jack. I love your caring heart, and your sexy body, and your sense of humor. I love that you take care of me the way no one else ever has. I love how much I laugh with you, and how right everything feels when I'm with you. I love you." She kissed him. "I love you." Another kiss. "I love you."

"Rosalie," he whispered, returning her kiss. "My Rosalie. My beautiful, sweet, smart, Rosalie. Here to stay."

"Here to stay," she echoed.

With Chloe headed to her friend's for a sleepover after the festival, Jack and Rosalie could barely keep their hands to themselves on the drive back to his place. They made it inside the house and Jack kicked the front door shut, and then hauled Rosalie into his arms, carrying her up to his bedroom. They were a tangled whirl of mouths and hands, clothes flying and hitting the floor until they were both naked.

"I love you," he said, unable to get enough of the way the words felt on his tongue. "I didn't think I'd ever say those words to anyone again, but I can't stop saying them to you. I love you, Rosalie."

"I love you," she said, weaving her fingers into his hair. He kissed her, soft at first, but it quickly morphed into something hot and hungry, need and love and lust spiraling between them. He buried his face in her neck, and she whimpered, clinging to him. He licked across her collarbones and then sucked a hard, pink nipple into his mouth. Her back arched off the bed, her name falling from his lips. He groaned, hunger for her, for *his woman* burning through him.

She was going to stay. With him. For him.

He bit gently at her nipple before laving it with his tongue, taking the sting out of the bite.

"Jack," she moaned. "I need you."

He kissed a path down her stomach. He could smell how turned on she was, and it made his mouth water in anticipation. His cock pulsed, pre-come leaking everywhere.

"Yes," she moaned, her fingers in his hair as she urged him lower. He chuckled.

"Needy girl," he admonished, holding back a groan at the sight of her pussy, pink and glistening for him. "Tell me what you want."

"Your tongue on my clit, now, please, God."

He used his thumbs to spread her lips apart, and she gasped. Her clit was swollen, protruding from its hood. Beautiful and needy and perfect. He pressed a gentle kiss to it and then settled between her legs, pushing her thighs farther apart. Exhaling, he gusted a breath over her pussy and then started kissing her thighs.

"Jack!" she gritted out, her fingers tugging at his hair. "Please. I need your mouth." Her hips shifted restlessly on the bed.

"Like this?" he asked, dragging his tongue up the center of her, just once. She moaned, her thighs shaking. His cock throbbed, his balls tight. "I could spend forever here," he said, licking her once more. "My face between your perfect thighs, making you come over and over again. Fuck, you taste so good. I'm addicted." He licked her again, and she practically screamed, grinding against him, her back arching, her thighs trembling. She was already so close. Fuck, so was he.

He sucked her clit into his mouth and polished it with his tongue. She thrashed and moaned, and he slipped first one, and then two fingers inside her, fucking her slowly with them as he worshipped her clit.

"Come all over me, sweetheart," he whispered, and she broke, her pussy choking his fingers as she squeezed around him.

"Jack!" she screamed, and he tasted the flood of her juices on his tongue as she came. Her thighs were practically wrapped around his head. "Jack. Oh God, Jack," she said, her body trembling with aftershocks as he eased his fingers out of her.

He rose to his knees, grabbing one of her ankles and laying it on his shoulder, spreading her open for him. "Need to be inside you," he said, his voice low and growly. Hungry. Needy. Rosalie grinned up at him, playing with her nipples.

"It's all yours. Officer," she added with a sexy smirk, a callback to their first night together that almost ended him right there. He fisted his cock and pressed it to her slick entrance.

"Fuck, Rosalie," he breathed. "Don't know how I'm gonna last. So tight and wet." He pushed in another inch and then retreated. "So perfect."

"Jack," she moaned. "Fuck me. Please. I need you."

He moaned and slid back in, going deeper this time. His hips burned with the urge to fuck and fuck, but he knew if he did that he'd lose control, and he wasn't ready for this to be over yet.

He sucked in a breath and then slowly, inch by inch, slid all the way inside. "Your pussy is so fucking good, sweetheart. So wet and hot. So tight around my cock." Pleasure raced down his spine and he slid out of her, and then all the way back in.

"Tight because you're fucking huge," she panted out. "I love the way you stretch me and fill me.

He leaned forward, coming down over top of her and kissing her as he started to move his hips, thrusting in and out of her, deep and slow. Her fingernails bit into his shoulders, the mattress creaking beneath them. He flexed his hips and then swiveled them, and she scratched her nails down his back, clinging to him, moaning, senseless. She fluttered around him, milking his cock.

"Fuck me hard," she said. "Fuck me so hard with your big cock that I feel you for days."

"Gunnnnnhhhh," he groaned, and he pressed forward, sinking even deeper. "You want me to fill this pussy up with come?"

"Yessssss," she hissed, and he couldn't hold back anymore. He started to fuck her, hard and deep, just like she'd asked for. Her cries and moans mingled with his, and she angled her hips up to meet his thrusts, the base of his cock sliding against her swollen clit with every thrust.

"Oh, God, Jack. I'm coming. I'm coming!" She screamed and then bucked against him as her pussy contracted around his cock, clamping down hard and triggering his own orgasm.

"I love you," he ground out, pinning her beneath him as he spilled inside her. He thrust again, more come spurting, and again, his orgasm seeming to stretch on forever. "I love you. Rosalie, I love you."

"I love you," she said, holding him close, hearts beating in alignment as they came down together, the future stretching out before them like a promise.

As of today, Rosalie was officially a fully fledged resident of Gossamer Falls, and she couldn't have been happier.

The day after the winter festival, she'd talked to Carrie, telling her that she felt it was time for her to take on new challenges. They'd had a hug and a little cry, but Carrie had understood. Trevor had been less understanding, not being able to wrap his mind around why she'd want to give up working for one of the biggest pop stars in the world, but ultimately he'd wished her well.

Not long after the winter festival, Carrie had decided to return to the city, and at first, Rosalie had gone with her so she could help with finding a replacement for her role and end the lease on her apartment. During the week, she'd worked and packed, and on weekends, she'd taken the train to Gossamer Falls where Jack and Chloe met her, or, if he was working, Autumn or Hazel. The weekends had always gone by too quickly, especially because they were always so busy with her looking for a new place and getting ready to move.

Now, with the first hint of spring in the air, she was saying goodbye to the city and hello to her new life with the man she loved in a town she'd come to adore. Last night, Jack had come up to the city with his truck to help her finish packing up her apartment. It was a furnished lease, so she didn't have much to bring beyond her clothes, kitchen goods, and other personal belongings. It also meant that she had no furniture and she'd have to work on furnishing her new place in Gossamer Falls, but she'd worry about that once she was there.

She and Jack had discussed moving in together, but had ultimately decided to wait. There was no rush, and Rosalie was very conscious of disrupting Chloe's world. So for now, she was renting an apartment on the ground floor of a large house on Fir Street. It was close to the little downtown, and a ten minute walk to Jack's. It was perfect.

"You ready?" asked Jack, loading the last box into the back of his truck, muscles bunching and flexing as he moved. She stood on the grimy sidewalk, looking up into the gray sky. Only a patch of it was visible with all of the buildings around them.

"Yeah. I'm definitely ready," she said, smiling at Jack. He grinned at her, and held open the passenger's side door for her, sneaking a kiss as she stepped up into the truck. "Soon, I'm going to be able to do that every single day."

She sat down and then pressed her forehead to his. "As much as I enjoy our phone sex sessions, I'm looking forward to being able to touch you every day."

The drive back to the city was calm and peaceful, and it

truly didn't feel like she was leaving anything behind. It felt like she was heading towards something. Towards her future. Towards where she was meant to be.

By the time they arrived in Gossamer Falls, the sun was poking through the clouds, casting gentle beams of light onto the sparkling bay. The snow had mostly melted, but the trees were still bare. For now. Soon, spring would bring everything back to life, and Rosalie couldn't wait to see it.

"Are you nervous about starting your new job on Monday?" asked Jack as he took the turnoff into Gossamer Falls.

She shook her head. "No, not really. Mostly just excited." She was taking over for Barbara at the food bank and couldn't wait to dig in. Barbara was staying on for the next two weeks to bring Rosalie up to speed, and then the job would be hers to run with. It felt good to do something that made an important difference in people's lives. The pay wasn't great, but she didn't need the money. Not only did she have a generous amount put away, but Carrie had given her a large payout when she'd left as a thank you for all of her work.

"You're gonna be great," he said. "I know it."

They turned off of Foundry Bridge Road onto Main, and then hung a right onto Chestnut. Two blocks later, Jack slowed the truck as he turned left onto Fir, and Rosalie gasped at what she saw.

The entire Shephard clan was standing in front of her apartment with a giant bouquet of balloons and a banner that said "Welcome Home Rosalie!" Tears sprang to her eyes, and her hands trembled as she fought to unbuckle the seatbelt.

"Did you do this?" she asked, turning to Jack, who had a soft smile on his handsome face.

He shrugged. "Your new friends wanted to welcome you. All I did was tell them what time we were coming back."

She leaned across the center console and hugged him, and then stepped out of the truck into the spring sunshine.

There were tears and hugs and sounds of celebration as everyone welcomed Rosalie, and Chloe gave her a friendship bracelet that said "I ♥ Gossamer Falls," which was Rosalie's favorite thing ever. Once the small celebration was over, everyone grabbed a box and started hauling everything inside. Everyone except Autumn, who was frowning at her phone.

"Everything okay?" asked Rosalie.

"I…" she shook her head, and a wide smile broke out across her face. "Hux is back."

Rosalie grinned and hugged her friend. "Go."

"Yeah?"

"Yes! Get out of here!"

Autumn nodded shakily and headed out. Rosalie knew that this was important to her, and it wasn't as though she had a ton of stuff to unload.

She stepped inside her new place, which was a bit bare, but cozy and homey all the same. The entryway led into the living room, which had a little fireplace and windows that looked out onto the treed backyard. She could already envision exactly how she wanted to decorate it, where she wanted to put the furniture, where she'd hang prints on the wall, where she wanted plants on the windowsill.

She turned in a slow circle in the middle of the empty

living room, pausing when she saw a framed picture on the mantel above the fireplace.

"What's this?" she asked, picking it up. It was a colorful illustration, done in comic book style of a man who looked a lot like Jack and a woman who looked a lot like Rosalie holding hands and facing each other in front of Pour Decisions while snow fell around them. Her heart pushed up into her throat. "Jack," she said softly. "Did you draw this?"

He nodded, a somewhat bashful expression on his face. "I did. I wanted to be the first to give you something for your new place." He moved closer. "Do you like it? It's to commemorate the night we met."

Her fingers hovered in the air over the glass, emotion clogging her throat and misting her eyes.

"I love it. It's the best thing anyone's ever given me." She couldn't stop staring at it. "It's so good, Jack. I had no idea you were so talented."

He blushed, making her want to tackle him to the floor. "It's nothing."

"It's not nothing. It's amazing. You're really talented." She set it down carefully on the mantel and wove her arms around his neck. "I love it. Just like I love you."

He kissed her, slow and sweet, and Rosalie's entire world narrowed to her and Jack in that empty living room. Empty but full of promise for the future that awaited. A feeling of perfect completeness filled Rosalie as she kissed Jack, and for the first time in her life, she knew she was exactly where she was supposed to be.

She broke the kiss, and Jack held her against him.

"Welcome home, sweetheart."

THE END

Thank you so much for reading Jack and Rosalie's story! I sincerely hope you enjoyed it. If you want more Jack and Rosalie, join my newsletter to get access to a super spicy scene (there are handcuffs and toys involved!). You can sign up here: www.tara-wyatt.com/newsletter.

Want to take another visit to Gossamer Falls?
Watch for GOOD LUCK CHARM,
Autumn and Hux's story, coming in summer 2024.
(Don't forget to join my newsletter to stay in the loop!)

ABOUT THE AUTHOR

Tara Wyatt is a contemporary romance and romantic suspense author. Known for her humor and steamy love scenes, Tara's writing has won several awards, including the Golden Quill Award and the Booksellers' Best Award. In 2018, she was a RITA® Finalist for her novella, *Until the Sun Sets*.

When she's not hanging out with your next book boyfriend, she can be found reading, bingeing something on Netflix, and drinking wine. Tara lives in Hamilton, Ontario, Canada with her husband, daughter, and the world's cutest dachshund.

Don't miss out on a sale or new release!
Join Tara's newsletter: www.tara-wyatt.com/newsletter

For regular updates and to stay in the loop, follow Tara on
Facebook: www.fb.com/tarawyattauthor

Visit her on Instagram:
www.instagram.com/taradwyatt

Follow Tara on BookBub:
www.bookbub.com/authors/tara-wyatt